I0819962

DEATH WATCH

TOM MARKERT

Book Design and Interior by Damonza

Printed in the United States
First Printing, 2025
ISBN (hardcover) 979-8-9933563-0-3
ISBN (paperback) 979-8-9933563-1-0
ISBN (eBook) 979-8-9933563-2-7

Acknowledgments

I want to thank many people who both inspired and encouraged me as I set about retiring from a hugely successful corporate career to spend a big chunk of my time writing books and movie scripts.

My first round of thanks goes to my family. My wife and four kids followed me around the globe as my career took off. In total, we moved fourteen times, including multiple international moves. My wife, Sarah, managed to keep the family on the right course through thick and thin. I can never repay her.

Thank you to my high school and college basketball teammates. We worked together as hard as we could. We overcame obstacles together that seemed insurmountable. We achieved so much including multiple championships, multiple trips to the NCAA tournament and more than our fair share of wins. But it was the camaraderie and brotherhood that stuck with me as the key ingredients to our success. Loved every minute. It motivates me today!

Special thanks to Candi Cross, an amazing woman and storyteller. Candi read the first draft of *Death Watch* on a long flight and couldn't wait to call with her enthusiasm. She encouraged me to stay the course and complete the novel, then performed her editorial magic on the characters and pace. I cannot thank her enough for the dynamic development and ultimately, helping to get it in the hands of readers.

Lastly, I want to thank all the writers who have come before me. Writing on the page is easy. Getting it into commercial book form is a different story. So many stars must align. Writers are a tough breed!

CHAPTER 1

Saturday, January 10, 7:15 p.m.

"You, sir. I can tell from the look on your face that you think this is a big pile of crap… a waste of time… a trick…"

"Oh, yes."

"You think we've planted people, right?" The man nodded affirmatively. "Well, let's start the evening with you."

Every performance followed the same pattern. The doubters and skeptics always easy to spot. Almost always young males. Almost always strong and fit. Always with an attitude that was so visible on their faces. It made the job easy. Win over a few obvious skeptics and everyone began to believe what they only hoped was true—that someone could read another's mind.

"And your name is?"

"Larry Regan."

"Mr. Regan, as you know, my name is Sampson, and I can catch glimpses of some of the things that you are thinking about. Not everything, of course, but some things. Now that we have established that, you think I am full of shit."

As had happened hundreds of times in hundreds of cities, this kind of interaction drew a huge laugh from the audience. The believers and skeptics laughed in unison, which served to relax the audience. It also allowed Mr. Regan to feel even more important. His chest puffed up a little broader, his smile more confident.

"Yeah, I really don't buy this mind stuff."

"Hmm… why did you come to the show?"

"My girlfriend." He sighed and glanced to his right at a twenty-five-year-old blond bombshell shifting with obvious discomfort. The spotlight flashed to her, illuminating how mortified she was.

It was time for Sampson to go to work.

"Ladies and gentlemen, for the next hour or so, I will get to know some of you quite well. I will not invade your privacy; I will not hypnotize you. I will merely ask you a question, touch you slightly and in most cases, I will sense your answer. Sometimes I can see glimpses of your future, and sometimes your past, and sometimes nothing at all. Believe what you must. Here are no mirrors or gimmicks. None of this show is planned. I promise you only some fun and a look at a world that most want to believe exists, but most do not believe exists. I ask you to participate if you want to and believe only if you want to…" Sampson inhaled deeply and surveyed the audience. He could sense they were ready to start.

Sampson's eyes drifted back to Larry Regan. Regan looked every bit as confident as just a few moments ago, and clearly was enjoying the limelight of being a part of a show. In short, the perfect specimen to start the evening off with.

"Okay, Mr. Regan. Let's just review where we are. You think I'm a hunk of shit." This, of course, has the audience roaring in laughter. "And you have no faith at all that I can sense your thoughts."

Regan shifted a bit on his feet but maintained his look of disbelief as he said, "Right. I'm sure you're not a bad guy, but this mind-reading stuff is just stupid."

"Hmm. You think so? Well, we do not know each other and have never met until this moment, correct?'

"Yup."

"All right, well where should we begin? How about a little wager?"

Regan shifted again. A layer of his composure faded, the look on his face becoming more serious. It made sense and happened every time. A challenge was now on the table. Some risk was now available, and Sampson's confidence began to unnerve Regan. "How about a fair bet? I have a one-hundred-dollar bill right here which I will wager against… let's see. How about a kiss from your girlfriend? But you probably can't okay that. Miss, would that be okay with you?"

Blond Bombshell's eyes widened, revealing a lustrous blue tint in the dramatic lights. They hinted at desire rather than disagreement. She offered a suggestive smile at Sampson, whose face stayed rock solid while urging his bottom half not to follow. "All right, Mr. Regan. Let's go. I will ask you three questions; specific questions that probably only you, or maybe your girlfriend, would know. If I get all three right, I win. If not, you win. Fair enough?"

"Yes," Regan responded as his head bobbed lazily up and down.

Ah, the fun part was beginning. Regan showed the first dripping of sweat. Victory. Then again, these goddamned lights were baking everyone. Regan's confidence was ebbing, and the risk to him was immense. The thought of his girlfriend kissing this loser in front of all these people was not good. *Why did I do this*, he thought.

"Okay, let's start with something not too hard, shall we? Mr. Regan, it dawns on me that I do not yet know the name of your girlfriend."

Regan started to blurt out the name, but Sampson hushed him.

"No, no. That will be the first question. If you will indulge me, could I touch one of your hands?" Sampson displayed his hands to the audience, wanting everyone to see that there were no wires, no gimmicks.

Regan paused and raised his left hand. Sampson held it like a delicate forest primrose. From the first touch, Sampson knew information would come in quick succession. There was always a type of feel from every individual and over time, distinguishable. Everyone he had ever met or touched could be read. The only question was how easily the information would come without shattering the audience's attention. This was going to be an easy one. Sampson closed his eyes and ordered his consciousness to flow down his arm and pass into Regan's body. The transfer was smooth as if a probe circled the brain of the man he touched. Like dazzling crystals gathering, the name lit up.

"Mr. Regan. Your friend's name is Kathleen, isn't it?"

Stunned, defeated and desperate to dart out, Regan nodded yes. As the color drained from his face as fast as water in sand on a hot day, he blurted, "You probably got that from the ticket." Others in the audience echoed some support, giving the young man a little more courage. "That's how it happened!"

"Hmm. Ya think so? Okay, we won't count that one." The audience thought that was fair as they always did, and it was time to move on.

"Mr. Regan. Let's try another one. Again, don't tell me the answer. What do you do to make a living?"

Sampson again closed his eyes while touching Mr. Regan and felt the answer, along with additional information, cross the connection they shared. "You sell cars, don't you?"

Flabbergasted, Regan only nodded yes. It was time to finish this and leave Mr. Regan with some sense of dignity. "To save time, how about I just tell you two more things about yourself that I shouldn't know, okay?"

This always struck the fear of God in volunteers; everyone's worst nightmare. Someone who can see into their past, their very being, and have the ability to reveal any indiscretion or embarrassing fact. It was a needless worry as Sampson had never—nor would he ever—cross the line of revealing explicit, private info. Tempting as it had been on many occasions, it was best to play it safe.

"Okay, we know you sell cars. How about we stick with that theme? Hence comes two more facts I have learned. You sell Volkswagens, don't you, and you work at Finnegan Volkswagen."

Whatever Regan wanted to believe was no longer an option. This man had done the impossible. He had looked inside another brain and found truth.

"Mr. Regan, I can tell by your expression I am right."

"Yes, but damn if I know how." A dejected Regan waited patiently to finish the bet: face further embarrassment of watching this know-it-all bastard kiss his girlfriend in public.

"Kathleen, if I may…" With that, Sampson reached for Kathleen's hand and kissed it. He sensed disappointment on her part, but to place any more affection would humiliate Regan and alienate the audience. The audience, as always, responded favorably to his sense of chivalry, and it was time to move along.

"Mr. Regan, thank you for participating. You were great." Sampson patted him in a man-to-man way across his shoulders. The audience gifted him a thunderous round of applause.

Relieved, Regan sat down and would probably never volunteer again for anything. Sampson had also learned from the slight touch of Kathleen's hand that Regan was about to get another shock. Kathleen had another love interest and in short order, he would be in search of another companion. He sensed tonight would be their last evening together.

As the applause built, Sampson looked approvingly at the audience and his watch. Only another thirty minutes of having to impress the small audience of Syracuse, New York. Then another city.

CHAPTER 2

Saturday, January 10, 7:30 p.m.

"It is cold out there," said the voice on the radio. And it was. A typical evening in Syracuse in the month of January, however. It had been snowing for four hours, temperatures were in the single digits with the wind blowing everyone to a freezing hell. A rotten, perfect evening for what was about to go down.

A solitary man sat in the truck marked "Niagara Mohawk Power Company" in bright blue and orange block letters. The heater labored to keep the truck barely comfortable. Behind the truck, under the canopy of Hancock International Airport and beyond the reach of the snow, stood a dozen bright orange cones surrounding a solitary manhole.

As the man reached to his right and grabbed a black lunchbox, he left the safe and warm confines of the truck and slipped past the cones and towards the already open manhole cover. He began the downward climb. The rusty ladder descended thirty feet into the darkness. Once at the bottom, the man opened the lunchbox and produced a portable flashlight, which yielded amazing light. He removed his coveralls and began to dress in yellow foul-weather gear that was waiting for him in a corner of the tunnel.

The cold made the change of clothing slow as the man's exposed hands lost feeling. Nonetheless, the intruder felt the slight delay and inconvenience was a good trade-off for the added element of surprise and secrecy that the snowstorm would provide.

The light illuminated a tunnel that headed north, and the man moved swiftly along it. Within minutes, a locked gate appeared. The intruder produced a key, opened the lock, and completed the journey in the tunnel, which culminated at another ladder. As the man climbed and reached the top, he pushed the iron manhole cover aside, and glared at the airport runways and gates in front of him. With no one in sight, he removed the entire cover, climbed out, and only partially replaced it. To a casual observer it would appear as though it had simply popped loose. To the intruder this was a part of his lifeline. If things did not go as planned, this tunnel offered him an exit to freedom. His ability to get in and get out of the tunnel quickly mattered. He was meticulous in his nature; his thinking crisp and raw; his mind bright.

CHAPTER 3

Syracuse Civic Center, January 10, 7:50 p.m.

Alan Grant was a fifty-five-year-old hulk of a man. At 6'6" and 230 pounds, the gray-haired man cut an imposing swathe. Grant had just completed a speech to a group of undergraduate students from Syracuse University, and his confidence was brimming. His aggressive stance on terrorism, mixed with a preacher's ability to captivate an audience, was a lethal combination. The audience ate up his message and style and were rewarding him with a standing ovation.

"Senator, you hit a home run," the young aide, Martin, whispered in the ear of the beaming orator.

The senator nodded in agreement and added, "I should have, son. Terrorism will only stop when we smack it in the face. Being nice and trying to negotiate is a waste of time. It's very simple—they push, we push harder. Americans love it because it is the right message. It is also the message that will get me elected as the next President of the United States."

Martin agreed and whispered, "Senator, we've got to go." With that, the senator waved to his flock for the night, walked off stage with poise, and stepped to a waiting limousine.

"Evening, senator," beamed the stout driver.

"Hi, Stan. How long to the airport?"

"Oh, only thirty minutes normally. But it's snowing hard, which you will see once we get outside the garage. You should plan on an hour, but we still have plenty of time to make your flight. Leave it to me, sir. You get comfortable, and I'll get us there quickly and safely."

"Sounds like a plan, Stan…no pun intended." Everyone chuckled at the soft humor. With that, the senator, aide, and two United States Secret Service agents assigned to protect the popular politician settled back in the sleek gray stretch limousine. The senator took a deep breath, and his thoughts were filled with his presidential run—six months ago yielded a long, long, long shot, and now, he was the leading Republican candidate. Serious enough that the government had afforded him round-the-clock protection. He liked the two agents, who seemed solid at what they did, although who was he to say? This was all new to him; new and exciting.

While his desire to become U.S. President was significant in many ways, it frightened him. He constantly asked himself if his training as a senator was sufficient for him to become the leader of the most powerful nation in the world. He always arrived at the same answer—*yes*! And even if there was some doubt, his ego and competitive spirit beat it back.

January 10, 8:15 p.m.

Sampson had finished another riveting show. Everyone felt good. No one was embarrassed, true to his word. He looked back to Regan, who was also applauding, and smiled. Regan's smile brightened as he nodded back at Sampson. The eye contact would soften his wounds and give him some confidence back.

Sampson retreated to his "dressing room", an oversize closet with a series of silver hooks on the walls, and a lone mirror over a desk. He changed, collected his check from an elated theatre manager, and walked toward a side entrance used only by the "stars". He laughed to himself. But he did feel like a star tonight. As he headed outside, pure white powder engulfed him. Then yellow as a taxi approached and started the treacherous ride to the airport.

CHAPTER 4

January 10, 8:17 p.m.

Emerging from the dark tunnel produced a great exhilaration. The cold and snow bit his skin as the goal of completing the mission licked his mind. He also knew he must move and behave as a normal employee of the airport would. He must not rush to complete the task. He must blend into the background. He must become a chameleon in a jungle.

He could see his target fifty yards ahead. Gate 13. It would be an unlucky number tonight.

The weather kept everyone indoors and without seeing a soul, the man climbed the stairs and stepped into the Jetway attached to a Piedmont Airlines Boeing 727. So far so good! He scanned the jet bridge and listened. The plane was deserted. Unbelievably and wonderfully empty. Too good to be true.

The intruder moved toward the rear of the aircraft. The plane was cold but without the nasty wind, it did not seem altogether bad. He felt the plane resembled a coffin with its tube-like shape. The intruder intended to be gone in only moments, so he dispensed with his frivolous thoughts and put his mind back on his work.

Once reaching the rear of the aircraft, he opened the door

to the restroom, which greeted him with the smell of disinfectant made to create "blue toilet water" to look like the color of cleanness. No telling how many asses sat there. Being a bona fide hygiene freak, the thought repulsed him enough to be distracted. Until he thought of all that cash awaiting him.

He set the black lunchbox on the floor, unclasped the handles, and opened the package. Inside was a small block of C-4 attached to a wire and a wristwatch-like device. The man pushed a red button for a green light to come to life. He picked up the package, walked to the lavatory waste bin, and slid the device to the bottom of the empty bin. He reached for a handful of paper towels, covered the device, and let the top of the bin automatically close. He slowed his breathing and exhaled with supreme coolness. He collected the lunchbox, ensuring he left nothing behind. Satisfied, he glanced at his wristwatch. *Time to go.* The intruder walked to the front of the plane, opened the jetty door and without ever being seen or noticed, slid back through the manhole cover and to the warmth of the awaiting truck. Lady Luck shined tonight! For him, at least.

CHAPTER 5

January 10, 8:25 p.m.

The gray limo crept into the *arrivals* area. The car was encrusted in snow and slush that had turned brown from the sand spread to help with traction in the streets of Syracuse.

The rear door opened, and the two Secret Service agents emerged. Both scanned the empty curbside area. Satisfied that conditions were safe, the lead agent confidently said, "Senator, you can come ahead now."

Grant and Martin entered the terminal. Inside the air felt warm and comfortable, and few people were milling around. The four men walked toward the ticket counter, found the first-class line, and approached a luscious Jessica Rabbit-like woman.

"Hello, gentlemen. How can I help?" She made eye contact with all four men, producing a gorgeous and genuine smile.

"Four of us traveling to Washington," the lead agent said as he handed tickets to the woman.

"Gentlemen, I will need to see your IDs." Each flashed passports, which the woman glanced at. Satisfied, she completed the process in moments, and handed all the paperwork back to the travelers. "Thank you, gentlemen. Enjoy the flight."

The senator smiled, but a sliver of anger passed through him.

Sexy Red didn't know me? The four headed to Gate 13. Senator Grant spoke quietly to Martin as they approached the security screening area, "That's not good, Pat. That woman should know me, for Christ's sake. I can't win if we strike out with the younger voters. Figure out an approach, or we will both be unemployed in November." Martin, the savvy junior aide, vowed to appease him, as he did with every order Grant barked. Some were nonsensical or outright stupid from his quick appraisal after working for two brainiacs—both boss women more capable of handling the U.S. presidency. But Grant had loads of charisma. No one seemed to give a shit about his floor votes or if he had sponsored or helped to pass any bills.

The lead agent flashed his badge to the older woman approaching him, and it had the desired effect. They were ushered to a private area used by law enforcement professionals.

"Ma'am, we are Secret Service. We are armed, and we have permits to carry the weapons on the plane."

The woman skimmed the badge and the permit and without a word, signaled them through. She was an ant in the whole army of counterterrorism and homeland security measures designed to, post 9/11, imagine the unimaginable and enhance defenses to prevent the ever-changing and growing threats to aviation security. The agent was shocked at how easy it was to pass through on a slow day due to the weather and cringed at how dangerous this kind of carelessness would be on a typical flying day. He motioned the senator through. They reached Gate 13 and found empty seating in the far corner of the waiting area.

Once seated, the senator pulled a newspaper from his briefcase and began to catch up on his reading. He had always enjoyed reading in his home in front of the stone fireplace in his study. The campaign was exhilarating and exhausting at the same time. He learned how to relax and enjoy precious time like this, even in an airport. The election was a long way off, and he needed to conserve his energy if he wanted to survive. So, for the moment, while an airport was not the greatest place in the world to spend time, he would relax and optimize the situation.

CHAPTER 6

January 10, 8:45 p.m.

Sampson thought the trip would never end while slipping and sliding, inching to the airport. But he made it, so to hell with being upset. He paid the cabby, adding a generous tip, grabbed his bag, and jogged into the barren airport. He did not see the man in the blue suit exit from a dark sedan and mirror his movements.

He approached the ticket counter. "Hi, my name is Sampson and I'm on the 9:15 to Washington."

The agent looked up, and Sampson sized her beauty up. He loved voluptuous redheads.

"May I see your ticket, Mr. Sampson." She maintained the smile.

As he handed it to her, their fingers touched, and Sampson caught glimpses of this woman in a romantic moment with a rugged-looking man. With an inquiring mind, and knowing this woman did not understand his gifts, he posed a leading question to see if the fish would bite. "Ma'am, you seem distracted," Sampson offered with faint concern.

The woman blushed and looked into Sampson's eyes. He felt her guessing, wondering if he knew, but then dismissed those foolish thoughts.

"Oh, I was just thinking about what I am going to do when I get off."

Sampson couldn't help himself. "I bet you can't wait for that moment to come. I hope you have a great time."

He smiled and left the bewildered agent wondering if maybe... just maybe... no... *maybe*? Sometimes his abilities were so entertaining.

Sampson walked toward the gate, cleared security, and began looking for a place to sit.

A short stroll across the waiting area and Sampson found an empty group of chairs. He hoisted his bags onto one and seated himself in the next chair.

After every show, Sampson found himself fatigued and sometimes packing a headache. Tonight was no exception and as he sat down, he closed his eyes and rubbed his temples realizing he felt more than tired tonight; he felt cold and alone, closed off from the world. He longed for companionship, but never found time to fit it into his life.

While Sampson had hoped for a nap, it was not to be this time. Still, the quiet period rejuvenated him enough that he sat up and began to scour his bag for reading material. There was nothing but the magazines he had already been through at least twice. As Sampson rose to find a shop, he spotted an abandoned *USA Today* on a table not thirty feet away. He had always enjoyed this paper. The articles were crisp and to the point. The sports section was thorough, and the paper was in color, not just black and white. *Perfect*, he thought. Another win tonight.

With his headache subsiding, and feeling energetic, he walked toward the paper. As he bent to gather it, his manners got the best of him, and he stared at a gentleman two seats away who was reading a hardcover book.

Sampson moved toward the man and gently tapped him on the shoulder. He was startled, as if in deep thought. Upon seeing the senator jump, both bodyguards leapt to their feet and dove forward into both Sampson and the senator. The force of the two men sent all four over the backs of the chairs and crashing into a wall.

That very moment, two things happened at the Syracuse Hancock International Airport that had not happened in a very long time: First, the gentleman who had unsuspiciously been tailing Sampson ran toward the mayhem and as he moved, slipped a firearm from beneath his coat. Second, a nearby police officer watching both the mayhem and the armed stranger, squeezed his microphone and shouted, "Code 66, Gate 13, critical!" This set off a rapid chain of events. Three other officers assigned to the airport and scattered throughout the complex raced towards the incident. Simultaneously, an announcement came over the public address system: "Would Mr. Oliver Orange meet his party immediately at Gate 13?" This announcement alerted the private security at the airport of a serious incident and raised the threat level as high.

Sampson stared in disbelief at what he was seeing. Two well-dressed men who had tackled him pointed guns directly at his head. While the tackle had caught him off guard, he had maintained his senses, and he knew enough right now to offer absolutely no resistance.

Another man appeared and raised a gun at these two suits. "Drop your weapons now. CIA!"

Just as quickly, two police officers totally baffled by the entire situation appeared with their guns raised and pointed at everyone.

The man who had identified himself as a CIA agent spoke first with authority, "Gentlemen, I don't know what this party is all about, but let's all get calm. Each of you lowers your weapons, as will I, and we will sort this gig out. I think we're all on the same team here, so let's not make any mistakes."

Perplexed, everyone began to co-operate except for the lead uniformed officer, a heavyset man in his late forties, with thin red hair cropped close to his head. "No, you will listen to me. The men who are wearing the uniforms here right now are the good guys. That I'm sure of. So, here is how we're going to play this out. Each of you set those guns down now… real slow… and then raise your hands. My officers are the peacekeepers here. This is my airport tonight."

In the same breath, everyone did as they were told. "Good. Good start. Now, one at a time, I want to see your identification, starting with you, Mr. CIA."

The agent did as he was told and showed credentials that identified him as Robert Becker with the Central Intelligence Agency. The uniformed officer studied the badge, squinting his eyes. "Looks real enough but stay put."

He then focused his attention on the two Secret Service agents. "You two are probably KGB or MI5 or some fucking thing, right?" the officer said with a menacing smirk.

The agent in charge smiled, "Well, pretty close. We're Secret Service to protect Senator Grant," he said as he pointed to the senator, who sheepishly hoisted himself from the floor. "We were stopping this man," he continued, pointing to Sampson, "who was preparing to do harm to the Senator."

"Harm? You call borrowing a fucking newspaper harm?" Sampson remarked indignantly.

"Shut up till I figure this out," the officer commanded. "Who are you?" he said, glaring at Sampson.

"My name is Sampson, and I am a normal person, a civilian, a citizen, not a cop or an FBI guy," he said, handing over his driver's license. The uniformed officer looked at the document and passed it back.

"Okay, everybody, here is what we are going to do. My partner is going to pat each of you down. Assuming you are clean, we are going to adjourn to a little room around the corner. I plan on verifying who everyone is, including the citizen with the driver's license and the big mouth."

Remarkably, everyone listened and obeyed. Everyone was patted down. No new weapons emerged, and they moved toward the small room only a few paces away.

"Lift the Code 66. This is under control," the officer uttered into his mic.

"Roger that," came the reply over the radio.

Once they got to the room, everyone sat down in silence. Outside, the snow was taking over the planet, so they were glad to be safe and warm for the time being.

A short time later, Commando returned and reported, "Okay, folks. An awful lot of this makes no sense, but you are all legitimate. Mr. Secret Service, you sure this guy wasn't just getting a paper? He is clean as a whistle. Has a lounge act. He's an entertainer."

Sheepishly, the agent responded, "Given he's not armed, I tend to think we were being too careful. My apologies, sir."

The senator added, "I would also like to say I am sorry to all of you. In particular, you, young man. I'll be glad to buy you a paper!"

Both men smiled. The senator thought to add, "I'm new at all this security stuff, but I want all of you to know I will make a great president, and I hope you'll consider voting for me."

Senator Grant, who had been silent throughout the ordeal, now owned the room, and all the tension escaped except for residuals from the stern police officer.

"One last question, Mr. CIA Agent. What exactly were you doing at the airport?"

"Oh, just catching the same flight, and I came upon the incident."

"Uh, huh." This did not jive with what he had seen. This man was watching the group. He was sure of it, and he had arrived for the flight far too soon to have been casually waiting. His instincts were aroused, but there was little he could do other than simply be suspicious.

"All right, folks. Go ahead and head for your flight gate. Most flights have been delayed indefinitely due to the weather. They are plowing the runways right now." *Thank God this is over*, the cop thought, but he remained intrigued with what he had seen.

The senator moved toward Sampson. "Sir, I am really sorry about this," he said as he extended his hand.

As Sampson made contact with the man's hand, what was shaping up as a bad day deteriorated fast. As Senator Grant gripped his hand, Sampson was struck by a blinding light only he could see. All sense of time and place disappeared. He sensed being in this abyss before. White noise fell around him. "Help?" "Blood?" "HELP!"

Then he saw a skeleton with rotting, smoldering flesh. But not a complete skeleton. It was missing a leg and an arm. He could smell the rotting flesh. He saw blinding light and felt excruciating pain in his face and head. Mercifully it lasted only a few seconds as he lapsed into unconsciousness.

The uniformed officer moved towards Sampson, using his walkie-talkie to summon help. "We need an ambulance now in the interrogation room. Man down. Heavy bleeding from the nose and mouth. Get me the paramedics." *Great*, thought the cop, *let's just make this the worst day ever.*

Sampson was lying unconscious on the floor, with blood pumping out of his nose at such an alarming rate that everyone sat there, transfixed, except the CIA agent. He moved swiftly, sitting Sampson up, and began to shake him violently. "Sampson, wake up, damn it, wake up!" He looked at the others and barked, "Get me ice, lots of ice, and two big bottles of water and blankets—NOW!" Two of the officers scampered away to meet the request. "Sampson, damn it. Wake up now!"

Sampson stirred and moaned. His eyes fluttered to dull life. Semi-conscious, fighting not to slip backward, Sampson willed himself toward the real world. Miraculously, or maybe not, the flow of blood eased as Sampson reached full consciousness. The officers returned with the supplies, and the CIA agent shouted orders again. "Pack his nose area with ice now. We've got to stop the flow of blood immediately. Cover him with blankets. With the blood he's lost he could slip into shock. Help him drink the water. He'll be thirsty and needs to drink right away."

The cop scratched his face. Either he was right with his hunch, or this guy was an ER doctor moonlighting as a CIA agent. Always go with the hunch. There was more to this, and probably the best thing to do was to let this play out, then stop the party and ask questions. Five minutes passed and Sampson reached full consciousness. The bleeding stopped. The floor was brilliant crimson everywhere. Sampson, still weak, drank the water held by a young police officer. He was thirsty—passionately thirsty—and as he drank, he felt his head clear. While too weak to stand, he could whisper his thoughts in barely audible gibberish. "The senator.... Where—*issss* he?"

Mr. CIA agent cooed, "Stay still and quiet." His concern was genuine.

"No. Who the fuck are you? Get the senator now!" Sampson's voice rose with hostility.

"Did you see something?" the agent asked.

Sampson's mind toggled between seductive fog and alertness. He peered into the eyes of the CIA agent. "*Please* get him. Somehow you know more than you should," he said pointedly. "He is in grave danger. Get to him now!" No time to succumb to sweet oblivion.

"How will he *die*?" the agent gasped in sheer horror.

Sampson was confused. He hadn't told the agent he would "die". Was he guessing, or did he know more? No time to worry about that now. "Don't know. Just get him, okay?"

The CIA agent looked to the uniformed cop. "Officer, stay with this man. Put the airport back on alert. Get more support down here post haste."

"Fuck, now you want to be in charge?"

"Look, indulge me. This is serious."

Too tired to argue, the uniformed officer complied. Once again, the cop barked orders into his microphone, prompting the officers to scurry, placing the airport back into high alert.

The CIA agent rose, retrieved his weapon, and sprinted in the direction of Gate 13, hoping to find the senator, knowing what he'd heard was the truth of the future.

It took only seconds until the agent spotted the senator and the Secret Service. Nothing amiss in the immediacy. "Gentlemen, we have a problem and I have no time to explain. Senator, your life is in grave danger. I don't know the who's, the how's, or the what's, so don't ask. We need to move now. I suggest we go back to the interrogation room. It's small but secure, and I've got more of the locals on the way."

The Secret Service agent made a quick call on the situation. "Senator, this man has been verified as a CIA agent. I suggest we move now. Stay in the middle. The three of us will surround you. Move quickly."

Senator Grant felt dampness in his armpits and beads of sweat on his forehead. He saw the three men shielding him, their arms tucked in their breast pockets, surely holding their weapons. As they rounded the corner, they were met by a small gathering of the press corps. Flashes went off, news cameras went live, and the shouts of questions overtook their ears.

The agents did not stop. They did not speak. Their training would not allow that. They scanned the crowd as they pushed through. The CIA agent was sure this was it. Lots of people, lots of noise, and an easy target in the kill zone.

Yet, nothing happened.

CHAPTER 7

A cluster of suits dashed inside the interrogation room. Someone slammed the door shut and locked it in the shuffle.

The CIA agent was the first to speak and looked directly at the redheaded cop with the attitude. "Any chance you fucks could help out a little? We were almost mobbed out there."

The cop had had about enough. "You told me to stay here, asshole. Besides, I got news for you. This is my jurisdiction, and you aren't leaving until we talk, and I say so. I saw you when this all went down. You didn't stumble on this. You were watching. Almost waiting for this to happen. So, you, sir, are full of shit, and you're on my turf right now."

The CIA agent was taken aback. The cop was good. No… maybe great. As trained as he was, he was made—and by a street cop. He smiled and looked into the eyes of the cop. "You're right. Things are not quite as they seem."

"Both of you shut up." The gravelly voice was that of Sampson, now sitting up, his shirt stained a deep red. "Tonight, I saw something I have never seen before, and I am scared. I make my living seeing the past and the future. I saw the senator tonight. *Dead*."

"That can't be. Here I am!" The senator felt a chill with these statements, but somehow, he believed this man.

"I saw your corpse, your skeleton, or most of it anyway. Your leg and an arm were missing. But you were dead. Pieces of flesh still clung to your bones, but you were dead. I saw death, and when I touched you, I felt death."

It was now the CIA agent's tum. "Did you hear anything or feel anything else?"

"No, just what I told you."

"Officer, we need full support here now. I want to get the senator out of here, but not until we've scrubbed the airport. Based on what I've heard, this is a threat that we cannot ignore. Call your bomb squad. Bring dogs. I want the airport searched quickly."

"I told you the feeling I had was imminent. What you are talking about will take hours," Sampson uttered. "I think I can walk now. Let me look around. Maybe I can narrow the field."

Everyone looked to the CIA agent for approval.

"Okay, you and I and that smartass local cop will do that. Everyone else, stay put. More help will be here shortly."

With that, the three left and headed back where the chaos had ensued, back to Gate 13.

"Listen, Sampson, and don't ask questions right now. Let your mind relax and try to make your thoughts blank." the CIA agent said gently.

"Have you seen any of my shows? That is what I do. How do you know that? Only I know that." Sampson couldn't understand how the man would know.

"Not now. We'll do that dance later. Let your mind go."

And Sampson did, and soon, he felt a twinge of death in the air. Much stronger as he moved toward the gate. "I want to go in there," he whispered, motioning to the jet bridge.

"I'll take care of that!" the uniformed officer barked.

Within seconds, the cop had a pimply-faced gate agent nearly in tow and told him to open the alarmed door. With the task completed, the agent scurried back to his post.

"I want to go in," Sampson muttered.

"Not so fast. I go first and the officer trails you. We do this by the book. Watch for trip wires, gunmen, who knows. Just be careful."

"There are no people on the plane. It doesn't feel that way to me."

They started down the jet bridge in single file and cautiously approached the plane. Sampson felt imminent death. The other men felt sweat trickle down the inside of their arms as they crept down the jet bridge, each expecting the unexpected.

As they neared the entrance to the airplane, tension reached a crescendo. Each step meant they were closer to danger.

The CIA agent plowed forward determined to complete the puzzle that remained in front of them. He was surprised that nothing had happened so far. He reasoned that an ambush involving people would occur inside the jet bridge and not the airplane. It seemed to him that it would be next to impossible for an assailant or group of assailants to flee an attack inside a plane. Most people wanted to live, and escape routes were limited from a parked aircraft. So, they were dealing with something else. He also knew to trust Sampson.

CHAPTER 8

January 10, 9:30 p.m.

The intruder disposed of the stolen Niagara Mohawk Power truck in an abandoned warehouse area he had scoped out days before. He parked the truck, packed up his few belongings, and gave the truck a last look over to ensure he left nothing behind. Satisfied, he moved to the back of the truck and removed a five-gallon can of gasoline and doused the cabin thoroughly. The intruder was a highly trained operative who knew how to destroy evidence. He knew the average thief would simply set the cabin afire and assume everything would burn. Chances are it probably would, but he would not take that chance. The entire truck had to be destroyed. The one extra step of stuffing a rag into the gas tank and lighting the fire from this point would ensure complete destruction. No evidence, no clues, low risk.

The intruder was the best in the business today. He knew it. He worked at it. He was as passionate about his work as a preacher with his submissive congregation. Only his business was not about saving lives.

The intruder struck a match and watched as the tank exploded, igniting the gasoline-soaked cabin. Within seconds, the entire shell of the truck was ablaze. Satisfied, the intruder walked in the snow-covered parking lot toward a tree-covered field that led to a McDonalds. He knew the snow would be a bonus to further eliminate any trace of his existence. Once he reached the McDonalds, he saw his rented, red Chevy Lumina parked under a streetlamp. He brushed the snow off the car and relieved to be out of the cold and wind, started the engine.

He reached for the cell phone, dialed a ten-digit number, and was routed to his assistant at the Pentagon.

"Mr. Whisnant's office."

"Hi, Maggie. It's me. Anything new?"

"Oh no, sir. All is quiet as usual. Are you ready to come back? I can order the plane."

"I am almost done with my meetings. Tell the pilot to meet me in three hours at the Albany airport." He judged the normal three-hour car trip from Syracuse to Albany in this weather might take up to four hours. It was an inconvenience to drive this distance, but he didn't want to take a chance of anyone connecting the agency with the aviation disaster that lay ahead.

"Maggie, put me on the secure line and ring me through to the President."

"Here you go, sir."

Whisnant heard the familiar sounds of beeps and boops as his call moved over to a totally secure environment. The call came into the White House, and directly to the President's private assistant.

"This is Millie Talisse."

"Millie, it's Wiz. Is Austin available?"

"Sure, Wiz. Hold on. I'll get him."

Millie had always liked this man. He was always pleasant, quite handsome and on numerous occasions, she had fantasized about their dating. However remote, she held onto the James Bond/Moneypenny dream. Besides the dream, she was also smart. Millie knew the one man in the world that Austin Feeney,

President of the U.S., trusted was John Whisnant. "Wiz", as he was called, had known Feeney his whole life. They had gone to high school and college together. Both finished grad school, and Austin Feeney had decided to enter politics.

Politics turned out to be an easy path for the tag team of Feeney and Whisnant. Feeney was gifted in his public speaking ability and had a way of winning over both his supporters and detractors.

Whisnant was the man behind the man. A brilliant strategist with a knack for not missing a detail. Whisnant laid out the directions and the plans. Feeney used his personality and people skills with the voters. Together, they conquered everything in their way. They started small by winning a congressional seat, and then later, a senatorial seat. Three years ago, the duo, aged forty-two, won the presidency. Nothing had been sweeter.

The phone suddenly came alive. "Austin, it's Wiz. I have just finished up here. Everything we wanted to do happened on schedule. It should pay results soon."

"Great, Wiz. I will be watching for the results. You coming back?"

"Yup. Should be back tonight. Late."

"How about a run in the morning? Then breakfast. We can talk more about your project."

"See you at 7:00."

"Over and out."

The connection went dead, but the brainwaves of both men charged up with contemplation of what would happen next. Neither man felt pity for those who would be harmed in order to ensure their private success.

Austin Feeney and John Whisnant were the two most powerful men in the world. They had no intention of letting go of this power until Feeney's second term concluded. Nothing could or would get in the way of his re-election.

CHAPTER 9

January 10, 9:47 p.m.

It was time to make their way inside the plane.

The CIA agent spoke quietly. "I will go alone from here. Stay put."

He moved cautiously into the cold, empty plane. The cockpit door was open, and no one was visible inside. The agent crept toward the back of the plane and there was no one on board. He moved swiftly back to the jetway.

"It's empty. Let's get out and wait for the bomb guys."

Sampson interjected, "I can't explain this and even if I did, you wouldn't believe me. I think... no, I feel, we don't have time. Let me look inside."

The agent sized up this young man. He knew to trust him from the tapes he had reviewed. "Alright, but we go with you and in five minutes, no more, we are out of there."

Sampson and the uniformed officer nodded in agreement.

Sampson took the lead and clearly felt something. A presence of danger. He moved down the aisle of the plane and stopped as he neared the rear lavatory. He knew the source of death was here, as the CIA agent and the officer stood by.

His face told the ominous story. The agent quickly assessed

the bathroom. Not too many places to hide anything. The obvious spot was the waste bin. He gently pushed the silver door open and searched for trip wires or booby traps. It seemed okay. He held his breath and pushed the door fully open. He could see a small device at the bottom, partially concealed by discarded paper towels. He peered inside. The agent was trained in explosives and immediately recognized the C-4 and timing device. He could see it ticking down from only three minutes and thirty seconds.

"Shit, shit…SHIT. You two out now and tell everyone to get away from the gate."

Sampson and the officer sprinted into the terminal and shouted for everyone to move.

General panic started, but people moved.

The agent ran his choices through his mind. There weren't many. If he left the bomb there, surely people would die. This was a lot of explosive material. No way was there time to get everyone away from the terminal. Plus, the combination of bomb and jet fuel from the plane. Only one choice. Grab the bomb and move it someplace safer. He knew C-4 was fairly stable, and he was only playing a deadly game of beat the clock. He grabbed the bomb and moved down the aisle toward the front of the plane and down the jetway stairs.

He peered at the timer and knew he had about a minute and a half. The snow was almost blinding. If he had time to think, he would also know how cold it was. He moved down the stairs and rushed forward. His plan was to get as far from the terminal as possible, gently set the bomb down, and run like hell. His experience portended he may survive.

Jogging through a foot of snow, he realized he was not going to get very far. He heard a rumbling behind him and turned to see an immense snowplow, yellow lights flashing, bearing down on him.

He raised a hand to signal the plow to stop. It skidded to a halt just feet in front of him. The driver rolled down his window.

He was a Black man, heavyset, and mad as hell. "What the fuck are you doing out here?"

"Get out of the truck now. Secret Service!" the agent ordered.

"Yeah, and I just fell off the turnip truck. Get out of my way, man."

"Look, I don't have time," the agent said as he removed his revolver and pointed it squarely at the man's head. It had the desired effect.

"Okay. I'm out," the driver said as he got down.

"Run to the terminal. Now!" And the man did, relieved this psycho in a snowstorm let him go.

The agent climbed in the truck, setting the C-4 on the seat next to him. He threw the truck in first gear and pointed the truck down the empty runway. He loosened his tie, strapped the wheel to the seat. He took off his loafer shoe and jammed it on the accelerator of the truck and sprang loose from the moving vehicle. The plow crept forward through the snow, with the agent doing his best to scramble in the opposite direction. He had glanced at the bomb timer just as he was leaving and guessed he had less than thirty seconds. As he counted to twenty-eight, he dove to the ground, covered his head and ears, and prayed.

As if on cue, the plow exploded with a monstrous roar. The blast sent debris everywhere and the agent heard missiles of shrapnel flying over his head. A sharp pain shot through his back, followed by a feeling of dampness. It didn't last long as he found himself drifting into blackness. Would he live?

Inside the terminal, windows shattered. Flying glass hit several female passengers heading to Chicago for a food convention. One was killed instantly; one would die later at Community General Hospital; and one suffered only minor cuts but would wonder her whole life why she was spared. There would be no answer and no peace for her.

The blast lifted ticket counters and slammed them against

walls. Three jet aircraft were badly damaged. One was overturned. Miraculously, there were only several small fires, which were extinguished by good Samaritans. Dozens of people wandered the airport, dazed and bleeding.

As the effects of the blast subsided, the local police worked to calm the crowds in the terminal. It was not working. Most were disoriented. Some tried to run from the airport. Others chose to remain under seats and tables waiting for another explosion. None would come.

Sampson had found his way back to the interrogation room, and gathered with the senator, two Secret Service agents, and a local police officer who was present when the explosion occurred.

The experience in the interrogation room was surreal. At the first sound of the blast the senator was literally thrown to the ground and covered by the Secret Service. Executive protection was their job, and they did it well. The windowless room had proven to be a good refuge from the carnage of the bomb. They could hear a shower of glass and debris launched against the walls of their shelter, but nothing penetrated.

Sampson looked at the officer. "We've got to find the CIA agent. With everything going on here, it will be a long time before anyone gets to him. How about some help?" Sampson knew he would get the help but chose to ask anyway.

"With the way today is going, why not." The officer shrugged his shoulders.

They moved back toward Gate 13 and the jetway. Both moved somewhat cautiously, although Sampson had a feeling the danger had passed.

Moving through the jetway, they reached the door that led to the ground near the aircraft. Sampson and the officer both took notice that the glass that at one time made up a window in the door was gone.

They moved swiftly down the stairs and were awestruck at

the sight of the airplane. The entire left side of the aircraft was peppered with debris. The most amazing sight was a plow blade embedded deep into the tail of the plane.

The officer was the first to speak. "Shit. Goddamn."

Sampson was equally dumbfounded. "This is unbelievable. We've got to find him quickly. It's so damn cold, if we don't get him soon, he'll be gone."

The snow continued to fall. Visibility was limited but it was easy to see the direction of the blast. Five hundred yards to the north, a fire glowed. Debris enclosed them. The smell of jet fuel lingered in the air, and the new snow which should have been pristine white was blackened. Both men assessed the situation and reached the same conclusion. Spread out and head toward the fire.

The men found the going tough. The snow was knee deep in places, and the wind was biting. Having left the warm confines of the terminal so abruptly, neither had thought to grab a jacket or gloves, and within minutes, both were almost numb.

The officer spotted something in the distance.

"Sampson, just ahead. I think I saw something move." He pointed straight ahead.

"I see it too."

They moved as swiftly as they could. Both were losing feeling in their feet. Both felt the prickles that warn you your body is in distress. Both ignored the warning.

They reached their target and realized within a couple of minutes they would never have found the agent. Snow had almost completely obscured his outline.

"Oh, nice to see you guys. Did you miss me?" the agent joked. The officer and the mind reader could do little other than laugh.

"Guys, we got a little problem here," the agent said. He tried to sit up, but he could only do so with assistance. Both men were aghast. A screwdriver had lodged itself deeply inside the man's back, and blood leaked at an alarming rate around the wound.

The uniformed officer once again took charge. "We've got two problems. Number one—you're bleeding pretty good, and we've got to do something about that; and number two—we will freeze to death out here if we stay much longer. And, oh yeah, as good as the Syracuse PD is, it will be some time until we got more help. So, we're on our own. This is going to hurt but we can't move you with that in your back. I think we need to pull it out, plug the hole with handkerchiefs, pieces of my shirt, whatever, and move you inside until we can get some professional help. You guys game?"

Both men nodded yes which was much easier for Sampson to agree to than the agent. The agent knew he was in for even more pain than he felt now.

"All right, Sampson, hold him still. I'm going to pull this damned thing out and as soon as I do, I'll stuff this handkerchief in the hole. Then we pick him up by the shoulders and get him inside as quickly as we can. One thing, we've got to keep pressure on the wound while we're walking. Ready?"

Everyone agreed.

"Here we go."

Sampson braced himself against the agent's shoulders as the officer pulled as hard as he could on the screwdriver. It came loose with a sucking sound. The agent screamed and then mercifully slipped into unconsciousness. Blood spit forth and the officer applied the cloth to the skin slowing, but not stopping, the staunch of blood.

"Shit. That had to hurt like a son of a bitch," the officer uttered.

Sampson felt sick to his stomach and dizzy. He stood up, turned away and vomited. "That was the worst thing I have ever seen," he bellowed with the despicable taste of bile.

"Yup, not pretty. In my line of work, we see this sometimes. It's always awful but you get better at dealing with it. Look, we've got to get him inside. This wound is bad, and if he doesn't get to the hospital right now, he will die. I'm sure of that."

Adrenaline raced through the men as they hoisted the agent carefully to keep the compress on the wound. The snow pounded down at an alarming pace. At times when the wind subsided, they could see the terminal. All three men were freezing yet struggled on. It took nearly ten minutes to reach the jetway. They tugged and lifted the comatose agent up the stairs. Within a few minutes, they reached the warm confines of the terminal and placed the agent on the floor near the spot where this whole ugly event had begun almost two hours ago.

"Sampson, I'll go get help. But he needs a couple of things. First, get him warm; I don't know how. And get his feet elevated. I will be back as soon as I can." Somberly he added, "He did some brave stuff today. Tell him to hang on."

The cop dashed down the terminal, leaving Sampson by himself to tend to the gravely ill agent.

It dawned on Sampson that everything he needed could be found on the damaged aircraft. Once again, although this time without fear, he ran down the jetway of Gate 13. He searched for pillows and blankets, which were abundantly available. He moved again to the lavatory of the plane. With no time to recall his earlier feelings, Sampson scrambled for a stack of paper towels. Arms full, he ran up the incline of the jetway.

He found himself shivering as he moved and realized he was soaking wet from his adventure in the snow. Cold as he was, there was no time to think about it.

CHAPTER 10

January 11, 2:00 a.m.

Whisnant's limousine pulled into the White House, and he was moved with expert escorts to the outer chamber of the executive office.

The President came out immediately to meet with him. From the look on his sidekick's face, something was terribly wrong. Wiz also knew that this room was microphone equipped and everything they said was taped. It would not be safe to speak until they entered the President's private quarters.

'Wiz, I don't suppose you've heard yet. I've just been briefed. An attempt was made on Senator Grant's life tonight…"

Wiz heard little else. *Attempt* meant failure. He had never failed at anything.

"Apparently a bomb went off. Grant is okay, but others, innocent others, are dead. The bomb went off at the airport and that's all we know right now. Grant is sure to call a press conference. It should play nicely into his terrorist platform, don't you think? Wiz, I will be back in a bit. I want to discuss this with you further then."

The most powerful man in the world stormed out.

Wiz was flabbergasted. What had happened? With the

resources of the U.S. government at his disposal, it would take only a short while to get at the truth. He picked up the phone and placed a call to his secretary at home. She would gather what he needed while he pondered a solution to this problem. He didn't care what time it was.

Sampson hurried to the wounded agent. He was concerned. His color was poor and his breathing sounded raspy. With the agent flat on his back, Sampson used the pillows to elevate his feet. He took a stack of paper towels and as he gently removed the blood-soaked handkerchief, dabbed the area with the fresh towels. The wound still pumped out blood, but it was no longer gushing.

Sampson cleaned around the area as best he could and put a fresh stack of towels flush against the wound, applying light pressure. With his other hand he grabbed blankets and covered the agent as best he could. Task complete, all he could do was wait and hope. Sampson was struck that he did not feel death with this man. Maybe a good sign.

In a few minutes, the officer returned with two paramedics and a stretcher. They went right to work in a flurry of lifesaving activity that Sampson did not understand since he didn't sense or feel near fatal. He overheard the head paramedic say that "it would be close". The screwdriver did not seem to have hit any vital organs, but it was a deep wound, and the loss of so much blood draining from the wound was a grave concern. If they could get to the hospital for a rapid transfusion ("big if due to the snowstorm"), the agent stood a chance.

The ambulance started to amble through the packed snow.

"Let's go find the senator and his entourage. We all need to go downtown and figure this out, Mr. Sampson."

What exactly *this* would be, only God knew. Hours before this cabinet of curiosities, Sampson was staring down the bombshell,

Mr. Larry Regan's yummy girlfriend in the audience of another hit show. His safety zone. His cushy blanket. But this. It could render him six feet under. Underground and underneath the goddamned precisely packed snow. Nature was always calculating and perfect.

They headed back into the airport and were awestruck by the damage. Glass, blood, carnage everywhere. They kept walking and amidst the rubble, spotted the senator sitting in a chair. He was flanked by the two Secret Service agents and a modest army of local police.

"Senator, I'm afraid I am going to have to inconvenience you a little bit longer. I still have work to do here but you and I, your security guys, and Mr. Sampson have some talking to do. I'll give you all a break tonight, but let's meet at 8:30 a.m. in my office." He handed everyone a card with the address. "Please don't talk about this until we speak with everyone. I will have reservations made for you at the Marriott, courtesy of the City of Syracuse. I am also assigning two officers to each of you until this is sorted out. They will take you to the hotel shortly. See you in the morning."

Their escorts did arrive in no time, and they walked out of the remains of Hancock International Airport and into an army of squad cars. The senator and his guards crammed themselves into one car, while Sampson occupied the backseat of another car. For the first time, Sampson had a few moments to think through what had occurred in the past couple of hours. Forget trying to make sense of it. A fight over a newspaper, the police, a vision of death, a bomb, a gravely wounded agent, a destroyed airport. And he was a character in this plot?

He simply had to look down at his blood-soaked shirt to realize this was happening to him and in his world.

But the needlepoint pricked. He had seen death when he touched the senator. He had to solve for that, which had never happened to him before. Yes, he could see past and present, and sometimes future events, but never anything this extreme. And what of the physical aspect of these visions? The bleeding from the nose and mouth felt like it would swallow him into oblivion. And it may have if the agent hadn't iced his face and quenched his thirst with haste.

The vision was powerful. Far more than he ever felt during his performances or from casual contact with a stranger. It was almost unimaginable to be able to predict death.

The entourage arrived at the Marriott. A gentleman in a red jacket, wearing a badge that said "Barry - Night Manager", approached the first car and handed the officer several envelopes. At once, the cars moved toward the rear of the property and parked. After a survey of the empty lot, everyone was allowed to exit the cars. They were whisked in a side door and led to an elevator, which took them to the tenth floor.

A young, squarish-looking officer with sergeant's stripes spoke. "Senator, you and your assistants will be in this suite. Plenty of room and three bathrooms. Mr. Sampson, you will be in this room, which you should also find comfortable. It's now 2:30 and we must leave at 7:45. So, you won't get much sleep. Make that REM count! There are bathroom kits in the room. Some of you could use some new clothes, particularly you, Mr. Sampson. If you would just write down what you need, we'll do what we can to find it. We'll be out here tonight. That's it. See you in a few hours."

Everyone left for their rooms as good soldiers. But what of tomorrow? What would they wake to, if the grace of shuteye came?

Sampson wrote down his needs and passed them to an officer before entering the hottest shower of his life. He had been chilled to the bone, and there was something that felt uncannily pure about scrubbing the blood from his arms and chest with scalding hot water. About five minutes into the shower, Sampson felt fatigue creeping over him. He turned off the shower, toweled off, set the alarm on his phone, and fell into a sleep as deep as a coma.

At 6:30, the alarm assaulted the whole of Sampson. He rose and was surprised to find a stack of fresh clothes next to the television. A pair of khakis, a button-down shirt, blue cashmere sweater, tube socks, a new pair of Reebok tennis shoes, and a green Ralph Lauren peacoat. Everything one might need in Syracuse in the dead of winter.

At 7:30 sharp, everyone was ushered into a waiting police van and began the short journey to headquarters. To everyone's surprise, the day was beautiful—10°, but sunny and no wind! The snow was a glorious white and glistened as the sun reflected upon it. Several feet of snow must have fallen.

Sampson scoured the van and was amazed at the fatigue showing on the faces of the senator and his guards. He wondered what he looked like but did not really want to know the answer.

As they arrived at an impressive steel structure, the Syracuse Public Safety Building, the van emptied, and all the passengers walked through a narrow, brightly lit corridor. The air inside smelled stale. The temperature was comfortable though. They were led to a comfortably furnished conference room with a long, mahogany table positioned neatly in the center. At the head of the table was the uniformed officer dressed in the same clothes as they had seen him in last night.

"Hi everybody, let's all grab a seat. There's coffee over there," he said, gesturing to his right. "All right. Well, it's good to get the band back together." Everyone chuckled. "Let's start at the beginning. We never did get to do formal introductions last night. My name is Sergeant Rich O'Reilly. I am a detective as well as a sergeant, and this is officially my case. I will tell you upfront that I don't think any of you are involved in causing what happened last night, or this would be unfolding in a very different manner.

Mr. Sampson, let me tell you what I know about you: thirty-four years old, never married, college education, and you have a small-scale entertainment gig. You read minds, they say. Never much believed in that supernatural stuff myself, but you make an okay living based on your tax returns. How's that for you?"

"Pretty good. But it's not really supernatural," Sampson said in a deadpan voice.

"Yeah, uh huh. We'll see. Okay. Next, Senator Grant: fifty-five years old, married for thirty years, with a twenty-seven-year-old daughter, an attorney who is unmarried. You are the front runner for the Republican Party nomination for President. The polls look good for you. Very good, in fact. And last but not least, Agent Carroll and Agent Grasse. Secret Service assigned to protect the senator. Long-term Secret Service. Probably thought this would be an easy assignment. You both check out fine. How's that?"

Agent Carroll responded, "Good, sir."

"Okay, so I am doing good. And guys this is with no sleep. You should see me when I'm rested. In fact, I bet you will."

He continued, "Last night was a disaster. Four people were killed; twenty-seven injured, five critical. One is a cop. That makes it personal to me. The CIA agent is critical. Lost tons of blood. He can't talk but I did put a call in to his superiors. Should hear something today. Time for me to stop talking and for me to listen."

He glanced at Sampson. "Sampson, this started with you. Tell me what happened and spare no details. All right, brother?"

Sampson swallowed some lukewarm coffee that tasted like motor oil. He looked at O'Reilly. "Hey, this is good. It does the trick. Wakes you the fuck up. Starbucks has a lot to worry about."

O'Reilly shot back, "Enough comedy."

Sampson got serious. "I finished a show last evening and came to the airport to catch a flight back to my home near Washington. I walked into the boarding area and realized I had nothing to read. I was going to buy a paper but spotted a leftover paper on a table across the way. I did not recognize the senator. I went to tap him on the shoulder to ask if this was his paper and just as I did, I felt like an NFL running back near the goal line. I went down hard."

The officer interrupted. "Accurate, gentlemen?" He glared at the agents. They both nodded in agreement.

"We scuffled. I lost. You showed up, and at some point, I remember shaking the senator's hand. As I touched it, it was like a lightning storm in my head. Green lightning, and I saw a skeleton… but it wasn't all there. I felt death. I felt the senator would die soon. That's all I remember. I went black. And I remember waking up with blood coming out of my nose and my mouth. And I was so thirsty. The agent we saved last night was putting ice on my face. The bleeding stopped and my strength came back, and the rest you know. We found the bomb."

"Senator, your turn."

The senator was all business. "Little to add. I made a speech at the university and was on my way back to Washington. I have already apologized to Mr. Sampson. We made an honest mistake as he reached for the paper."

The lieutenant liked this man; he could have blamed the agents. That would have been easy. He stood up for his guys, used the word 'we', shouldered the blame. In truth, the agents had screwed up. Sampson should never have gotten that close to the senator, O'Reilly reasoned. This man would be a good leader. He'd have to remember him at election time.

O'Reilly chimed in, "Senator, not great news for you. I'm pretty sure you were the target. Light load expected on the flight. No one famous, no one rich. I'm pretty sure you were the target. It was also professional. We found a baggage handler dead in a closet. His keys were gone, and he was naked except for his shorts. The killer took his uniform and got on the plane; put a big fucking bomb in the bathroom, which we found, as you know. If that plane had been anywhere near on schedule you, senator, would be toast."

The room was stonily silent as everyone realized how close they had come to death. No one had connected the dots until now, and the realization horrified them.

"There is one piece that doesn't fit. Why was a CIA agent watching all this unfold from the background?"

"I can help with that answer." Behind them a slight man with a noticeable limp had quietly entered the room.

CHAPTER 11

John Whisnant was seated in the private quarters of the President of the United States. He was sipping coffee as Austin Feeney stepped into the room and closed the door behind him. No words were exchanged as Austin crossed the room and poured himself a cup of decaf.

Satisfied with the taste, Austin spoke first. "So, what happened?"

"You won't believe this, we've got reports a psychic found the bomb," Whisnant uttered.

"Huh? You've got to be kidding? That's hysterical." The President laughed under his breath.

"Austin, I'm telling you that's what we know so far. Supposedly some pissant little sideshow act 'felt' the bomb and the locals got it off the plane."

"When will you know more?"

"Soon. The locals are interrogating right now. But it doesn't change the obvious. We failed. I failed. There's no risk. They won't find anything to tie us to this. The important thing is what do we do now. The polls have Grant beating you. It is down to you and him, and there is no third choice. I think we still have to eliminate him as a threat."

"Maybe." Feeney had a devilish grin on his face.

The man with the limp moved into the room toward an empty chair. "Sargent, please excuse my interruption."

"Christ, this is a circus, but if you can help with this case, it is not an interruption. Sit down. Tell me your story."

"Yes. My name is Dr. David Ellison. I am a Doctor of Medicine and a research scientist with CIA. In fact, I have run for a long period of time, a project, highly classified and very well-funded, that has to do with the… well, the… paranormal."

"Uh, doc, could we try and put this in English?" the sergeant insisted.

"Yes. So sorry. We are working with the science of the mind. It is intricate, you know. But we have made some amazing progress."

"Doc, I'm sure there is a point here, somewhere?" The sergeant was now becoming annoyed.

"Yes, yes, there is," the little man fumbled. But he remembered no man could tower over his intellect, certainly not some foul-mouthed, cliché cop. "You see, we have developed chemicals, or formulas if you will, that allow the brain to change somewhat. Our goal was to work toward enhancing brain capacity. It was all very clinical, and we weren't quite sure where the road would lead us. About ten years ago, we stumbled upon a combination of chemicals that allowed the brain, in some unexplained fashion, to act as a receptacle for the thoughts and visions of others."

The room was dead silent. Everyone was on the edge of their chairs, and no one dared to move, least of all Sampson.

"Mr. Sampson, you were, or rather are, a part of our program. About five years ago, you were a CIA operative. You were recruited into our program; you volunteered along with eleven other men who met our criteria. We injected a… well… cocktail into your brain, as well as the others'. A miracle occurred. Each of you could read the thoughts of others. Not every thought but many of them. We studied you, our experimental group, for weeks, and the progress was remarkable. The ability to read others' thoughts grew stronger day by day. We were all so happy, until one day one of our subjects was reading another's thoughts, and things went horribly wrong."

"What went wrong, doctor?" This time it was Senator Grant who interjected. O'Reilly scowled at the senator to remind him he would do all the questioning.

After hearing the assessment of what his life had constituted over the past several years, Sampson could no longer feel his face. It was weightless. Not comprised of real human matter, it seemed. Though he scrambled to find it in his rattled mind, he had no basis to object or deny what he had just heard. He didn't remember volunteering for any program of the sort, but his endurance training and always living on the edge of the next phenomenon had kept him above normalcy. *Sampson, you did this to yourself, didn't you?* he drilled silently.

"That subject was able to read too deeply and seemed unable to let go of the other's thoughts," Dr. Ellison continued in the low voice of a campfire storyteller. "The subject convulsed. You could see bulges protruding from his head. Quite grotesque. They would pop out and pop back in. Within seconds, the subject began profusely bleeding from the mouth, nose, and ears. He died almost instantly. We found out in an autopsy that his brain had grown to twice its normal capacity. Literally, at the end, his brain had exploded inside his head."

The men grimaced.

"Hold up, doctor. What cocktail of mindfuck are we talking about? What is mixed in with Sampson's brain mush?" the sergeant queried.

Dr. Ellison weighed his options. Let the cat out of the bag to a few losers with the IQ of a gnat who wouldn't be able to understand anyway or perhaps tell Sampson in private. After consideration, no one deserved to be let in on his coveted book of secrets. "I'm not at liberty to say, sergeant. Of the eleven men that we started with, nine followed the same path within days. We tried to stop this. We did; we really did, but we were unsuccessful. Nine men, young men…" The doctor looked down and shook his head back and forth in a frenzy. "I take the blame for this."

"Doctor, two men are unaccounted for," O'Reilly pressed. Who would "volunteer" for such a program? What was in it for them? "I call bullshit—"

"*Please* let the doctor finish," Sampson pleaded. The sergeant stepped back and pouted like a toddler.

"Yes, well, one is at a private institution. He also suffered a ruptured brain but did not die. There is not much of the man left. The other, well, Mr. Sampson, is you."

"Doctor, who funds this research project? Why am I just hearing about this now?" Senator Grant quipped.

"The men who died were CIA operatives. It was quite simple to tell their loved ones that they died LOD… in the line of duty. The risk is expected and anticipated in that line of work. As for the funding, various government agencies contribute; some knowingly, others… well… with a budget as big as the government's, it's not hard to find the money. Elements of the stories you hear about the government paying $1,000 for a toilet seat are true. It's a way to hide the truth about where money is going. At the end of the day, no one questions the CIA. Too risky. Too much to fear."

Sampson said, "Doctor, assuming you are telling the truth, why am I alive?"

"Hmm, sheer luck I suppose. As we realized what was happening, and how quickly it was happening, I decided to try various protocols to stop the process. But I am afraid it was like throwing darts at a dartboard. We had no facts; just educated guesses. You were given another experimental drug. One which wipes out all memory in your brain. Much like amnesia might.

You retain all your motor functions such as talking and walking, but you lose all memory of the past—friends, family, lovers. My thought was, if you could forget that you had this ability to read others' thoughts, maybe your mind would relax, and this crisis would pass. And thank God it worked. You did forget everything, for a while anyway." Sampson gasped. "You won't like this part, Mr. Sampson. We then spent months, through various psychological techniques, slowly implanting a false past into your brain. You have no memory of your real past. Everything you remember was built for you at CIA. Cruel, I am sure you think, but it was the only way we could give you a life back."

"You mean I am something you created? You stripped away my real life and gave me another reality you thought would be nice? I'm not an avatar, a machine, a bot..." Sampson was on the verge of panicking, falling under the load of everything in the past twenty-four hours like the weight of all the Apex Regional Landfill was threatening to suffocate him.

"Yes, I am afraid so. But it was done with honorable intentions. Nine of your colleagues died horrible deaths. It seemed the best alternative at the time. Mr. Sampson, I will remind you, you consented to this. 'I did not want to keep you locked in a laboratory forever. We decided to complete the mental programming; wipe out current memories—everything to do with this project—and implant a goal into your brain to encourage you to be a mental performer, a psychic if you will, but a psychic with little ambition to reach the heights and notoriety of, say, a David Copperfield. In other words, we wanted you to use your talents, but not in a way that might call attention to yourself. And that has been working well until recently. You don't know this, but all your shows have been attended by CIA. I have been to most; disguised, of course. You have been followed and watched twenty-four hours a day since you left my care."

"That explains the CIA spook at the airport. I knew he didn't just happen on this." O'Reilly had been right. He beamed with pride.

The doctor continued, "You are right. Agent Becker was doing his job. As we have watched your shows the past few months, Mr. Sampson, we have grown alarmed that we are seeing an uptick in your ability to read. Initially you seemed able to see only superficial information. That level of depth has grown. From what I have heard of last night I am now most concerned. Your ability to 'see' is growing. And with that, I am also afraid your personal risk is growing. This is the pattern we saw with the others."

O'Reilly said, "So, what Sampson saw last night wasn't an accident. It was a result of this testing you've been doing on humans."

"Yes and no, sergeant. I accept full responsibility for what happened. We, or rather I, thought what we were doing was totally safe. I was wrong, and I have lived with the death of those young men on my conscience since it happened. I can't change the past, but I accept responsibility for it."

"Yeah, that's a sad song, doc, but where do we go from here?"

Dr. Ellison walked over and rested his hand on Sampson's shoulder. "I need to take Mr. Sampson back to CIA and my laboratory. We need to determine a way to minimize his visions. We must not let them escalate."

"Guys, I'm jumping in here," Sampson asserted. "Since it is me we're talking about, I'd like to have some say. I want to find out about my real past. Not what you've planted in my head. And I have no desire to be experimented on. I will go with you, but I will not be a prisoner. I will come and go, and leave, as I see fit. Those are my terms."

"Accepted," said the doctor. "This entire conversation must stay among us for purposes of national security. I'm sure you all understand the risk should the press get a hold of this."

The interrogation lasted another three hours. At that point

Sergeant O'Reilly was convinced that no one in this room had anything to do with the bombing. No further information could be gathered.

"All right folks, you are all free to go. Use some caution. Senator, this bomb was meant for you, babe. Don't be sure whoever did this won't try again, and soon. I suggest you be real careful. Mr. Sampson, thank God you showed up last night. You saved many lives, and you should be proud. You also showed great courage in helping find the bomb. You, sir, also have another issue. I don't know if you saw the morning papers, but the *Post Standard* reported that a psychic saved the day. The press are everywhere and want to meet you."

"No." The doctor halted the conversation. "We must go now and work on this problem while we can."

Senator Grant said, "Sampson, I want to say thank you again. You saved my life, and I am very grateful." They briefly shook hands. "I'd like to have you out to dinner. Would it be okay if I called you?"

"Sure, sir, I'd like that." *What the hell, new and powerful buddies*, thought Sampson.

They exited the room with caution before trailing off in pairs.

In the White House, the two friends reached the conclusion that Senator Grant must be eliminated. His challenge for the Presidency was just too large, and they could not risk losing that at any cost—human or otherwise.

"Wiz, let's get this done! The miss in Syracuse cost us a couple of points for sure. No second chances this time." The President's face became hard, and with a stern look, he said, "It was also stupid for you to have done this yourself. Too much damned risk."

Wiz did not take kindly to any sliver of criticism. However, it was up to him to set the record straight. He boiled inside, but he couldn't exactly pulverize this man in front of him. Wiz breathed evenly until he was calm. "We won't need another chance. I'll give you the details in the next couple of days. Sit back and enjoy the show, pres."

The President had no choice. "Fine. I've got some things to do, which will get us some of those points back."

CHAPTER 12

Sampson and Dr. Ellison boarded a flight from Rochester to Washington, D.C. They had learned that the blast from last night's explosion had left a crater forty feet deep in the main runway. The FAA had closed the airport indefinitely. Rochester was the closest major airport. Two more people had died from the blast than originally reported to the police. Only pieces of bodies had been found. They believed they were baggage handlers. It would be hard to be sure.

Sampson didn't know how much to hate Ellison. If everything had been true, and he had volunteered, that would take some of the blame off Ellison. His initial impressions of the doctor were positive. He hesitated and lightly touched the doctor's hand. The doctor did not object. He could see his thoughts… genuine concern, remorse, unhappiness.

"I do not blame you for verifying the truth with your gift." The doctor's words caused Sampson to jerk back to reality. "I hope you know now I am telling the truth. I want to fix this mistake. I can't change the others."

"Doctor, tell me what we will do."

"Inside the Pentagon is my laboratory. It's small. I'd like to start as soon as we land."

"I can't. I've got a show tonight."

"I know."

"What do you mean, you know?"

The doctor smirked. "I mentioned that we were watching you. We also controlled your shows, or should I say, the bookings of the show. Your agent is an agent. We cancelled today's show."

"Shit." Sampson chuckled. All this was simply unreal. He was thirty-four years old. Did he have a family? If not, how could he have kids and keep them out of danger? His musings were getting strange now. *I can't have a fucking family with this bizarre reality!...But I want kids.* "Shake it off, man," he whispered to himself.

Dr. Ellison was not without compassion. But for the most part, he led a life of intellect and research. The book of emotions had been closed in his undergrad days after a soured relationship with a cute party girl who never studied. "Mr. Sampson, we didn't want you to get big and famous. Too much risk. We only booked you in small spots and some really out of the way. You did get calls for bigger shows, but we said no. I am sorry."

°So, you controlled my livelihood also? I never understood why I couldn't go big."

"You will always have your needs taken care of. We needed to study you in a controlled environment." Ellison was genuine in his words. But where would all this lead? If Sampson cared for luxury before, he didn't know it. His middle-class bills had always been paid.

The plane arrived in Washington. They were met by a limousine driver and headed straight to the Pentagon. The experience was surreal for Sampson. But he was frightened of death, and he knew he had been close last night. He must get at the truth. That notion consumed his thoughts.

Senator Alan Grant boarded a flight from Griffiss Air Force Base later that afternoon. The plane had been sent by the President of the United States, who politely expressed his sorrow for what had happened last night and wished his opponent well. Grant knew this was a political ploy, but there was no graceful way out and frankly, the private aircraft was a comfort to be welcomed right now. He called and thanked the formative opponent while sipping on his complimentary Johnnie Walker Blue. He was glad to be able to collect himself over a stiff one before landing, hopping in a limo and being met with his wife's emotional interrogation.

She squeezed him tightly for a long time. "That really scared me, Alan."

"I know, me too. I am in the mood for a hot bath, a beer and a nap. Care to join me?"

"Hmm. Best offer of the day." They headed into the house holding hands.

There would be no bath or beer for the Secret Service. They had almost lost a man last night, which was a cardinal sin. They would meet to review the incident and strengthen their go-forward plan. They held no illusions that this would not happen again. They were trained to expect it, and they respected their training.

O'Reilly found his way over to Community General Hospital and was shocked to see the CIA agent sitting up and eating red Jell-O. "How's that taste?"

"Like shit but after yesterday, I thought I'd never taste again. So, I guess it tastes good." "We never did formally meet. I'm Sergeant Richard O'Reilly. Syracuse PD."

"Yeah, I could tell by the flat feet." They chuckled. "I'm Bob Becker. CIA."

"Tell me something I don't know. We learned a lot while you were napping."

"Napping? Is that what you call it in this Podunk town." The comment was made with a huge smile, and clearly meant to be funny, not biting.

"You know it's hard to be a sheriff in Podunk." It was obvious the two men enjoyed each other's company.

"Sheriff, I want to say thank you. I heard you and your side-kick from the psychic hotline dragged my sorry ass back. The doc says it saved my life."

"Too much paperwork if you died. It was easier to drag you back."

"Yeah, uh huh. Well, thanks anyway."

The sergeant hated to end the banter, but he needed to make sure he collected the final pieces of the case information. "We had the pleasure of meeting Dr. Frankenstein… I mean Ellison, and he filled us in on the laboratory of horrors. How much of this do you know?"

"Most of it, maybe all of it. I know this though, the doc is a good guy, a solid citizen. He fucked up and he knows it. More than that, he accepts his responsibility. He really thought there was no risk… not that his superiors gave him much of a choice."

Questions and fragmented answers filled their space, and O'Reilly learned little else. He was glad to see that Becker would be okay and in fact, was healing way ahead of schedule. He hoped they would have the opportunity to meet again.

Sampson and Ellison were whisked through the gates and the security of the Pentagon. They parked in an underground lot and walked briskly to a set of metal doors. Ellison passed a card through a reader and a voice sounded, "State your full name for voice verification."

"David Jefferson Ellison."

"Access accepted."

The door clicked open, and they passed into a brightly lit, slender tube of a hallway.

Sampson noticed security cameras trained on them, moving with precision as they moved.

"Security is pretty good here, as you might expect."

They reached a door and once again, Ellison swiped his card, and again the voice, only with a different message. "Dr. Ellison, welcome. Please place your index finger on the screen for identification." Ellison did as he was told, and the door clicked open.

The laboratory was like something from "Star Wars": computer screens blinking, ten or more men sitting at terminals banging madly at keys. And in the center was a screen like you would find in a movie theatre. The main room appeared to be connected to a series of smaller rooms. Each contained its own windowless metal door.

"Sampson, I'm sure you are tired, but it is very important that we start right away. The room on the right is an ordinary examination room. We'll start there with blood pressure, heart rate. I expect to find nothing, so that will be quick. Once we complete, we'll move to Phase II."

"Doc, from my point of view you must know this is all a bit surreal. I'm not sure, but I think I should hate you." Sampson stretched out his long, taut arms above his head to feel the muscles pull. He needed a way to relieve the tension escalating. He was now deep into some bizarre world behind locked doors that he had no way of breaching if the shit hit the fan. No mental or physical strength he took pride in having. Sampson had no choice but to trust the doctor and cooperate, so at least he could see the sunshine at some point today. His Hebrew name meant "sun" after all!

"Perhaps you should. But right now, let's focus on you. I want to make sure we control this power before it's able to control you. After that you can hate me if you so choose."

The physical exam was completed in three hours. Whatever the cocktail had done to alter Sampson's mind, it had not changed his physiology in any detectable way. At least none he had found so far. The doctor pronounced Sampson "healthy". It was time to start to understand more fully what Sampson was capable of.

"Sampson, tell me about your powers. Start as far back as you can remember. Tell me everything. Every detail is very important."

"I don't remember exactly when it started and up until yesterday, it was all pretty tame. It is almost as if I can intercept others' thoughts. Sometimes I must concentrate to get them, and at times, not. I find the thoughts come easier and more quickly if I touch something they've touched or stand where they've been. The clearest pictures come when I touch them, or even just lightly brush their hand. It's almost like an avalanche of information and pictures coming at me. I sometimes really have to concentrate to break apart the images to make sense of them."

"Tell me about yesterday."

Sampson hesitated. "That is a tough one. I had a very good show in Syracuse. Visions came easily and I caught a good audience. When I checked in at the airport, I accidentally touched the hand of the woman who checked me in, getting some personal thoughts, intimate thoughts…"

"Perk of the job, huh?" laughed Dr. Ellison.

"Yes, it does come in handy with beautiful women." They both laughed. "Anyway, you've heard what happened. I touched Senator Grant and I saw death, a skeleton; missing limbs; flashing light, or maybe it was lightening; a green flash of color. But more than the usual, I felt death, or maybe it was danger. It was powerful. I felt sick and then I think I blacked out. I woke up. I remember blood coming from my nose and mouth. I was lightheaded. Someone gave me a drink. I was very thirsty. That helped, and someone put ice on my face. I felt better. Faster than I thought."

"Okay, go on. Once you felt better, then what?"

"Not much. We went to find the bomb."

"What led you to the plane?"

"Don't know. I felt a… hmmm… I didn't realize it then, but I knew the threat was there, felt it was there."

"Have you been able to do this before?"

"I don't think so."

Dr. Ellison cusped his miniature hands and took a deep breath. "As we guessed, your abilities are growing. I might as well tell you what I suspect and give you some history. I am afraid this will not be pleasant. Your colleagues went down a similar path, although it happened much more quickly than with you. Their powers grew, and it's almost as if the human body can only take so much. The risk, you see, is that you see something powerful, and can't let the vision go in time. The longer you see it and the longer you focus on it, the more it damages your body. That causes the bleeding. The bleeding is what killed your friends. What we have to do is focus on figuring out how to make sure you can let go when you need to let go. Sounds easy, but nine strong men were not able to do it. The visions are strong, and it seems like they are compelling—almost like a good dream that you don't want to end. Trouble is, if you don't end it at a certain point, it will kill you. The trick is how to end it. That we must work on together."

"Doc, how is it that I recovered so quickly?"

"You are strong, and you naturally heal quickly."

"I sense there is more."

"Yes. And we'll get to it at a later time. But none of this does any good if you can't let go in time. And the stronger the vision, the harder it is to let go."

"Can you help me with that?"

"Oh, I think so. We have some techniques that worked before. The next couple of days will be important. First, though, you must rest. We have a small apartment in the next room for you. A shower, couch, fully stocked refrigerator, TV. Everything a man could need or want, and all courtesy of Uncle Sam. Relax today and sleep well tonight. We will start at 8:00 a.m. tomorrow."

CHAPTER 13

The evening edition of the *Syracuse Herald Journal* told the same story as the *New York Times* and the *Boston Globe*. At latest count, eighteen people had died in the blast at Hancock International Airport. The blast had been heard five miles away. Every agency was involved in trying to solve the disaster and not one clue existed. Only two things seemed to be certain: Alan Grant, senator from Maryland, and very likely the next President of the United States, seemed to be the target; and an unknown psychic had saved the day. On the front page of each paper was an enormous photo of Sampson. He was being labeled a modern-day superhero.

The release of the story caused panic with those in the know. The CIA knew they now had a problem. An experiment on a man had given him powers. This could never be allowed to get out. Worse yet, Sampson would now be a target by many foreign governments and fringe groups looking to exploit his talents. This could be dangerous for the United States and Sampson.

The whole mess was dumped in the lap of Steve Etkind, a sector head with the CIA. Dr. David Ellison reported to Etkind, but rarely did the two meet. Etkind was trained as a field agent and that was his passion. This laboratory stuff was of no interest to him. He had indeed received a promotion to sector head not long after his predecessor was blamed and took the fall for the death of the nine agents assigned to Dr. Ellison. He did not like or dislike Ellison; he just had no interest in his work at all. He hoped within a year to be out of this job and into a bigger job closer to fieldwork. He felt Ellison's work offered him no upside and substantial risk. But this would be visible upstairs and, if handled smoothly, could accelerate a promotion. This would be reason enough to watch him like an eagle.

John Whisnant was plotting his next move. His years of competitive athletics had taught him that some days you just don't get the breaks. But he also knew that the senator must now be eliminated and quickly. The press would be kind to Grant for a period, and with the elections closing in, he and Feeney couldn't afford this opponent to be on the field much longer.

As he drove down the boulevard in his sleek gray Jaguar XJU, he became excited as he realized how powerful he had become. He was the number two man in the free world. He had dated models and actresses, along with his boss. Being single and in this position had its benefits. And all the women had a spark, but the best, without a doubt, were the professionals. They were uninhibited and would do things the models couldn't even think of. He decided when he was done with his meeting that he would phone his old friend, Binky. Binky managed fifteen of the most pristine and expensive professional women in the business. Binky was always glad to accommodate a high-ranking government official. He knew at some point that there was a chip he could cash. And the businessman in him saw the motivation that his girls felt when given the option of fucking a celebrity. After all, the girls were like everyone else. Spending time with a celebrity was exciting. And while the girls would never talk about any action outside of their own intimate group, they loved to talk among themselves. These were the professionals who worked five days a week and made a quarter million dollars a year—tax free. The tricks were safe, and no funny stuff allowed. The clientele, only the rich and famous. Binky had been brokering high-class whores for five years and had never had an incident. He was convinced he never would. Wiz remembered all the details Binky had shared and could not help but think this was a solid business.

Wiz reached his destination—a stunning five-bedroom home in a posh section of Washington. He parked and rang the doorbell. Within seconds, he was greeted by a well-built man with a crew cut. "Colonel, nice to see you."

"Wiz, it's been a while."

Wiz had known Colonel Bob Cates for several years. They had met casually at a social event and developed a professional relationship. Cates had been a Navy Seal and highly decorated. He had led a small team that eliminated 'problems' the U.S. was having with small, misbehaving nations. He retired as a full colonel at age forty-five and was now doing private work for the U.S. government and, Wiz believed, others. Cates could be trusted.

"What can I do for you Wiz?"

"Bob, it's a big one. I'm sure you are familiar with Senator Alan Grant?"

"Huh… kind of hard not to be."

Wiz detected a slight drawl he had not noticed before. "Yes, he is gaining some notoriety that we are not thrilled with. Bob, we really wish he wasn't such a good competitor. Thought you might be able to help us with that?" There was no need to come out and be specific. Both men knew the game and the score.

"I assume you would be in a hurry?" Both men continued the charade. "Soon is good."

Cates reached down to a small pad and wrote "\$1.0M Cayman National XJ21602".

Wiz scanned and memorized the information. Cates lit a match and burned the small piece of paper.

"Colonel, nice to see you. Perhaps we could have dinner?"

"Sure, call me."

Neither man had any intention of eating with the other, but it was a convenient way to end the meeting and part amicably.

Wiz left pleased. The job would be done and done well.

Cates immediately moved to action, which was his way. He grabbed his burner phone. A man answered the phone.

"Yup."

"Jimmy B. You have a very fine set of phone skills," he said sarcastically.

"Ah, Colonel, only the best for you." Both men chuckled.

"I am assuming this is not a social call, and you know we are not in a secure situation," Jimmy B stated.

"Roger that." The colonel catching himself slipping back into combat jargon. "Here is what we need. Three dogs and a trainer; pure breeds; good night vision. And soon, say twenty-four hours. I understand an order like this will be expensive. Is it doable?"

"Sure, Colonel. I will pick the dogs myself."

"Outstanding. Let's meet at MH 1800 hours in two days." The code was well understood by both men.

"Roger that."

With that, the call concluded. The colonel knew Jimmy B would come through. He was very good. Also a Navy Seal, he was the prized lieutenant of the best commando team to serve under Cates. They had formed a very strong personal and professional relationship during their service together. Both had deep respect for one another.

Cates's request had been simple enough. Three mercenaries, with strong talent and capable of working effectively in the dark. They would meet at the Marriott Hotel, which was a prearranged point at 6:00 p.m. in two days. Not much time. Not much time at all. Just the way Cates liked it.

CHAPTER 14

Wiz drove straight to Binky's residence and place of business. Binky's was not a bar or a hotel as one might expect. Instead, it was an apartment building with secluded underground parking, eighteen units in the building. A two-man private security force would meet all visitors (as well as dissuade any unwanted visitors) and stood at the ready as the elevator doors opened.

"Hello Mr. Whisnant," a burly-chested and muscular man in his thirties uttered.

"Hi, Peter. I'd like to see Binky."

"No problem, I'm sure. Let me check." The men slipped into a doorway off to the left.

Waiting for the man to return allowed Wiz to reflect on the magnitude of the business that Binky ran. Each of Binky's girls had their own apartment. Each unit was a two-bedroom. One bedroom was their own; the other is where they entertained. The apartments were theirs free of charge as long as they worked for Binky. Most girls would work five or six years and retire. Most retired very wealthy, and young enough to find a mate that they could love and raise families with. These were all college-educated women—smart, bright, attractive, and expensive. Very expensive and worth it.

The door that the guard had entered suddenly opened and

a big man, 5'11", severely overweight, and sporting a full beard, waddled forward with his hand extended. "Wiz, nice to see you. Glad you could come by."

As they shook hands Wiz said, "It's good to see you. I thought we might chat a moment."

That was a signal routinely used by the clientele to signify they wanted to discuss the options that might be available to them.

Binky ran a well-scheduled house of ill repute. His 'girls', as he called them, would only work five consecutive days or nights. None of them was allowed more than two encounters a day. He required them to be fresh and rested at all times. As he told them, quality was mission critical. Men didn't want quantity; in fact, just the opposite. For most, one time was plenty. Each of the girls was schooled by Binky. Never once would he personally touch them, but every day they went to his 'school'. What was known to only Binky and his girls was that each room was equipped with a series of cameras and microphones. Every unique movement, every moan and every movement were captured on film. Each day, religiously, Binky would review what he called the 'game film' with the girl, and only the girl, involved in the act. They would discuss her performance. Binky would make suggestions and recommendations on how to improve. Both would assess the things that the gentlemen liked and disliked during the session. All this information was compiled and stored on a computer database by person. With each encounter, the profile was updated and improved. In the files were the likes, loves, and dislikes of 500 of the most prominent men from around the world.

Binky had had only two incidents that threatened his business in five years. One had been a congressman who drank too much and had trouble not talking about Binky's operation. That had cost Binky $110,000 to eliminate the problem. The congressman simply disappeared one day. Binky didn't know what had been done to him and didn't care to know. The problem vanished.

The other incident had involved one of the girls about a year ago. Jennifer was gorgeous as a tall, leggy, blond with an ample 36D chest. Very popular with the gentlemen, but one who questioned everything Binky did. In particular she loved to question, in front of the other girls, the salary he paid them. Slowly, she was turning harmony into an angry town meeting. He could not and would not tolerate this. One hundred thousand dollars later, her headless body surfaced in an alley. The head was never found, and probably the girls knew this had been the work of Binky. Not a pleasant thought, but sometimes everyone needed a reminder. Anyway, since then, no uprisings in the hen house.

Binky asked Wiz to take a seat in his office and through a side door, entered an anteroom with a two-way mirror that allowed him to look into his office without being seen while tapping the keys of his computer to pull up the file of John Whisnant. The file told him much about the sexual habits of John Whisnant. He had been here many times, and his range of sexual pleasure was broad. He preferred dark-haired, tanned women. Generally, he would stay only sixty to ninety minutes. Upon seed spilled, it was always a swift exit. Now, he had been known to be a bit rough at times with the girls, but no injuries left.

With that information, Binky matched the desires to who was available. Two good possibilities: Carolyn, a red-haired beauty; and Bryce, a black-haired knockout. Both were excellent in every way. Tough choice, but Bryce would be a better match. This was an important man, and Binky wanted to be sure he enjoyed himself. He phoned upstairs to Apartment 13.

"Hello Binky. Are you coming up?" the woman teased.

"No. I'd like to, but you've got work to do. Pull up John Whisnant on your screen, love.

He's important. How's fifteen minutes?"

"I'll be ready."

"He'll be there shortly. Have a good time."

Both parties hung up the phone. Binky closed his laptop and reentered his office.

"Good news, Wiz. Bryce is available. You've not spent any time with her, but you will find her irresistible, I'm sure. She's in 13. My fees have not changed. Wire the money to the normal location. I know you know your way around, so go now. You mustn't keep this beauty waiting."

"Thanks Binky. I'll see you later." With that, he headed upstairs to meet his fantasy for the day.

CHAPTER 15

Sampson and Dr. Ellison had worked for almost two days on a series of techniques designed to help Sampson break free of a vision at an appropriate time. It had all been theory, with no way to practice. Elements of his past—memories and skills—were beginning to come back. This was normal. Once a subject was informed of his past, the memory of things past often began to come back. No one fully understood the drug, but the doctor knew to expect this.

Without notice, Sector Chief Steve Etkind, Ellison's boss, burst through the doors.

"Doctor, I know we have not spent much time together. Don't take that to mean I think your work is unimportant. It is important." A lie but probably effective. "I am up to speed on this Sampson thing. I need you to get these visions under control. This could really help our government, as I am sure you have figured out. I want to be briefed daily; more often if necessary. Any questions?"

"Uh, no. I guess it's nice you're involved."

"Yes." He really didn't like this man. He was weak. "One other thing. Senator Grant wants Sampson at his house for dinner this Saturday night. You and I are going to make sure everything goes okay. A thank you for saving his skin, I suppose. I will pick up you and him on Saturday at 5:00 sharp. Issues?"

"No."

The mighty Etkind stormed out, and everyone could breathe again, especially the doctor. Etkind rattled him. The man was a creep.

Cates had spent the past two days learning everything he could about Senator Alan Grant.

Seemed like a nice guy. Cates had heard him make a speech where he denounced terrorism against the U.S. and vowed to fight back. Cates was impressed. But he knew he wouldn't be able to vote for him; he would be dead. With limited time for research, he focused on the basics. The only sure place to kill him on this tight timeline was at his home. He pulled out maps of the area and arranged for weapons. His basics covered, it was time to head out to meet the troops.

He checked into a suite under the name of George Isaac Joe, paid cash, and went to his room. He clicked on the TV while he waited. An old "Rockford Files" was on. He always liked Jimmy and Angel.

Promptly at 5:00, everyone showed up.

"Colonel, you haven't lost your sense of humor. G.I. Joe is how you check in these days." Jimmy B clearly thought this was funny.

"I try hard, Jimmy B." The two men embraced.

"Colonel, I would like to introduce you to three very fine men. The tall gentlemen there is Pat, this is Trevor, and this is Ben."

All the men extended their hands, and the colonel eyeballed them while shaking hands. His assessment was positive. All the men seemed physically fit, and he trusted Jimmy B and his judgement. There was always some element of risk in trust but there was no choice for this event.

"Gentlemen, I am Colonel Cates. This is my mission. Have a seat and I will give you the details."

The men filed in and were seated at a round glass dining room table. Cates positioned himself at one end and Jimmy B at the other.

"The target is Senator Alan Grant. The timeline is two days. Security on Grant is heightened due to the Syracuse incident. We will do the job at his house. We will do it at night. My goal is Saturday. I have all the road maps with me. One of you needs to sort out the best ins and outs."

"Pat, you take that," Jimmy B stated.

"Yes, sir," Pat said affirmatively.

The colonel went on, "Next, we need the blueprints for his house. Can't do it conventionally by stopping by Town Hall. We need to get them tonight."

"Trevor, that's yours," Jimmy B dictated.

"Aye, sir."

"Lastly, I need someone to meet tonight with an arms supplier. We'll need good equipment. Night vision scopes, rifles, and hand weapons; normal operational equipment I should think."

"Ben, by process of elimination, that's you." Jimmy B ordered.

"Yes, sir."

"Here is the number to call. He'll give you what you need and put the tab on my account." Clearly this impressed Ben, and that did not go unnoticed by the colonel.

"Jimmy B, you and I go out tonight on recon. I've got the stuff we'll need. We'll need to learn everything we can in just a few hours. Like the old days, huh, soldier?"

"Oh, yes, colonel. Oh yes." Both men smiled.

"Good, okay, let's hit it. We reconvene back here at 0800. Good luck, gentlemen."

The men spaced their departures to avoid any suspicion. The colonel and Jimmy B were the last to leave. They exited the Marriott and reached a black Ford Taurus the colonel had rented with false identification. Totally untraceable if need be.

"Jimmy B, I found a spot on the map to put the car. We'll have a half-mile hike in the woods to reach the edge of his property. It's a big house. Acres of property. Very secluded. Appears, from the maps anyway, to have lots of cover."

They made idle chit chat on the drive to the property. They arrived at 2130 hours and hid his car in the designated spot. In the trunk were camouflage fatigues, boots, gloves, face paint, infrared headgear, and two pistols with silencers, each with three clips of ammunition.

They suited up in silence, applied the face paint, and started the trek toward the house of Senator Grant. The night was cloudy and cool. The temperature in the forties. No moon visible, which was an added advantage. Cates estimated the trek to take an hour. The woods were thick. They would need to be very cautious. Even if it took longer, no matter. A mistake at this stage would jeopardize the entire operation. Cates would treat this as a life-and-death situation. They donned night gear, sophisticated infrared technology that allowed a person to have pretty good vision in the dark. It was a bit clunky to wear but the positives far outweighed the negatives.

With amazing stealth and with the aid of the compass, they moved deliberately through the woods. They came upon small animals as well as two deer out foraging for food on the cool night. The terrain was rough, but not as challenging as other places the two men had been in their career. They covered the distance in forty minutes and reached the edge of the clearing to the senator's estate.

Both men surveyed the property, Jimmy B utilizing only his headgear and Cates using infrared binoculars. Both men wore earpieces and while communication was to be kept to a minimum, it was available should they need it.

Even from 500 yards they had learned much already. No dogs; that would help. Two Secret Service agents visible guarding the perimeter of the house. Cates was certain they would find more. Following the close call in Syracuse, unless the Service was nuts, they would be overprotecting right now.

The two men split up. Cates heading right, and Jimmy B left. They agreed to regroup in this spot in two hours. In that time, they had discovered more in two hours than would be imaginable to an untrained soldier. Without a word they completed the trek back to the car in thirty minutes. Once certain no one was watching the car, they emerged from the cover of the woods, removed their camouflage, and started the journey back to the Marriott.

Trevor and Pat had already returned. Their work was spread out on the glass table for examination.

The group gathered around the table. "Gentlemen, let's start. Jimmy B and I learned a great deal. First off, good cover approaching the house. Relatively easy in-and-out access. Five hundred yards from clearing to house. Some cover; mostly maple trees. The yard is well-lit, particularly near the house. We counted two Secret Service on general patrol. We then split left and right. I found one more agent… interesting… he was in a tree. Night scope about midway between the house and the woods. I was able to see in the house; nothing special. I'll leave that to Trevor. Jimmy B?"

"Sir, one more guard on my side; general patrol. The alarm box was on my side. Fairly new unit: battery backup, so killing the power won't do it. Easy enough to take out though. Probably would need two minutes, no more."

"Trevor?"

"Sir, I have the blueprints. Standard house. Living quarters on the first floor. Full basement that is partially finished. Sleeping quarters upstairs. Six bedrooms."

"Good. Thanks soldier. Pat?"

"I have all the maps, sir. I will need more time to study them, but preliminary read is good. Multiple access points. Good mix of primary and secondary streets. Highway access within five minutes. Sir, I had time, so I located the local police station as well as the nearest state trooper barracks. The locals are twelve minutes away, and the state almost twenty. I saw a shift change with the locals. Looks like three cars. The troopers are only a small substation; probably only one or two cars anywhere near the house. No sheriff presence within thirty minutes."

"Superb field work, soldier." Cates was impressed with the initiative this man showed.

"Sir. We have what we need. Five Glocks, each with two clips. Two Browning rifles with night scopes, five military knives, five stun grenades, night goggles with infrared for all of us, full camouflage suits, boots, and night paint, communication gear. All appears to be in good shape. All, of course, untraceable."

"I bet you did some damage to my credit card."

"Significant, sir." He smiled as he uttered the words.

"Thank you, soldier, I'll remember that at Christmas."

Everyone laughed. The humor had broken the tension that had gradually built.

"We will spend the rest of the day getting ready. I am a stickler for detail. We will acquire the target on Saturday night. Not late; early evening, right as it gets dark. The Service won't expect that. I checked the senator's schedule through my sources and as best as I can tell, he will be home. If we find this to be untrue, we go on Sunday. Let's get to work, gentlemen."

CHAPTER 16

Sampson and Ellison spent Friday continuing to find ways to control the visions. Both had reached the conclusion that little could be done medically to limit the effects of the visions. Surviving any future incidents depended on Sampson simply 'breaking free' early enough to survive. This would be difficult to do, particularly facing very powerful visions. But they would practice for as much time as they had together.

Ellison had been surprised all along that Sampson was so cooperative. His life had been robbed from him, volunteership or not. He was aware of the fate of his predecessors and surely this weighed on his mind. Yet, he moved on. They were pleased much of his past memory was returning. Ellison knew that, over time, they would all return. Sampson seemed to view that as a gift; Ellison felt it was returning something to its rightful owner.

Sampson's ability to see beyond the normal continued to impress Ellison. Ellison wondered how much more the ability would grow. But mostly he wondered how he was going to keep Sampson alive. That dilemma became the source of his nocturnal panic attacks. This was his fault and his problem. He would not let another man die for his foolishness.

Friday would be a busy day for the good senator. He was rested and would be making his first appearance since Syracuse. He had deliberately stayed quiet and secluded since the incident; partly because he knew he had little to share with the press, partly because he had been shaken up by the incident and was cautious at this stage of the campaign to avoid any display of weakness to the American public.

The senator awoke refreshed, showered, and left the house for his office at 7:00 a.m.

Martin handed him a cup of coffee, and they started the dance. "Sir, big day. As you know, you have a major fundraising speech tonight at the Hilton. I'm almost done with the speech. You and I will review on the car ride over. I'll make sure it is brilliant!" Both men chuckled. Grant always liked the way his brainiac aide emphasized the word, *brilliant*, which was usually a few times a day.

"Thanks, Martin. You really do good work. As you know, I have asked Sampson to join me for dinner on Saturday. I was hoping you could join us?"

"Yes, sir. Thank you for asking." Martin felt honored… and eager. Since this campaign had ramped up, he was living on lukewarm meals in brown containers courtesy of every app imaginable.

"I'm also going to ask Susan to join us."

"Sir, it sounds like fun. I hope your daughter can make it."

"Yes, me too. *I don't see enough of her*," the senator whined in an exaggerated fashion.

The day flew by. It was impossible to run a campaign and be a senator. Grant hated the tradeoffs. Usually, his staffers would shoulder enormous burdens to allow him to campaign. He regretted this. There was no choice, however. But he would remember them if he made it to the White House.

Showtime arrived and they jumped into the limo. Dinner was planned for 7:30 and he wanted to be there to greet as many as he could at the fundraising dinner. He half-heartedly read over the speech, made a few changes, and pronounced to Martin that he was ready to go. Martin was always amazed at his ability to see a speech once and deliver it flawlessly. Charisma and memory. If only the campaign could operate on this alone.

They arrived and like an iRobot Roomba sweeping through the room, Grant moved to personally meet as many as he could. Everyone was struck by this genuineness. "A true man of the people," as the press called him. Politically he was considered a moderate. In truth he did as his heart told him to do. Unlike most in politics he had alienated very few. Even those who did not agree with his decisions admired his honesty, his dedication, and mostly, his caring attitude and behavior.

Grant continued to work the crowd. Though he never felt like he was "working" anyone. He felt as though he was meeting people, exchanging ideas, and almost always enjoying himself. He had not been in politics very long. Following his graduation from the U.S. Naval Academy, Grant had spent eight years as a fighter pilot. It was a peacetime stint with Grant never once actively involved in any real-time conflict situations. Many of his peers at the time regretted a lack of real combat, but Grant did not. He valued life and would use force only when necessary. Reaching his decision on how best to combat terrorism had been difficult for him. He preferred a more peaceful solution, but he knew no terrorist understood the word, *peace.*

Following his military stint, Grant had entered the workforce and taken a job in sales for Procter & Gamble. The job requirements ran parallel with Grant's skillset, and he was an instant success. Clients loved the young man, and within ten years, Grant was running the entire sales force for a large P&G division. Six years ago, a friend had suggested that Grant consider a run for a vacant senate seat in Maryland and contacted the Republican Party. They were interested, and everything was set in motion. To his disbelief, he won by a landslide, and resigned from P&G.

Grant attacked Washington much the way he had attacked P&G. Hard work and one customer at a time. His style and his success had paid off. In four years, he had earned a reputation that others might spend a lifetime trying to achieve. He had earned the national spotlight with his reform policies on the Welfare and Social Security Systems. His plans were aggressive but based on reality, and the American public as a whole had supported them. Alan Grant had veritably burst on the scene.

All fundraisers followed a pretty normal pattern. Filthy rich people and corporations paid an outrageous sum of money for the pleasure of a pretty average meal, which was almost always steak or chicken, and a cartload of cheap carbs. The food was a facade for an opportunity to hobnob with celebrities and politicians and network with peers. It was a chance to tell your friends you had dinner with a bigwig or a big-wig-to-be. Before dinner you would be welcomed by the person or company sponsoring the dinner. And of course, after dinner there would be a few warm-up speeches and then the big address.

It was now time for Grant to take the podium, and he was welcomed with thunderous applause. As things quieted down, he began to speak. "Ladies and gentlemen, I want to thank you for coming tonight. I know you all have families, and you are very generous to spend your time at this event tonight. I promise I won't keep you from your families long."

Martin smiled broadly like a proud mother from his seat on the dais. Three or four sentences and the audience was already in love.

"I have a wonderful speech prepared for this evening but at the risk of giving my aide, Martin, a heart attack, I'm going to call an audible and just speak from the heart."

Martin's smile stiffened. *Cameras, cameras, keep your cool!* He silently said to himself,

"No, senator. No audibles. Audibles are very risky. This campaign does not need any risk." While he was troubled, he never let it show on his face. There was nothing he could do to stop this, so he resigned himself to a roll of the dice.

"As most of you know, I was nearly killed a few days ago in Syracuse. Many others— mothers and fathers, sons and daughters—were killed. This was an act of terrorism; of that, I am sure. The site of the blood and carnage will never, ever leave my mind. Terrorism is an act of cowardice. As you know, I have introduced legislation to guide America in dealing with terrorism. If I am fortunate enough to earn this party's nomination for President and find myself elected, I want you to know I will work hard in this area. Several of my opponents believe terrorists should be dealt with gingerly. They use the word 'negotiate'. It is my experience that you deal with the class bully hard and fast or you will be tortured for a long, long, time.

Terrorists are no different than a class bully. Their mission is to take what they want, do what they want, and they don't care about our rules or, as we saw in Syracuse, they don't care about life. Unacceptable! Unacceptable! Unacceptable!"

As he said the words he pounded the podium, and the audience burst into applause. A chorus of approval that sang for several minutes.

"When I reach the White House, we will fund antiterrorist groups. We will seek out those who would hurt our citizens, and we will punish them. No matter when or where they are caught, they will be subject to our most severe penalties. Jail time will be long, parole rare. Capital punishment will be mandatory for the most serious crimes. We will also strike back at the terrorists. If we find conclusively that a country or a splinter group has caused pain to the U.S., we will strike back with force. I do not want to hurt innocent civilians, and I will do everything in my power to avoid that, but we must, must be aggressive in this area. Force is what they know. Negotiating is just a word with no meaning to them."

The adoring audience crammed for a spot in the palm of his hand, and he continued for fifteen more minutes on different topics.

Much to Martin's delight, Grant strayed very little from the original speech. But the effect of the spontaneity was enormous. He could see it in the faces of the audience, and he could hear it in their applause.

Following the speech and the handshakes, Grant sought out Martin. He knew his assistant's ego would be a bit bruised. "Martin, what did you think of the audible?"

"Sir, no more audibles. I nearly shit my pants." Both men laughed. "But as audibles go, it was good. No, it was very good."

CHAPTER 17

Saturday arrived in a flash for everyone. Wendy Grant began her shopping trip to the market early. Being a senator's wife meant lots of time alone. To pass the time, Wendy had taken many classes and over time, became a fabulous cook. What started as a hobby was becoming a wonderful and extravagant obsession. She spared no expense. Le Creuset and cases from every region of rosé all the way.

She knew they were expecting Sampson, a Dr. Ellison, Martin, Ellison's tough boss, Mr. Etkind, his wife, Sarah, and to her pleasant surprise, her darling daughter, Susan, was available and would also be attending. That made eight in total, counting them. She also knew there were five Secret Service agents protecting them, and she always made sure to have enough goodies for them. They were nice men and women, always showing her a soft side, and while she dreaded thinking about it, they risked their lives to protect Alan. So that meant thirteen in total, a pretty big, small dinner party. Perfect!

Wendy decided on a hearty menu to celebrate life. Her husband had almost died! Chilled shrimp with a spicy horseradish sauce and pepper brie as an appetizer, spinach salad with warm bacon dressing, Cornish game hens served with an apple stuffing, mashed potatoes, baby carrots and for dessert, Alan's favorite, hot

Southern bourbon pecan pie with a scoop of Haagen Dazs vanilla ice cream. Sounded like Thanksgiving to her. Perfect!

Susan had agreed to help with dinner and would arrive early this afternoon. Wendy found all the ingredients and returned home. While many would dread an afternoon of cooking, she couldn't wait. Couldn't wait to watch everyone stuff themselves. Couldn't wait for all the compliments. Her equally sentimental mother had taught her to be a dutiful wife that made sure every meal was nothing less than delicious.

The party was scheduled and rescheduled three different times to accommodate the senator's ever-changing calendar and availability. Finally, they agreed that a 5:30 p.m. start would be perfect for cocktails and hors d'oeuvres and dinner would begin promptly at 6:15. It would be chaotic for Wendy until dinner was served but with Susan at her side, she knew she could pull it off.

Cates and his men had completed their planning and were preparing to leave at 7:00 p.m. sharp. The men were mostly silent, each thinking through their assignment. Cates was proud of these men. They seemed sharp and he was convinced tonight would go letter perfect. He felt a rush of adrenaline as he thought about the evening. It felt good.

CHAPTER 18

The guests arrived on this chilly evening, and the house was filled with a tantalizing aroma from the food being prepared. One by one, Senator Grant introduced them to his wife and daughter. Sampson, Ellison, and the Etkinds were the last to arrive and all were greeted with great warmth by the senator.

"Mr. Sampson, our guest of honor, this is my wife, Wendy, and my daughter, Susan."

As Sampson reached to shake their hands, he was awestruck by the beauty of Susan. She looked to be in her late twenties, with wavy blond hair, and striking ice blue eyes under stylish, blocky Prada glasses. He felt himself smitten. He hoped she could see all of him clearly through those glasses, including his instant worship.

Sampson shook Wendy's hand and reached to greet Susan a bit clumsily. Knowingly and somewhat embarrassed by it, he concentrated a bit, wanting to find out more about her. He was surprised by what he sensed. She was attracted to him physically, which he could see in her face. Her thoughts revealed that she did not believe in the supernatural and that his claims of reading minds were phony. He let go and broke the connection. His curiosity had gotten the better of him and he was simultaneously ashamed and encouraged like a first crush. There may have been dozens, but with merely puzzle pieces of the past yet to line up, the concept of lust, love, even life was a fog lately.

Wendy moved everyone into a well-appointed, English country-like family room that smelled of fresh leather and wood. Flames greeted them from the fireplace.

Sampson found his way to a leather chair in front of the fire, sat down and nearly died of comfort. The leather was like butter.

Everyone munched on Wendy's edibles and drank with pure abandon. Life was happy and cozy. About a half an hour later, Wendy invited her guests into a swoon-worthy dining room.

After a series of celebratory toasts, the relaxed group dove into the feast. Wendy timed how long it took to receive a stamp of approval from one of her guests. Five seconds. First bite. A win. The habit of keeping track meshed with her OCD. Only her daughter knew how intense it was. She had experienced the brunt of it first in childhood with the most neatly packed lunchbox full of ribbons and colored packaging while her friends had brought normal snacks in well, careless packaging by overwhelmed parents or nannies. Her mother wanted Susan to report back if the teacher took notice of her preparation skills. She also knew Wendy would be up wiping down the kitchen not one or two but three times to purify everything once again for the next occasion.

As one might expect, topics always drifted back to politics, but in a warm and friendly sort of way. Everyone had opinions and everyone expressed them in a civil manner over fine California chardonnay.

Sampson's eyes continued to dart to Susan with a life of their own. Much to his disappointment, she was seated at the opposite end of the table. A message perhaps?

But the conversation had allowed Sampson to learn a great deal about her, and he liked it all. Never married, exercise fanatic, a partner in a small law firm specializing in medium-level criminal work, likes to travel, only child, and bad eyesight. Some type of glaucoma. Those eyes were so damned pretty though. *Interesting.*

CHAPTER 19

Cates and his men had departed the Marriott on schedule and were in the process of positioning themselves around the senator's house.

"Colonel?"

"Go."

"Colonel," the voice of Jimmy B. came through the microphone. "A few more than we expected. Looks like a party. I make out seven or eight from here feeding their faces."

"Maintain position. Work towards more accurate assessment. Out."

Damn, Cates thought. He had hoped for less casualties. More people meant more time and greater risk. Well, no matter. These men were trained soldiers. Those inside the house would be no match for these men. Once the agents protecting the senator were eliminated, the rest was a walk in the park.

Cates reached for the mic button. "Men, we are a go. Stay with the plan. Eliminate everyone in the house. That is all."

Inside the home, dessert delighted, and Wendy took a bow. She and Susan ushered everyone back into their family room for Brazilian and Columbian coffee and liqueurs ranging from Grand Marnier Cuvée Louis Alexandre and Stambecco Tiramisu to

Micil Connemara Irish Cream and Cotswolds Cream. Everyone's eyes widened over the display that Wendy presented on an Albee art deco brass cart. Sampson wanted to forget about his mushed mind and just hang out with the Grants. After all, he had points after saving the man's life. It was a nice thought.

Grabbing a colorful assembly from the cart, Susan plopped down next to his chair on the floor with her back to the fireplace. "I love a fire on a cold night." She removed her glasses and sipped the dark cordial.

"Me too. I'm glad you came over. I was disappointed we didn't get to talk at dinner."

Susan looked very serious, and Sampson was afraid she was going to tell him he had no chance. "I really want to thank you for saving my dad. He means the world to me, you know."

He was melting in his chair and fumbled for words. In his best Western imitation he said, 'Why, thank you, ma'am."

She smirked and he silently cursed for making a fool of himself. Did he know how to flirt? *Get a grip, man!*

"You seem like a nice person, but I just don't believe this supernatural stuff." She stiffened.

"Oh, I know."

With antagonism in her voice she responded, "What do you know?"

Sampson was flustered. "Well, I don't know exactly. Oh hell!" Opting to tell the truth he said, "I do know that you don't believe me about my abilities. I sensed it the moment we shook hands."

"I don't believe that."

"Hmm… a challenge." Sampson's outlook brightened. He could impress and convince her sooner than later. "Think of your favorite spot to vacation."

"This is a waste of our time," Susan challenged.

"Humor me. Remember I'm a guest."

She giggled. "Well, Mother would kill me if she thought I was being impolite to a guest!"

All right. I'm thinking." The thoughts came easily.

Sampson reached for her hand. "White sand, beach, gentle waves, hammock with a book."

Susan looked stunned. She was thinking of her last trip to Grand Cayman, and damn if he didn't get it right! As her eyes drifted back to Sampson, she became alarmed. His face was pale, and he was staring into space. Was that blood she saw trickling from his nose? His color drained. She touched his arm, which was cold and damp. As she shook him, she said, "Sampson, are you okay?"

He blinked and a part of him came back to reality. In a raspy voice he whispered to Susan, "Get the doc and Agent Etkind."

"If you are trying to scare me, please stop."

He looked directly at her, and she could tell this was no joke. "Susan, get them now!"

Sampson stayed focused on his vision. He felt death, a cold breeze that chilled his skin. The green lightening came and went, and he saw a man's head explode from gunfire. Seconds passed and he saw another man lifted off the ground by a wire wringing his neck; the neck turned crimson, and he was released to the ground. Sampson began to feel weak, and he knew from his training that he must now release his vision. It was difficult, but he shook his head, cleared his thoughts, and rushed back to the real world.

He took a breath and realized he had a minor nosebleed, which he dabbled with a Kleenex. As he looked up, he saw Etkind and the doc, as well as the senator staring at him. "They're here now. They've killed two guards."

Etkind spoke first, "Are you sure?"

Dr. Ellison jumped in, "He's sure. What do we do?"

Etkind began to utilize his field training. "Sampson, any idea how many there are?"

"No. At least two."

Etkind ran the options in his mind. They were in deep, deep shit. That much he knew for certain. By now everyone had gathered around Sampson. Etkind commanded, "We have little time. Please listen, they don't know we know what's happening. We need that advantage right now. So, everyone put a smile on now. They may be watching. Senator, do you have any weapons?"

"A shotgun in the upstairs bedroom closet."

"Good. We'll need that."

"Flashlights?"

"Yes, several."

"Okay. Senator, go and get the gun and as many shells as you have. Remember they may be watching. Everyone, keep smiling and moving normally. Keep the gun below window level or cover it."

The senator moved toward the stairs.

"Wendy, would you get the flashlights? Susan, would you get some knives—the bigger, the better."

Etkind grabbed his cell phone and furiously punched numbers. The crowd listened intently. "Bluebird one. Code orange. Senator Grant's estate. Agents down. Unconfirmed. We are under attack. Notify Secret Service and locals."

A moment passed and a voice crackled back. "Rangers scrambled ETA twenty. Unable to raise Secret Service on your grounds. Locals notified. Good luck. Out."

"All right, we need to assume that the guards are dead." This panicked the group. "We'll have help in twenty minutes. Special forces rangers. We need to be ready. Sampson, I've got two weapons. You take one. Unfortunately, I've got only one extra clip; eight shots. Use them smartly. Senator, we're dead if we stay here. We won't last twenty minutes. Any ideas where we could go?"

Senator Grant thought hard before speaking. "The lake. It's a quarter mile or so. We have a boat. We would all fit. It might buy us the time we need. There is a short path that leads from the basement door. I know it like the back of my hand. We can do it in the dark."

"Okay, best option. Let's move to the basement. Remember, casually, two at a time. Is your circuit breaker box down there?"

"Uh huh."

Etkind thought to himself he would need a miracle to survive this. They had reached the darkened basement without incident and were huddled against a wall. Sampson and Grant had positioned themselves in front of the group.

They never saw the intruder. His first words scared most of the group to a new height. Ben stepped forward and uttered, "No one move. Put the guns down."

In truth, Ben would have preferred to simply start shooting. But in the darkness, he was unsure how many weapons were present. Once the guns were down, he would shoot the men first. Etkind knew this also and was preparing to raise his weapon to try to take the man out. Just as suddenly, the intruder went down with a thud, and behind where he had stood, was the figure of Susan. "Asshole."

"Nice going, Susan. Where did you come from?" the senator asked.

"Dad, I went to find something to fight with. I thought this axe handle would do nicely.

Seems like it did." She smiled.

The doc stepped forward. "Sampson," and he gestured toward the downed man.

Sampson knew instantly what the doc was implying, and he reached down and touched the soldier's hand. Nothing came, and Sampson was forced to bear down on his concentration. Flashes emerged. Faceless. Four… five. A leader… maybe two. He could see them moving outside. A rifle, headgear? Sampson broke the connection. There was little to learn.

Etkind had bound the man's legs, hands, and mouth with duct tape. He looked at Sampson.

"Sorry, Steve, four… maybe five guys. They have rifles and something on their heads. Night vision equipment. Shit."

They took off the man what they could. Etkind took the earpiece from the man. He doubted they would risk the radio, but it was worth the try. The man carried two handguns. Etkind gave one to Susan. "Any idea how to use this, ma'am?"

"Yup. I've taken lessons. I own one just like this."

The senator, with Wendy hanging onto his waist, gasped, "Susan?"

"I meant to tell you, Dad. I did," she said sweetly.

"We'll talk about this later, young lady," he said furiously.

"Alan, women need to protect themselves too!" Wendy whined.

The family was shushed. Etkind continued to assess their situation: One intruder down. Sampson had some training, but he was unsure how much he could count on him. The senator might get a shot or two off. Susan, okay, she was a tough broad. The others would be of little help. Probably four more intruders.

Five or six minutes had passed since their pleasant night became an assassination plot. Fifteen minutes before the professionals would show up.

Sampson seemed edgy. "Steve, there is danger in this house now. I can feel it clearly."

Steve could see, even in the dim light, that Sampson was bleeding from the nose. The doc saw this too and moved to Sampson. "Let it go now." He shook Sampson until he let his grip go.

Dazed, Sampson whispered, "They are here, very close. Approaching now."

Etkind ordered everyone to the far corner and instructed them to get down behind boxes or anything they could find.

"Sampson, you and Susan stay with me. We have to preserve our surprise element. We can only use the guns if we absolutely must. I think what they will do is this. One guy will check the basement; we must surprise him. It's pretty dark right now and in a second, I'm turning off all the lights. Susan, you stand by this switch. Turn it on when he reaches the floor. But you must stay behind this box until the last moment. Wait… can you see?" He hated to ask the obvious.

"I have the most powerful glasses on in the world."

"Nuff said," Etkind whispered. "Sampson, take the Glock. Get behind the furnace and position yourself for a clear shot. But only, and I mean *only*, if l miss. Understand?"

Sampson nodded and moved behind the dirty, ancient furnace. Susan concealed herself near the light switch, which Etkind flicked off. The basement was washed of light, and everyone could hear the faint sound of Etkind moving to an unknown position.

Within a minute, although it seemed longer, the basement door opened and closed. Then a clicking sound. Susan thought she would scream. She held her position and dared not to expose herself. She listened intently for a clue as to his position. She tasted sweat from her lip. And then she heard it. A foot very close. A foot gently scraping on concrete. He was on the floor. Her right hand moved toward the switch. She felt it and pushed it upward, sending bright light into the room.

The plan had gone perfectly, which was now clear to everyone. The soldier had entered the darkened basement wearing night vision equipment. When Susan lit the basement, the intruder was temporarily blinded by the flash of light, which gave Etkind time to make good use of the axe handle. The intruder shouted a muffled scream, which was halted within a second as Etkind slammed the axe handle down on the gunman. No further noise.

Etkind wasted no time and bound the man with the duct tape. Not a soul in the room was anything but amazed with this field agent.

"Okay, time to go. I think we are still undetected. We're going to make for the lake.

Sampson, grab the night vision gear and his weapons."

Sampson did and was surprised to see a handgun with a silencer, which he handed to Etkind. Etkind thoughtfully looked at the weapon.

"Everyone, move toward the door." As they moved in one direction, he moved toward his prisoners and fired one round into the foot of each man.

As he turned back to the group, he could see their faces looking strangely at him. Particularly his wife. "Look, they will find them in the next few minutes. We can't have them untied and coming back after us. They will, I assure you. I shot them in their feet. It won't kill them, but they will not be able to hunt us. Sampson, you go out the door first with the senator. As soon as it's clear, everyone else move fast. No noise. I'll be behind you eventually. Senator, get to the boat and get as far away as possible. If I am not there, go without me. I will slow them down."

"Steve, no." It was the agent's wife, who hadn't spoken all night, and she was openly crying.

His training had just taken over and he had forgotten his wife was even with him. He regretted that immensely. She needed comfort, but there was no time. "I'll be fine," he said matter-of-factly. "This is what I do. We can talk about it later. Sampson, go now." He kissed his wife and moved off.

Sampson unlocked the door to the basement and moved silently up the stairs and into the opening. The cool night air felt strangely refreshing. He could see his breath and he knew his training was coming back also. He raised his weapon to his chest and scanned the outside area. Nothing was visible. He was startled as a hand touched his shoulder. "Sampson." It was Etkind. "It's clear out there." He touched the earpiece now in his ear. "Three in the house. They know something is wrong. Get them out now. Fast as you can."

Everyone headed out the door and Etkind relaxed a bit when they passed the clearing and reached the woods. They stood a chance now. But he knew from his training that they would only move as fast as their slowest person. He feared that might be his wife. No matter. He was resolved to slow down the intruders or stop them himself altogether.

He bolted from the house to the woods but did not follow the group. He moved to his right and inched along the forest. Within a minute, he came upon his quarry. The Secret Service agent lay in a pool of blood illuminated by the pale moonlight. His head was nearly severed, and his face bore a pained expression that Etkind would never forget. He looked at him with great sorrow, but his feelings would have to wait. To the man's left was the rifle with a scope that he had hoped to find. Ammunition was in a small box in the man's rear pocket. Etkind knew the man's communication device would not be of help. He was certain that the soldiers had taken at least one, and any attempt to use them would only help the opposition.

He took the rifle and ammo and moved back toward the woods and positioned himself directly in front of the path. Now he would wait. Within seconds, two men emerged from the basement. Etkind followed the lead man with the scope, sighted him, and squeezed the trigger. The man went down. A second shot took down another intruder. Etkind suddenly felt a searing pain in his own shoulder and fell to the ground as another bullet bit into the tree next to him and exploded into the bark.

Etkind crawled deeper into the forest, not losing sight of the path. As he inched along, he felt nauseated, drowsy, and every movement sent his body into spasms of pain.

"You did pretty good."

The voice startled him, and he looked upward into the eyes of Jimmy B. Jimmy B pointed a handgun at the forehead of Etkind, whose thoughts moved to his wife. God, he hoped he had given her enough time to escape this lunacy. The gun sounded and Etkind felt no more pain.

"Steve, Steve." Sampson began shaking Etkind. He could see the blood and knew time was short.

One eye fluttered and opened, looking up at Sampson. "Thought you could use some help. I took care of your problem." He nodded toward a dead Jimmy B, who lay beside Etkind.

"Shit, I thought I died."

"Not yet."

"Sampson, there is one more."

Before they could discuss this any further, a thundering noise roared from the sky and brought spotlights from two black Ranger helicopters illuminating the property. The sound was deafening, and the wind from the rotors was ferocious. Sampson wondered what children thought during wars when some of these monsters roared into their villages.

CHAPTER 20

Cates was concealed near the house in a row of pine trees and spotted the approaching Rangers. He knew his time was short. He was glad he had eliminated the two wounded soldiers in the basement when he did. They were good men, but he could not risk witnesses and the men were hurt. They would require a hospital and a doctor, and that was too risky. Cates slipped unnoticed into the woods and moved back to the rendezvous point. He was disgusted with himself. He had been beaten. He had lost. He had failed.

Nearby, Sampson watched as the helicopters set down. They were quickly approached by a small platoon of men who bore down on Sampson and Etkind. Etkind weakly reached for his identification, which satisfied the soldiers.

Sampson said, "This man is wounded and needs medical attention. A group of our people are by the lake including the senator. They are armed and scared. Be careful. We took out four of them. We think one is missing. We don't know about the Secret Service."

"One is dead....I saw him five hundred feet to our left." Etkind lost consciousness.

The Rangers made fast work of their task. They evacuated

Etkind immediately, searched for the missing gunman, but had no success and left a secure scene to the federal agents.

Sampson spent the next four hours with the others explaining what had happened. The FBI told him it was a miracle he was alive.

Cates drove carefully back to a parking lot at Dulles Airport. In the lot he parked the car the men had used to get to the senator's home. He jumped in another rental car and left the lot. Two minutes after leaving the lot, he heard an explosion and knew the car was ravaged.

Cates drove for an hour, making sure he wasn't followed. He stopped at a pay phone, punched in a series of numbers and was connected directly to John Whisnant.

"The mail was undeliverable. We tried but couldn't get through."

"Okay, I'm disappointed. We'll speak again."

The connection ended. Wiz was stunned. He knew Cates had failed and could not believe that. This man had never missed. Dozens of missions in far more challenging circumstances and never a miss. Why now?

Wiz, as competent as he was, was beginning to lose some confidence. The senator and this Sampson guy were more than lucky. No matter. The game was not over. There would be another round, another very decisive round.

CHAPTER 21

The press picked up the story and it made for sensational news with all the key plot points, including a captivating headline: "Murder and Mayhem at Senator Grant's Estate: Psychic Present, Senator Survives Another Attempt on His Life".

Senator Grant was being made into a cult hero with the American people. He gave a short interview in which he denounced terrorism and vowed to continue his personal mission of eliminating it forever. He spoke of the fear he felt for his family and loyal aide during the siege. He spoke of the courage of his wife and daughter, and of all the people at the dinner party. He said this was what Americans were made of. His rallying cry against terrorism grew extraordinarily strong with the American people.

He did not speak much of Sampson. They had all agreed that calling attention to his powers would only serve to further endanger Sampson. The senator praised the courage of Agent Etkind. Etkind's wound was serious, but he would recover. Lastly, he praised the Rangers who came and swept away the last of the criminal element. He ached for the agents who died.

By the next morning, the American public all knew of the senator. A CNN poll had statistically projected that, if an election were held today, Grant would win by a landslide over the incumbent, and generally well-liked President, Austin Feeney.

The President could not believe what he was reading in the morning paper. His efforts to eliminate the man only served to fuel his popularity! For Christ sakes, after he read this stuff, he would vote for the man too! Austin Feeney, the most powerful man in the world, was losing.

He sat in his office alone and pondered his problem. Somehow, the senator was a man of nine lives, or was this Sampson guy really the luck? He did not at all believe this "see the future" shit, but no one could be this lucky or this fortunate. *No one.*

Austin reasoned another imminent attack on Grant was a poor idea. Sampson had to be taken out, plain and simple. Whether he believed it or not, he could not risk the chance.

Like a shot, it struck him. Why not use the terrorist thing against the senator? And why not line his pockets at the same time? He reached for the intercom button.

"Millie, get Wiz here now!"

"Yes, sir." *He's not all like himself,* she thought.

Within two minutes, Millie reported to the President that Mr. Whisnant would be there in twenty minutes. He asked her to rearrange his calendar to allow for a two-hour meeting uninterrupted.

When he did arrive, Wiz looked haggard, somber, frustrated. "Austin, I'm sorry about what happened." Apologies did not come easy for John Whisnant, but this one was more than warranted.

"Let's work the problem, old buddy. Can't change the past."

Wiz was surprised to find Austin in such good spirits and with such high energy. It reminded him of high school, in the locker room at half-time of a basketball game. The team had played badly and were trailing by twenty-two. Everyone was down, ready to give up. But not Austin. He worked his teammates into a frenzy, and they played a flawless second half and won the game by fifteen points. He had provided a victory, carried the team on his back, and delivered on the promise. Wiz saw that same attitude today, and it was infectious.

"We have to leverage his stance on terrorism, take advantage of it. His position is clear—an eye for an eye, harsh punishment. Our position is softer. Negotiate, but don't infuriate. His position is more popular today, but I've got a thought on how we break his back with the American public." Feeney smiled devilishly, deep in thought, and then continued. "Grant is talking tough on terrorists, right?"

Wiz nodded agreement.

"Suppose a terrorist splinter group crops up that wants to take the senator on. They consider it a challenge, a goal. Suppose this terrorist group chooses to target a highly visible sector of American business, one that has deep pockets and affects the lives personally of most American businesspeople, as well as the general public."

"Keep going. I'm intrigued, Austin." Wiz listened intently.

"Wiz, let's target the airlines. To send our first message to the good senator, let's knock down a commercial flight. I'm sure you can scrounge up a stinger. Take down a flight from the ground and find a way to blame Grant. Then negotiate with the big five airlines. Tell them we want $10,000,000 each, or one of their air ships goes down. Have the money wired to the Caymans. You know the drill. Just don't let it be traced to us. My guess is all five will pay. No matter what, we win. Most will pay, and we have money for life. More likely, the American public will turn against Grant, I get another term, and we have a lot of money to retire on. It will work; I know it. Figure out the details, and don't wait too long. He's got momentum for now."

Whisnant pondered the proposition. It could work. Taking down a planeload of people was not a pretty thought, but this was business, all business. *It could work*, he thought, and he could afford all the whores and bourbon on the planet. "All right, Austin." The men shook hands, and Wiz departed.

Over the course of the past few days, not much was learned about the attack on the senator. With no survivors, and an obviously professional group of assassins, little hope existed within the FBI that this case would be solved.

Agent Etkind's wounds proved to be relatively mild. He lost a great deal of blood, but the bullet had entered and exited without causing any damage to vital organs. He would be on his feet in a couple of days.

Sampson continued to work with Dr. Ellison on the depth of his powers. Remarkably, he was able to exert more and more control over his ability to see. But Sampson could also tell the doctor was still very concerned about his ability to shut off a vision.

"Sampson, we have done all that we can do in the laboratory. You have a stronger will and more ability than the others before you."

Sampson was relieved to hear this. "Does that mean I can go back to my life now? Or should I say, what's left of it?"

Dr. Ellison looked up at Sampson with soft, sorrowful eyes. "No, I'm afraid you can't. You have been in all the papers. You know that. The Agency has a very real fear that, at a minimum, you could be a kidnapping target or worse, an assassination target. As of last week, you are back on the payroll of the CIA. You and I will continue to work together, but you have been assigned to Agent Bob Becker. You remember him from Syracuse?"

The doctor reached in his drawer. "Here is your weapon and CIA credentials. You may need them, my friend."

"How is he?"

"Fully recovered. A little sore, but back to work tomorrow.

He's your new boss. You both are assigned to Senator Grant full-time. They want you to protect him and solve the case."

"Where am I supposed to live?"

"The U.S. Government is your new landlord. Tomorrow, they will show you your new place. It's a nice, secure building. You will have two guards with you at all times until things really calm down."

"I don't get a choice, do I?"

"Nope, not if you want to stay alive. Give it a try for a while anyway. CIA kind of grows on people."

They both smiled. Both men understood that this was the way it had to be.

"Doc, I've got a favor to ask. I've been cooped up here for a while. I'd like to go out tonight."

"Alone?"

"Not exactly. I was thinking of giving Susan Grant a call. I started talking to her at the party. She seems nice, and she likes me." The doctor offered a wry smile. "Besides, have you ever seen anyone other than Aaron Judge swing a bat harder than that?"

"No, uh-uh. Look, you call her. If she can go, we'll figure out a way to break you out of here." The doctor would have to call in favors, but this man deserved a break. "I'll figure it out," the good doctor reasoned.

Sampson retreated to his quarters and plopped down in a chair. He felt excited about calling Susan but for the first time in many years that were becoming clearer, was actually nervous about making a call to a woman. In the end, mind won out over body. Sampson Googled the name of her law practice and retrieved Susan's office number. Only then did it dawn on him that he worked for the CIA now. He probably could have made one call and had her phone number, social security number… her bra size. For God's sakes! Sampson chuckled at his stupidity.

Sweaty palms and all, he dialed the number, and reached

the receptionist who forwarded his call, presumably to Susan's assistant. "Ms. Grant's office. May I help you?"

"Is Susan available?"

"May I tell her who's calling?"

"Just tell her I am returning her call to the Psychic Hotline."

"Hmm, okay," and Sampson was put on hold.

A moment later, the line came alive with a smoky, mischievous voice. "Hello."

"Yes, I'm returning your call about a dream date."

"Ah, Mr. Sampson," Susan uttered with a playful tone. "I was wondering if I would ever hear from you again."

"Well, I thought maybe we could go play paintball tonight, and you won't need your axe handle."

She giggled a throaty laugh, "I always carry my axe handle."

"All right. I was wondering if you would have time for dinner and maybe a drink tonight with me. I promise no one will attack us."

"Is that a promise?"

"As best as I can tell. Come on, say 'yes'. It took all my courage to call you."

"Why? Are you afraid of me?" He hated it and loved it at the same time. She was torturing him. He remembered this from high school. The women hold all the cards, but he decided to play along.

"Yes, you scare me. You're the daughter of a senator, maybe a President. You're a successful lawyer, you're kind of cute, and I love your glasses."

"What do you mean, 'kind of'?"

"Well, you're cute, actually damned gorgeous in my view."

"So, this is about you!"

Oh, this was torture! "Of course. I'm not calling to make you happy. I want me to be happy, and it would make me happy if you said you'd have dinner with me."

"Who's buying?"

"I'll buy."

"Deal," she laughed.

"Thank God! I was out of clever lines."

"Fooled me. What time, where, and what should I wear?"

"I'll pick you up at 7:30, and I would suggest something low cut, black if possible, and some pumps."

"A little too much detail. A girl knows how to dress."

"You asked!"

"Yes, leading questions are not a good idea for you."

"I'm through. Text me your address please!"

"See you soon. Bye!"

The phone went dead, and Sampson came alive. His energy level soared, crackling with all the possibilities.

Sampson found Dr. Ellison and relayed the good news that the doc had already anticipated. Two agents would accompany him in a bulletproof stretch. They would handle the reservations at an appropriate place, which would allow for his privacy and security.

CHAPTER 22

Wiz arranged to meet with Colonel Cates at an out-of-the-way diner west of Washington.

When Wiz arrived, the colonel was sipping hot coffee with a scowl on his face.

"Wiz."

"Colonel."

"Look, Wiz, I screwed up. I'll finish this on my own; no cost to you."

"Hold on, colonel. No one is pissed here. The senator had more than enough help with this Sampson character. I am beginning to believe in his abilities. The CIA says it's real, some experimental drug. Anyway—new game plan. We're not going after Grant. Better yet, we're going to work the terrorist angle against him. What I want you to do is knock down an airplane from any of the big five airlines. Make it a jet with a light load of passengers. Big, visible explosion, maybe a surface-to-air stinger? We're then going to play the terrorist angle against Grant and blackmail the airlines at the same time."

Cates's outlook brightened with this naughty plan. "This should be a better angle. How soon?"

"Right away. Let's work out the details."

The two men ate a greasy, bad meal, and mapped out every detail along each bite.

Cates estimated two days to acquire the weapons and a day to plan the event out. They settled on four days from today. Ironically, both men laughed when they simultaneously selected the location—Syracuse. Why not? That's where all this started.

The men left at different times with full discretion.

Wiz was full of tension. He knew taking down a commercial airline had to work. Three strikes, out. He felt pressure. He needed a release. He punched in Binky's number and was pleased to be put right through to the man himself.

"Binky, I'm free for the next couple of hours. Thought I might stop by."

"Wiz, always glad to accommodate. Come on by."

"See you in about half an hour."

Binky loved his job. He fired up his PC, entered Whisnant and presto, up came all of Mr. Whisnant's love fantasies. He matrixed that with his stable of women, and up rolled Carol, the redhead, again.

Twenty-five minutes later, Wiz arrived, and Binky escorted him up to Carol's apartment.

She met them at the door.

"Carol, this is John Whisnant. Wiz; Carol." They exchanged a brief handshake, and Binky quietly departed.

Carol was petite, with flowing red hair and pine forest green eyes. She resembled actress Renee Olstead. Curvaceous body from hell. Wiz soaked it all in. Now, this was a fox! He wavered between not wanting to touch one hair on her head, she was such a specimen of beauty, and wanting to plow into all that lusciousness.

"Would you like a drink?" Her voice was soft, adding to her allure.

"Sure. Bourbon; neat."

Carol moved to a wet bar and poured a large bourbon in a handsome tumbler. As she strode toward him, he felt himself growing hard. But it was a conflict of emotion. He was ready to fuck this woman like there was no tomorrow, but he could not mentally release the pressure he felt inside his head. He had never failed like this before; in fact, he had always won. He couldn't shake Sampson from his head.

Carol sensed his distraction. "John, how about a nice massage after your drink? I'm really good at that. Once you're relaxed, though, you belong to me."

"Don't talk down to me." He ran a hand into his head of wavy, jet-black hair. Not a grey hair sprouted up surprisingly, given his tense lifestyle.

Carol was surprised at his reaction. Usually, men liked that line. In fact, his profile suggested this would, and in the past had been, a turn-on. *Oh well, retreat*, she thought.

"I'm not. I'm sorry."

He suddenly grabbed her and forcefully kissed her. Carol did not like where this was heading. This man was mad, and she would have to be careful or he would hurt her.

"Go easy. We have all day. No need to rush a good thing."

"I want you now."

Before she could answer, he picked her up and carried her to the bedroom. He sat on the edge of the bed, and she came to him. He kissed her breasts through the silk shirt and suddenly and forcefully ripped her blouse off her. She was wearing no bra. Just as quickly, her pants were off, and he admired her gorgeous body. He stood, and she worked his shirts and pants. What happened next totally alarmed Carol. He threw her on the bed and plunged inside her. The pain was excruciating as he relentlessly thrust in and out of her. He passionately kissed and bit her neck. She prayed Binky was watching and would stop this. Wiz's frame was all hard muscle. It hurt so much she thought she might pass out; she knew better than to scream. He was nearing climax, she could tell. She hoped this misery was almost over. Without warning, Wiz arched upward and grabbed her neck when he gave one final thrust. As he exploded inside her, he tightened his grip on Carol's neck and snapped her spine. It was the most glorious climax of his life, and he stayed inside the corpse for several minutes.

As Wiz grew hard again, he decided that this was the best fuck of his life, and it deserved a second round. He re-entered the dead woman's vagina and within five minutes, satisfied himself more plentifully.

As he uncoupled from the woman, he found himself once again feeling in charge of his destiny, his old confidence levels having returned. He knew he would have to clean up this mess, but that would be a problem he could deal with in a few minutes. For now, he planned on a hot shower.

Binky had tuned in in time to see what happened. But as he ran through his options, he knew he had none. If he ran down and tried to stop the attack, Wiz would know about the camera. That would jeopardize his life and certainly mean the end of his business. No, he would have to watch and wait for Wiz to make the next move. He waited only seconds and witnessed the brutal killing, on top of the animalistic act on the obviously dead woman.

Wiz emerged from the shower, dressed, and used his cell phone to make a call to CIA. Satisfied, he next picked up Carol's phone and rang Binky's private line. Binky forced himself to wait for the third ring and put on his best show.

"Yes?"

"Binky, it's Wiz. Come up to Carol's.

"Sure. When would you like me? Everything okay?"

"Yup, come on up now."

"Okay, on the way." Binky hung up the phone and prayed

to God. No time to think about this. He knew he would have to think on his feet.

Within two minutes, Binky entered Carol's apartment. "What's up, Wiz?"

"Carol. We were making love and I think she had a heart attack. She just died."

Binky was amazed with the path this was going down, but he knew he had to play this one out. "No way! She was always healthy. Are you sure?"

"Yes, she's dead. We have a shared problem here that I intend to clear up for you. I… well, we… can't have this handled through the normal channels. I've called the Company; in fifteen minutes, they'll be here. *Poof!* Problem gone, my friend."

"Wiz, I appreciate this. I really do. You are doing me a big favor here. I really owe you." "I know. But you're a friend." Wiz clapped him on the shoulder and urged him to go back to business. "Just keep everyone inside their rooms and quiet for forty minutes."

Satisfied with his performance, Binky left quietly and retreated to his office to watch the progress on TV. What he saw amazed him. He had heard of CIA "sweepers," but thought it to be only a rumor. In thirty minutes, they had removed the body, vacuumed the apartment, stripped the bed, wiped down every surface, and even removed the covers of the drains, cleaned them, and then poured gallons of Drano down them.

Binky thought, *shit, this death was erased.*

Job completed, the lights were turned off, and they were gone. But the work of the sweepers was not yet done. They had retrieved clothing from her closet, along with shoes, purse, and light jacket. In the van they cleaned the body thoroughly, first lightly scrubbing all her skin and hair, and finally, douching the vagina to remove sperm and other means of tracing DNA. The woman was then dressed, hair dried, makeup applied, and carefully dumped in an alley with her purse, but with all her cash gone. This would be another unfortunate, big-city incident.

At the same time all of this was going on, Sampson's limo was pulling up to Susan's apartment. He straightened his new clothes. More Ralph Lauren thanks to Dr. Ellison, who appeared to have a thing for the classic American designer. Sampson walked up and rang the bell, followed by two agents who stayed back at a discreet distance. As the door opened, Sampson was awestruck. A goddess stood in front of him. She was dressed in a little black dress and wearing sexy pumps decorated with what appeared to be spikes. "Wow! You look hot."

"Thanks."

"Except for one thing."

She looked at him, disappointed and pouty.

"I asked for low cut. That neckline is not low enough."

"Uh-huh. Well, we do what we can. If you behave tonight and I agree to see you again, I'll work on the cleavage."

"All right. Sounds fair."

"Come on in. Your friends too."

Everyone entered her quaint apartment. He was taken by the decor. The walls were white, which afforded an open, airy feel. Dark hardwood floors were covered with elegant Persian rugs. And he was particularly taken with the artwork Susan had chosen—modern watercolors by Alfred Birdsey. Birdsey had passed away, but his daughter, equally talented, had resumed her father's work.

Sampson could not contain himself. "Now this is nice." He envisioned shopping for interiors together. *Oh my god, you goof!*

The CIA agents, Sampson noticed, positioned themselves discreetly, and were pretending not to be listening. Sampson knew they were taking in every word.

"Sampson, would you like a drink, or should we be going?"

"Well, we've got two problems." Sampson lowered his voice to a level only Susan could hear. "First, if we stay, I may never leave. Second, we've got reservations in just a couple of minutes downtown. How about we get that drink at the restaurant?"

"That will work. I'll grab my coat, and away we go."

Susan, Sampson, and the two agents left the apartment and headed towards the limo. Dr. Ellison had chosen Saporito's, an upscale Italian restaurant with lots of private candlelit booths. They shared everything as longtime lovers, laughing and flirting with every bite. Sampson brushed her hand a few times and felt pure electricity. Did she? Her ice blue eyes sparkled in the candle-light. After ninety minutes, the agents nearby were signaling for Sampson to wrap up the tryst. No bill was delivered, but one of the agents dropped a $100 bill on the table for the server.

The journey back took them through some of Washington's poorest neighborhoods, which they were seeing now, as well as the most affluent, during the latter part of the journey. As they rounded a bend in the road, they came upon a significant amount of police activity. Blue and red lights lit up the evening sky. The limo halted in a line of automobiles, which numbered twenty or so, passing the activity one by one, taking turns to view closely whatever had slowed down their busy lives.

Sampson could see the agents in the front of the limo. He saw the activity ahead had raised a caution flag for them and as they inched forward, their heightened awareness level.

As they approached the scene, Sampson was overwhelmed by a feeling of death. His stomach felt queasy, and he wanted to run from the area, but something stronger beckoned. Something made him want to get closer. He closed his eyes and concentrated on a feeling. Darkness… mostly darkness. He could sense a girl, a girl in trouble. He smelled fear and then death. He had to learn more.

"Susan, I'll be right back," he huffed and threw the door open before she could respond.

Sampson began sprinting toward the lights. He could hear the car pulling over, and he was sure he heard one of the agents say, "Sampson, what the fuck?"

As he neared the police line, he removed his CIA identification. He knew this would get him only so far, and the rest would be a crapshoot. Police and the other ancillary agencies typically hate each other. He had heard it described in the past as 'healthy competition gone haywire'. He flashed his badge at the first officer, who nodded and allowed him to pass. In his periphery he could see the other two agents sprinting in his direction. He knew that once everyone was together, he would have no shot at eyeballing what he came to see.

Sampson deliberately walked toward the activity in the alley. His plan was to keep his head down and hope that he could approach the scene unnoticed before his two bodyguards closed in. So far, the plan was working. He made eye contact with the last uniformed officer, who nodded slightly, allowed him to pass. He could see the target now. A body. Female, young, fire read hair, dead. She was calling to him. He could hear a faint cry.

Several men surrounded her, including a medical examiner snapping pictures. Two men in plain clothes examined the area around the body. Both saw Sampson approaching and just as one raised a hand to stop him, a commotion started further back. The two agents were arguing loudly with three uniformed officers. This distracted the detectives enough that Sampson was able to kneel near the body. He touched her hand, which opened a portal to a series of images.

He could see a man, but not his face, only darkness. Sex. He heard the man wail in pleasure, and he felt cold death after that. He steadied his concentration, but all that came was a phrase, "Please, Binky."

Was Binky the killer? He needed more, and bore down on his concentration, oblivious of his surroundings.

He could hear a voice in the distance. "Sampson, stop. Stop. You are killing yourself." He felt himself shaking, and realized it was not him shaking himself, it was Susan shaking him.

"Sampson, please stop."

As he came back to the real world, he could see Susan crying and looking right at him. *Why is she crying?* His head cleared and he could see the reason for her concern. Blood streamed out his nose. He felt lightheaded and laid back and closed his eyes. He could feel a cloth at his nose and strangely, he knew the blood would stop. He would survive this.

"Okay, what the fuck is going on here?" As Sampson opened his eyes, he could see two detectives plus his bodyguards staring down at him.

Susan replied, "The man has a nosebleed."

"Well, do it somewhere else. You're fucking up my crime scene. Why don't you spooks get the fuck out of here?"

Sampson extended his arm and was able to get to his feet and walk with a little help.

The group moved without a word back to the limo. Sampson was helped to his seat and sat weakly upright.

"Mr. Sampson, you can't do that. You know that you compromised security, sir. Not only for you, but for her as well." The agent had a very serious look on his face as he looked at Sampson and Susan.

"You're right. I was wrong. I'm sorry."

Sampson looked at Susan and her eyes were red from crying, her face a bit puffy but beautiful, nonetheless. "Sampson, I've sort of lost my appetite for a nightcap out. Let's go back to my place. You can shower and rest."

Weakly, he shook his head, "Yes."

Susan looked toward the front of the limo. "Boys, take us back to my place, okay?"

The agents shook their heads, furious at what had transpired. The trip back to Susan's home was brief. Sampson was able to navigate into the apartment under his own power. One of the agents left to purchase a pair of sweats and a T-shirt to replace the blood-soaked clothes of Sampson. Susan led Sampson to a bathroom. She pulled fresh towels and a washcloth from a cabinet and dug a fresh bar of Dove soap from a drawer.

"I think I'll burn your clothes."

"Good idea."

"Why don't you holler when you're through? Your new clothes should be here by then." It appeared that he wouldn't need to shop for his own clothes for a while! Her eyes took on a serious tint, and she perfected her frames to show a little more command. "You scared me tonight. I thought you were dying. And the thought of that dead girl… one of the worst things I've ever seen."

"I'm sorry about tonight. Really sorry. I'll make it up to you."

"Promise?"

"Promise."

"All right. Apology accepted. Get in the shower. You look like something from a Frankenstein movie."

Sampson was feeling better and couldn't resist another chance to spar with Susan. "Susan, I'm pretty weak and probably should not shower alone."

"Maybe you should take a bath."

"Do you have Mr. Bubble?"

"No, of course not."

"Well, I can't take a bath then."

"I see. I can understand that."

"I think the shower would be fine, as long as someone was with me."

"I'll send in one of the bodyguards."

"No, no. They need to protect the house. You'll do in a pinch."

"You're cute, but annoying. I have a rule. I don't kiss bloody men." She tossed a towel to him, turned, and closed the door behind her as she left.

Sampson muttered loud enough for her to hear, "That went well!"

The blood washed easily from his skin, and he felt revitalized and refreshed. But as he toweled, Sampson remembered the man howling on top of a curvaceous body. Smooth, fair skin. *Binky. What a fucking name.* Before investigating, he had to cater to the new woman of his dreams. Sampson found Susan's hairbrush in a drawer. He wrapped the towel around his waist and opened the bathroom door. He was pleased to find a blue Nike sweatsuit, white crew socks, and a pair of stylish On Cloud tennis shoes. No Ralph.

He dressed and made his way to the kitchen. It was easy to find. He could smell eggs, bacon, and his favorite breakfast food—corned beef hash—cooking on the stove. Susan was perched over a range top preparing a feast.

"How was the shower?"

"Okay. I almost fainted because no one would stay with me, and I had trouble soaping my back."

"I hate it when that happens."

"So… you can cook as good as your mother?"

Susan laughed heartily, thinking of Wendy's obsession with all things cooking and entertaining. "You don't want to say that. She's rather obsessed with food, the presentation of food and social graces, handed down by my French grandmother. Personally, I prefer dive bars and diners, but don't tell her I said that!"

Sampson sensed some interesting family history. And what of his? Still to be determined.

The agents were eager to enjoy the food and accepted the invitation. Susan served out equally large portions for the four of them. She brewed coffee, which perfectly complemented the meal. Everyone ate in silence. Susan sensed the anger of the agents melting away. She was glad. About midway through the meal, Sampson broke the silence, "When we finish, I want to go back to CIA."

The blond-haired agent wryly smiled at Sampson. "Well, sir, I figured that. Actually I have orders to bring you back."

"Hmmm. I see."

"Actually, we were supposed to bring you back a while ago, but I figured you needed some time with your girlfriend."

"He's not my boyfriend," Susan retorted.

"Could be if l wanted to be," Sampson laughed.

The agent started laughing, "Okay, sorry I mentioned it." They all shared a laugh, which served to break the tension.

Sampson leered at Susan and smiled at the agents. "She really wants me. We did have a nice dinner before all the… mayhem."

Susan stood up to clear the plates. "Why don't you boys go do your spy stuff? Us lawyers need to read our briefs. There won't be any sleep."

"Briefs. Hmm…" Sampson muttered.

"Get out. You're a child."

"Adolescent, actually."

The agents shook their heads. Susan cleared the plates with some help from Sampson. The agents had returned to the living room, leaving them alone in the kitchen. Sampson suspected this was deliberate.

"Susan, thanks for tonight. Sorry I ruined your night out."

"I had fun. I've never been taken to see a dead body on a first date."

"Sorry. The plan was Italian food and a long make-out session."

"Another time."

Unexpectedly, Susan stepped toward Sampson and kissed his lips. He felt fire and wanted more, and he sensed she did too. But not tonight. The timing was wrong, and he wanted her so badly he could not risk losing her by moving like a snake. He reminded himself that something this good would be worth a significant time investment.

"You didn't ask me if you could kiss me," Sampson stated playfully.

Susan arrogantly chuckled, "Oh, did you mind?"

"I usually make the first move. I'm an action kind of guy. You've probably noticed." "Well, Mr. Action, you're a little slow."

"Careful, I may have to spend the night."

"Now that is a frightening thought."

Sampson's voice took on a serious tone, "I… would like to see you again. Can I call, say, tomorrow?"

"Sure, Mr. Action. I'd like that."

"Would you like to kiss me some more? I am your boy toy."

"Get out. You're insufferable."

"Ciao, Baby."

"Loser."

The ride took only a short while, as much of Washington was now in bed. Sampson could not believe it was the middle of the night. He felt so alive and so happy. Suddenly, memories flooded in of his first girlfriend in high school; tenth grade. He sat next to her in Earth Science. They had talked. Eventually had a date, and ended up in the back seat of his father's Buick. He remembered the moment like it was today. The first kiss was deep, and new, and wonderful. The taste and smell of her perfume… *Charlie*, he thought — $2.99 a gallon on sale at Wal-Mart.

Sampson was elated to remember clear scenes from his life.

As he left his dream world, he realized they were already at CIA, and the car was stopping. They moved from security point to security point and ended up in the conference room. To his amazement, Dr. Ellison and Agent Robert Becker were present. Nighttime was the right time for so many activities.

The two men smiled at one another. Sampson said, "You look different without the snow and the bombs."

"Yeah, you too."

"So, I work for you now. Small world."

"I'm glad to have you. You saved my life, you know."

"Aw, shucks, it was nothin', boss," he said with a poor Southern drawl.

"Oh, yes it was. I had a big hole in me. What was it? The docs couldn't tell. It did bleed when you pulled it out."

"You had a screwdriver in you," Sampson replied.

"All right. Let's jump into this thing. I'm up to speed, and maybe a little further ahead. Tell me about the incident tonight."

"We were going by the crime scene, and I had to see it, or her, I guess. I touched her and I saw and felt her last few thoughts."

"She was a robbery victim; already got a preliminary M.E. report."

"No, that's not right… it was not a robbery."

"Sampson…"

"Bob, she was murdered. During sex. Her neck was snapped."

"What?" Bob gasped. "That is some sick shit."

"I'm telling you I'm right. She was hoping, no, praying, that someone named Bink or Binky would help her. He didn't. It was a guy, who killed her during sex. One snap. Very swift. He was on top of her. He didn't choke or beat her. I couldn't see his face. I didn't get anything else, but that's how it happened. This robbery thing is bullshit."

"You know, if I hadn't been with you in Syracuse, I wouldn't believe you."

"Bob, why would I lie?"

"I don't think you would or did. But someone here is lying. How could the M.E. make that claim? You wouldn't miss a broken neck… unless you were told to. That does happen in our business, but not often. And it's usually someone or something important."

The doctor fidgeted in his seat. "I'll leave you two to this work. I'm afraid it's straying outside my area of expertise."

Becker knew otherwise. He knew Dr. Ellison knew enough about the Agency to know where and, more importantly, where not, to stick his nose. The less you know, the better off you are at CIA.

"Smart man, the doc," Becker said.

"Good man. He's kept me alive. I have a little control over these things now. I was pretty close to the edge in Syracuse."

"Yeah, I read the file. Look, you and I have to talk. Something is wrong here. Too many coincidences. Syracuse and the attack on Grant's mansion are linked to Grant. How does this dead girl fit in?"

"I don't know. But she's a part of this. There is a connection."

"Okay, suppose I buy that. Not that I have much of a choice since I don't have anything else to go on. What else can you tell me?"

"Nothing. I've told you everything. Bink or Binky is about the only clue. He's the link to the guy who killed the woman. What do we know about this woman?"

"That's another mystery. She had no ID. Fingerprints were negative, and she does not match any missing person's report. I saw her picture; gorgeous and exquisite like a movie star. Seems to me she'd be missed. Definitely not a vagrant."

"Prostitute? Ties with the sex picture you saw."

"Maybe. But no drug marks and again, she was just too clean.

Also, the other flaw in your story was that she was negative for sperm samples."

"I'm losing some credibility."

"This smells of CIA—dead girl, no one knows who she is. Without your intervention, she is a statistic that closes tonight. Given workloads, and the fact that no one is claiming her, means that case will shut tonight and never open ever again."

Sampson looked exasperated. "We've got to find Bink or Binky. It's the only lead we've got."

"Yup. I'll make the inquiries myself. If this is a CIA insider, the less folks who know, the better."

After two days, however, not a clue had emerged.

CHAPTER 23

Colonel Cates had waited three hours in a field just a tenth of a mile outside of Hancock Airport in Syracuse. He had gauged that, at about sunup, the airport would become busy. Lying in the field he was invisible. His camouflage suit blended in perfectly with his snowy surroundings. His face had been carefully painted as well. He had never been spotted in Vietnam amid the war, much less in Syracuse, or Podunk, New York.

Obtaining a Stinger surface-to-air rocket had proven to be difficult and far more expensive than he ever planned. But he paid it and was fully prepared for what lay ahead. Under cover of darkness, he had carefully loaded the weapon, and it lay nestled against him now.

Cates had easily obtained a flight schedule off the Internet. He wanted a bigger and more visible target, which eliminated the commuter flights. He also had a modest conscience, and his training had told him to minimize casualties. He selected a Mohawk Airlines Boeing 727 bound for Pittsburgh. The flight was a 6:15 a.m. departure which, given the winter timeframe, meant nearly complete darkness, allowing him to slip away without notice, like the warrior he was.

With binoculars Cates could see the jet push from the jetport, and watched as the force of the starting engines blew the fresh powdered snow from within its wake. As the jet taxied to the far end of the runway, Cates could feel his pulse quicken just a bit. As the whine of engines began, Cates sat upright and prepared the weapon. He would hit the airplane directly above his head just after takeoff. The momentum of the jet would carry the debris well beyond him and would create the disturbance he would need to move from the scene. He could hear the jet rev up its engines at the far end of the runway and begin gaining speed rapidly in his direction.

He could see the jet beginning to leave the ground as it rose upward. Much as a kite catches wind and takes flight, the plane began a gentle ascent and at the precise moment it was overhead, Cates pulled the trigger and listened to the elegant hint of a missile rising upward.

At that very moment, Sampson sat bolt upright in his bed at the laboratory. He and Bob had worked almost nonstop since the death of the girl, and he had been in bed only moments. Barely conscious of what was happening, he saw the image of a white plume of smoke leading to a plane and… heat, death, noise, screams, a devastating fireball. The image went black. Then he could see a white field, and huge chunks of blackened metal, a brown suitcase, and a metal coffeepot, falling to the ground and into the snow. Then there was silence; total silence, and he could see an airport silhouetted against the white snow. Familiar… oddly familiar.

He let the vision go, or it let go of him. He stood up too quickly, blood rushing to his head, and he fell to the ground. Sampson crawled to the door and screamed. He could see Bob, but blackness surrounded his vision. But he fought. Amidst a choppy breath he whispered, "Bob, it's fucking Syracuse again. A plane is down."

"Oh my god," was all he heard.

The execution of Mohawk Airlines flight number 113 was flawless. The stinger had struck its wing, ignited both fuel tanks, and fell a quarter mile away from Cates. As quiet and unnoticed as a church mouse, he left the field.

CHAPTER 24

Agent Becker wasted no time. He checked the information wire, but there were no reports. Who would he call? Syracuse—that cop, O'Reilly. A prick, but best available. He called the Syracuse PD and was put directly through to none other than O'Reilly. "O'Reilly, this is Bob Becker, CIA. Remember me? You saved my life."

"Yeah. I'm busy."

"Sarge, humor me. Are there any problems at your airport this morning?"

"No."

"I know this is crazy, but would you check?"

"Agent, you CIA spooks bug me."

"Forget the CIA. Do this for me."

"Fuck you. Hold on." Less than a minute passed, and an out-of-breath O'Reilly returned. "We have reports of a bird down, goddamn it! If you fucks had anything to do with this, I swear to God, I'll hunt you down."

"Calm down. We didn't. We are on the same side."

"How'd you know then?"

"A tip. Just got it." Becker lied but thought this to be easier than trying to explain Sampson repeatedly. "Sarge, I'll be back to you. And thanks." The line went dead.

"Sampson, it's bad. It's what you saw. A plane went down! I called that cop we met in Syracuse. O'Reilly was just getting the call."

"I want to go there."

"Done." Becker picked up the phone and barked, "I want the Challenger fueled, pilot ready. Destination Syracuse. The airport is closed, but there is a military base nearby. That will do. Wheels up in minutes." Sampson was amazed at how the CIA machine moved when it had to. "Let's go!"

Sampson nodded in agreement, and they moved to a waiting limousine and began the ten-minute trip to the airport. In the limo, Becker went straight to other business. "We did a full check on the names Binky and Bink. The official channels gave us shit, absolutely nothing."

"I sense there's more."

"Yup. The unofficial channels gave us more. If we've got the name right… and it appears to be 'Binky'… it's a brothel. He runs a brothel, not an ordinary brothel, mind you, but a brothel, nonetheless."

"No way! That explains why that poor woman was trapped underneath a monster."

"The clientele is the interesting part, however. Upscale; way, way upscale. He caters to the ultra-rich and famous, including politicians… big politicians. The place is supposed to be extravagant and 100% discreet."

They reached the airport, boarded the Challenger, and were airborne in less than two minutes. The flight to Syracuse would be only thirty-one minutes.

"Bob, what you told me in the car fits. So, finally we've got a link. Now we've got to figure out a way to exploit this."

They spent the remainder of the trip in silence, both men with their minds racing, trying to sort out the next move. The plane landed at the Air Force Base in Syracuse, where a waiting car and two additional agents met them. After brief introductions, they were whisked to Hancock Airport.

As they approached the entranceway to the airport, they were waved away by a uniformed officer until Agent Robert Becker produced his CIA badge. "Officer, we need to get to the scene immediately. We're meeting Officer O'Reilly." Becker anticipated that, with all the confusion, the officer would not check with O'Reilly, and he was right.

"All right. Straight ahead. Park as far to the right as you can. We're still getting emergency equipment."

"Thank you."

They drove ahead, passed the spot they were asked to park at, and pulled as close to the scene as possible. Sampson found the moment funny, "We love to piss people off, don't we?"

"Yeah, and we're good at it. Let's go," Becker said.

The group had dressed for the weather. It was cold and blustery. Another raw Syracuse day. Agent Becker was slightly out in front of the others and was prepared to run interference from the locals. They rounded the comer of the building and came upon another checkpoint. Becker and the others produced their IDs, signed a logbook, and moved ahead before any questions could be asked. As they rounded the last turn, they were struck by the carnage. The smell of jet fuel permeated the air. Charred wreckage. A big chunk of the fuselage lay in an open field. Debris of chairs, briefcases, luggage and, worst of all, bodies and parts of bodies, covered the landscape as a macabre horror scene.

"Just what I fucking need, the spook patrol!" O'Reilly had come up behind them. "I meant what I said," O'Reilly glared at Becker. "If you had anything to do with this, I'll hunt you down and kill you!"

Sampson stepped forward between the two men. "We didn't. I give you my word. We want to find out who did this every bit as bad as you do."

"Fair enough for now."

O'Reilly did not like the CIA or the FBI, or basically anyone for that matter, but he was smart enough to know that this would be a complicated case, and the resources of the CIA would help. He also didn't care who got the credit for the case. "Plane went down at 6:55 a.m. about an hour and a half ago. No survivors. Tower saw something leave the ground and hit the plane. It exploded. We think it was a missile. We're pulling the Air Traffic tapes or, should I say, the FAA is handling that? If it was a missile, and we think it was, it hit a fuel tank. The whole thing went up in a big kaboom. You can see what's left."

Becker jumped in, "Any group claim responsibility?"

"Nope, not yet, but we'll have a flock of them soon, as you know."

"Thanks, O'Reilly." Sampson felt an urge to walk the area. 'Would you mind if we looked around?"

O'Reilly liked Sampson. He could tell he wasn't being a prick; just trying to get his job done, much like himself. "Go ahead. Anyone gives you any trouble, tell them to go fuck themselves, and then see me."

As they parted company, Sampson walked away from the wreckage and toward the airport. The snow was deep and had already filled his loafers. He stopped as he felt pain in his head. He knew this was the spot where the devastation began. In front of him he could see an outline in the snow; much like an angel outline kids make in the fresh, fallen snow. He could feel the presence of the man who did this. Like unique pheromones, he knew he'd felt it before at the senator's house. Same man. Pictures flashed in his mind. He bent down and touched the snow outline. He saw a glimpse of a face. He could feel death still. But he let go. He sat in the snow, a handkerchief to his nose.

"You okay?" Becker stood behind him.

"Yeah. I will be in a minute." Sampson dabbed at his nose. "I saw him; at least some of him. Enough to make a start, anyway." Sampson suddenly felt something. Instead of death, this time it was life… a young life. Something was clinging to life here, nearby. Maybe. "Bob, get O'Reilly."

"What is it?"

"There isn't time. Hurry!"

Becker sprinted off and returned with a flushed O'Reilly. "What is it, spook?"

"Have you accounted for all the passengers?"

"No. You can see the fucking mess."

Sampson struggled with how to approach this. He couldn't tell him everything; there wasn't time. "O'Reilly, I know you don't like us, but I need your help. Someone, I think, is alive here."

"You're nuts. The place is a death zone."

"Please. There isn't time." Sampson shook his head back and forth.

"Where is this… person," O'Reilly asked.

"I'm not sure… I'm just not sure."

"Would you guys please get out of here?" O'Reilly said menacingly.

What a moody bastard. Apparently, he needed a Susan in his life too. Sampson moved forward and put his face two inches from the bully. "Someone's alive, I'm telling you! I'll find the person, or you can lock my ass up. I want you to clear this field right now. They'll listen to you. I will take full responsibility."

O'Reilly hesitated. He did like this kid… kind of. There wasn't much downside. Everyone was dead. The disruption could be blamed on the CIA. Why not. "All right, kid, but it's your ass."

O'Reilly moved toward another officer and muttered something. The officer returned with a bullhorn. "Okay, listen up everybody. Shut up! Shut up!" The crowd quieted enough. "I need everyone to stop what they're doing right now." As he looked around, he could see many workers were ignoring him. "Goddamn it, pay attention! Stop what you're doing right now and move to the building on my left. Move!" And they all did as they were told. O'Reilly walked to Becker and Sampson.

"Okay, I did my job. Now what?"

"Stand here with Bob." Sampson could see the looks of confusion and fear on peoples' faces. He wasn't sure how to proceed himself, so he started just walking methodically and slowly amidst the wreckage. He touched what he could. Occasionally he would get vague images of death. Nothing, damn it! Was he wrong?

As he reached the far end of the crash site, he sensed something faint. Sampson could tell from the lack of footprints in the snow that this area had had little traffic so far. As he moved through the debris, the sense became stronger, stronger. He turned over charred wreckage, moved seats that were strewn together. He was amazed at what he saw. An entire section of the plane buried in the ground. Sampson could see a good twenty feet down. It would be the most horrifying experience of his life. He could see seats with passengers' bloody, burned bodies. The smell was putrid. Yet, he knew something lived. He climbed down, trying not to step on bodies. Death everywhere. He turned over cushions and climbed deeper. Not only could he feel life, but he also heard a whimper in the furthest corner. He scrambled down, moving everything in his way.

As Sampson moved a blue blanket, there she was. A small girl, maybe three years old, still fastened in her seat. She looked up, weak and frightened. Her skin was cold to the touch.

"Hi, I'm Sampson. I'm here to help you. What's your name?" He waited, not expecting an answer.

"Becca."

"Becca. That's your name?" They both managed a smile. "What do you say we get out of here?"

Sampson unbuckled the toddler. He could see no injuries, but it would be best to be careful. The girl scrambled to her feet and clung to Sampson. "I bet it was scary for you down there, wasn't it?"

"Becca scared." She wrapped her arms around his neck and little knees across his chest.

"Becca, hold on tight and we'll climb out of here. How about we get a hot dog and a milk when we get out?"

"Hot dog."

How the hell did she survive? Only survivor. But her body was small and in the back of the plane. Angels fluttered around some. He firmly believed this. He also wondered about her parents. They were probably on the plane, which made her an orphan. Sampson pushed the thoughts away and scaled out of the hole. It was a difficult climb, all jagged edges and body parts. Becca did not make a sound. Probably shock.

As he took the final step out, he secured his grip on the child. Rather than continue the tight cling, she looked forward but kept her right arm wrapped around Sampson's neck.

"So far so good, Becca."

"Good. Good." And the girl smiled up at Sampson. She came into the view of the workers who were huddled to the side of the building.

"Good God!" O'Reilly mumbled. He could see cameras flashing and news crews whirling into action.

"He ain't bad, is he?" Becker uttered to grumpy O'Reilly.

The scene was surreal. Workers broke into cheers and applause. Someone had emerged from this disaster. It was what every rescue worker lived for and hoped for. Everyone's spirits lifted, including little Becca. She kept her grip on Sampson's neck and beamed. A pair of paramedics rushed forward with a stretcher. As the paramedic reached to take the girl, and Sampson loosened his grip, the child began to scream and shout, "Hold

Becca! Hold Becca!" As Sampson re-established his grip, the child's sobs subsided.

The paramedic said to the girl's new guardian for the hour at least, "Look, she's got to get to the hospital, and it would be better for her if we kept her still. She's probably in shock, and maybe a bit hypothermic. Who knows what else. How about taking a ride with us?"

O'Reilly had come up alongside, "Go ahead, spook. We can wrap up here."

"Will you tell Bob?"

"Yup. Oh, by the way… Sampson, nice work. You're still a spook, but I'm okay with it." Sampson laughed.

Little Becca looked at O'Reilly and said, "Spook."

This caught O'Reilly off guard. But he looked right at her, "Yeah, that's Sam. He's a spook."

Becca looked puzzled, "Spook?"

The paramedic looked impatient. "Hey, Lewis and Martin, can we go?"

"Yes."

Sampson, the two paramedics, and the lucky girl walked thirty feet to the ambulance, boarded and amidst lights and sirens, drove off.

CHAPTER 25

Less than three hours after the crash, Cates placed a call to the homes of the CEOs of the big five airlines. It was a recorded message utilizing the world's best technology. It would not be traceable, no matter what the best minds in the world tried.

"Good evening, gentlemen. This message is going to the CEOs of the big five airlines. You know who you are. Today at 6:55 a.m., Mohawk Airlines flight 113 was shot down in Syracuse by the Freedom Fighters Alliance. This is to show you Americans that tough tactics like those shown by your Senator Grant are bullshit. We won't and can't be stopped. But you can stop us from harming your airline and your passengers. To ensure this, you are to wire $10 million U.S. to Swiss Account #111121347602USB within three days. If we receive your payment, your airline will not be harmed. Feel free to contact the FBI. They won't find us. We are cleverer than them. They will tell you not to pay us, but it is your decision. If you pay, we will not harm your aircraft; if not, well… three days, gentlemen, and no more."

Cates could only imagine the confusion this would cause. Each of them would carefully weigh the decision. Of course, in the end, they would go to the FBI, and he would be forced to shoot down another plane. But all the better. More attention would be thrust upon Grant, and in the end, they would pay.

Ten million to an airline was nothing. He didn't know precisely what Wiz would pay him, but he know it would be handsome. Wiz knew better than to mess with him. That would be dangerous—deadly, in fact.

Becca would not leave Sampson's side or his lap all the way to the hospital. The paramedics determined the little girl to be in good shape. Her blood pressure was good, no apparent external injuries. They would have to wait to get to the hospital to see about internal injuries. The only concern was her temperature, which was 96.8 degrees... cold. They had her wrapped in blankets and boosted the temperature inside the ambulance.

Becca continued to cling to Sampson, "Are you feeling okay, kid?"

"Kid!" she shouted back.

"Oh, you want to play words?"

"Words."

"Can you say, 'hot dog'?"

"Dog."

"No, you missed 'hot'."

"Hot."

Everyone laughed. It helped them all. The death they had seen needed to be replaced with something good, and a child's laughter would be that medicine.

They arrived at the hospital, and an orderly reached to take Becca from Sampson. "NOOOO!" she screamed.

Sampson said, "Look, she's a little attached to me right now. How about I carry her where you need her?"

The young orderly objected, "No, that won't work. It violates policy."

"Policy, huh." Sampson became indignant and flashed his

CIA badge in the face of the orderly. "Fuck policy. This is a government matter."

Before the orderly could respond, Becca said, "Fuck!"

"Oh, shit. I've got to watch what I say."

"Shit!" said Becca.

Sampson looked at the orderly, who seemed amused. "For the time being, I'm in charge of her. I'm not leaving her side until the local police get here. I want a doctor now to see this child. She's a witness to a horrible crime." Sampson knew this was a stretch, but he also knew the orderly would buckle as this began to sound more official.

"Yes, sir. This way."

They were led to a curtained examination room, and within a couple of seconds, a woman introduced herself as Dr. Sarah Axel.

"What's wrong with your daughter? The orderly said it was urgent."

"It is urgent. This little girl survived a plane crash this morning. We need to know if she's okay."

The doctor appeared puzzled. "Who's 'we', you and your wife?"

Sampson realized this woman had no information. "No." He produced his badge, and he noticed the doctor take a step back. "I'm CIA, as you can see."

"Yes, I'm not blind." *Snappy*. Sampson also began to take notice of her beauty, which was extraordinary in a vampiric sort of way. Small in stature, maybe 5'2". Athletic build, a sculpted body. Translucent skin, thick, dark hair and dark eyes. *Gothic doctor.*

"Doc, my name is Sampson. I'm sorry we got off on the wrong foot. I've had a kind of a bad day."

"Bad day." It was Becca. They both laughed.

"Is she yours?"

"No, but I'd take her."

"Becca." She did it again.

"Yes, Becca, I'd take you." Sampson smiled at her.

"We're trying to find out about the parents now. Not sure if they were on the plane." "Oh, well, let's look her over. Sampson, would you take off her clothes?"

"Huh? How?"

"Try the buttons and the snaps. That seems to work best."

"Uh, huh." He fumbled with them, and eventually they came loose.

Becca became a bit more cooperative and lay on the examination table. After about half an hour, the doctor deemed her as healthy. Her temperature had come up, and she was fine.

"Agent Sampson, she looks tired. I'm sure she'll want to sleep soon. I want to observe her for a while. We must be careful of shock. We're going to move her to a room right now. I've arranged for a private room."

As Goth Doc finished speaking, a friendly female orderly in her early fifties entered the room with a wheelchair.

"Becca, if it's okay with you I'd like you to take a ride with this nice lady. She's going to take you to a nice room."

Before Becca could object, Sampson jumped in, "Becca, it's okay. I'll be up to your room in just a minute."

Remarkably, she agreed, and boarded the wheelchair with a smile on her face. No sooner had she left then in came Agent Becker and O'Reilly. Becker didn't look so happy. "She okay? The kid, I mean."

"She's fine, Bob. I'd like to introduce you to Dr. Sarah Axel. This is Officer O'Reilly. He hates me. And this is Bob, my boss. Dr. Axel is treating Becca."

O'Reilly scowled.

Following the odd greetings, Becker jumped in. "Doctor, would you stay for a moment? Sampson, the news is bad for the little girl."

"No. Tell me both parents weren't on the plane."

"No, they weren't, but just as bad. She's an orphan. She was on her way with a caseworker to an orphanage in Pittsburgh. She has no relatives. There were no other survivors on the plane."

A nurse burst into the room, "Doctor, you and the others should see this." They moved to the next room in time to catch part of a special bulletin on the television.

"… amid the wreckage today there was a miracle. While all were thought dead, a psychic brought in by the police…"

"Bob, how?" Sampson screamed.

"… his name is Sampson. Watch the footage," and they did. There he was moving, touching, and eventually climbing into the hole, and emerging with a tiny child. "… this man is a hero, and his name is Sampson."

"Wow, I'm really impressed," cooed Dr. Axel.

"I'm not. You won't understand this, but it complicates my life."

"You'll live, Mr. Hero."

Bob jumped in, "Doc, is the girl okay? Can we go now?"

"No, she needs some support right now. She's attached to Agent Sampson, and I think for a couple of days, she needs him. Besides, what's the plan for her?"

"Not sure. I'll notify Child Protective Services," O'Reilly said.

"Great! She lives through this shit and ends up in a foster home. Great world we live in!"

Becker broke in, "Look, Sampson, you stay here with the kid. I'm gonna go back with O'Reilly and see what we can come up with. I'll arrange rooms at the Marriott. Adios."

As they left, Sampson followed Dr. Axel back to Becca's bedside.

"Becca. Miss me?" he talked to her like her longtime caretaker.

"Miss."

"Boy, do I have a way with women!" Sampson beamed.

"She does seem to like you, that's for sure," Sarah said.

"Hey, there's a lot to like!"

"Maybe. Anyway, play with her for a while. I want to keep her awake for a few hours. I'll be back."

As Sarah left, Sampson began an easy ritual of talking and playing with little Becca. It was a special time for him, and he wondered why he had gone all these years without a wife and children. Seems like he had missed so much—way too much.

As he finished a long spat of contemplation, he was startled as Sarah came back, and more startled to see the clock. Almost 4:00 p.m. They had played for three hours, and it seemed like only minutes!

Sarah sensed his startled look. "What's up?"

"Nothing. I just had the best three hours that I've had in a long time, a very long time."

"That's nice." She motioned him to a corner of the room. "I'm going to give her some medication that will make her drowsy and probably sleep. It's important. We can feed it through the IV." Sarah went to a nearby cabinet, produced a syringe, and gently tapped into the IV. Within five minutes, Becca was peacefully asleep. Sarah and Sampson tucked her in.

Sampson lightly kissed her forehead. "Amazing kid."

"Yes, and very lucky." She looked more directly at him, which caught him off guard. "Would you like to have dinner tonight? I'm off in a few moments. Syracuse has some good spots. I'd love some company. I promise to get you back before she wakes up."

Sampson thought it over only momentarily. "I'd love to."

"Before we go, I've got to ask. Is this psychic stuff for real?"

"Afraid so. Want to see?"

"Yeah, I guess. What do I do?"

"Hold my hand and think about what you'd like to do tonight. I'll do the rest." She lightly held his hand and concentrated on tonight. Sampson found himself happily surprised. He was having similar thoughts.

"Ready?"

"Yup."

"I'll give you two hints... *room* and *service*."

Sarah turned beet red. "Oh, God!"

"Don't 'Oh, God' me. I had the same thoughts."

"Oh, God."

"We're adults." He smiled, and she relaxed. "What about her? Is it okay to leave?" Sampson was very concerned.

"She'll sleep a long time. Besides, I'll have my pager. If she wakes up, we'll come right back."

"All right. Shall we go, and where to?"

They proceeded to the Syracuse Marriott, a hotel Sampson remembered well. After they checked in, Sampson wandered to the gift shop and picked up some essentials: two toothbrushes, two hairbrushes, two mouthwashes, toothpaste, a razor and shaving creme, and a big, red Elmo.

"That for me?" Sarah said.

'"No, you get a toothbrush, though. This is for Becca."

"That's it?"

"That's it."

They took the elevator up and entered the room. '"Not bad. There is a minibar," Sarah said.

"Thank God! If you don't mind, I'm going to take a shower and then we can look at the menu, if that's okay." Sampson studied her face for approval. What a naughty doctor. Then his mind drifted to Susan. He wasn't the player type. Either way, he and Susan only had one dinner date! Well, dinner date and a dead body.

"Okay with me. Is it a big shower?"

"I imagine it's very roomy. But it would be a good thing to check out. I'll let you know if the hot water works."

"Okay," she cooed.

Sampson left the room and stripped down in the bathroom. He started the shower, and the hot water felt wonderful on his skin. As he closed his eyes, he felt something suddenly grab his ankles. He came instantly awake, ripped the shower curtain open, prepared for the worst. But there would be no worst. In front of him, a sight of milky white skin set off by black body hair. She looked Eastern European.

"Gotcha," she chuckled.

"Yeah, you did. You scared me to death!" Sampson smiled.

"I'm a doctor. I'll save you." She stepped in and felt the hot water envelope her body. They began to kiss, lightly at first, then with intensifying passion. Their hands explored each other, and Sampson felt himself being guided into her. She was delicious to his senses. Her smell, her movement, her taste. Within minutes, they both erupted with a series of moans and passionate movements.

"So, do you do this with all the CIA guys?"

She smiled and slapped him playfully. "Some, but not all."

"How about we towel off and order dinner? I saw two of those ugly terry cloth robes in the closet."

"Ugly, but they'll do."

They had natural, free-flowing conversation. Sampson learned that she was unattached, with her job leaving little time for men or anything else. She had grown up with five older brothers, which likely developed her hard exterior. But she loved helping and healing people. She mothered a cat and two goldfish only. She was also poetry in motion in bed. He learned that several more times before his alarm went off at 6:00 a.m.

Sampson was the first to wake, and he playfully nudged his partner and did his best Rocky imitation, "Yo, Adrian, time to get up."

"Oh, shut up. And hold onto your mind-reading job. You won't make it as a comedian."

"Hmm. I thought I was pretty good."

"How about a hug?"

"Do I get free medical care?"

"I'd be willing to do a one-time inspection of your body."

"Okay, it's a deal."

They both laughed and fell into one another's arms. Thirty minutes later, they were showered and arrived at the hospital by 8:00 a.m. when Becca was just waking up. Sampson was relieved that she would see him as she awoke. "Hi, kid."

She beamed brightly, yawned, and rubbed her eyes.

"Sarah, before it gets crowded here, I wanted to tell you how much I enjoyed last night. I hope we can see each other again."

"Me, too." She kissed him lightly on the cheek, and went to examine Becca. After a twenty-minute examination, Dr. Axel finished up and pronounced Becca fit as a fiddle. "She's just fine. Nothing wrong, Sampson. She can leave today."

"No," he asserted.

Sarah was startled. "Hey, why are you mad at me?"

"I'm sorry. It's not you, it's me. She has nowhere to go but to an orphanage. I don't like that. Look, could you keep her one more night? Call it observation," Sampson pleaded.

"Yes, but what will that do? Prolong the inevitable?" Sarah turned her head down.

"Maybe, but it will give me some time to figure something out." Sampson gave his best forlorn look.

"Okay, consider it done."

Sampson now had a hot doctor and a hot attorney, with her senator father, in his corner. He thanked his lucky stars. And then there was this little girl whose heart he did not want to break. Sampson gave her a little squeeze as she left the room. Before

Sampson could reach the bed, Becker walked in and looked glum faced.

"Nothing to be had at the crash site. It was clean, professional. But it was a terrorist group. They called the CEOs of the big five airlines demanding $10 million each, or more shootings for those who don't pay. The terrorists say your buddy, Senator Grant, is to blame. They don't like his tough stance. I say, 'Fuck 'em'; I like what he stands for."'

"What are the airlines going to do?"

"Don't know. You and I will be meeting with the five CEOs this afternoon in Washington."

"When are we leaving?"

"About an hour, give or take."

"Bob, I figure the CIA owes me a couple of favors, wouldn't you?"

"Yes…"

"Well, I'm cashing one in. The kid is going with us."

"No. No way. Can't be done." Becker shook his head.

"Oh, why not? Come on. We'll call her a witness. She might need protection. Look, she's an orphan. I'm going to figure something out and until then, I want her with me."

"If l had time to argue, you'd lose, but I don't. Get your friend," he winked as he said it, "To get her ready."

"What's the wink for?" Sampson caught on. He knew about he and Sarah last night.

"I am the CIA." He burst into laughter.

Saying goodbye to Sarah was awkward and uncomfortable. Sampson didn't feel certain he would see her again.

CHAPTER 26

Within ninety minutes, they were airborne. The flight was quick. The CIA had arranged for Becca to stay at a small safe house in suburban Washington. Round-the-clock sitters and guards would ensure her happiness courtesy of the U.S. government.

Sampson would stay as often as possible, but he knew he had to solve this case. It couldn't wait. Lives would be sacrificed. Sampson was sure of that.

As soon as they touched down, they were met by two nondescript black sedans. The first would transport the child to the safe house. The second would rush Bob and Sampson back to the Central Intelligence Agency in Langley, Virginia. Luckily, Becca was sleepy for the journey and once handed to the federal agent, offered no resistance.

"Take care of her. She is a special package." He surrendered the child to the female agent.

"Oh, I will, sir. Don't worry!" the young agent shot back. "Will I see you tonight?"

"Yes, but I don't know when. I'll call."

"Okay."

Sampson's heart tugged at him at the sight of Becca's departure. He had a fatherly instinct, and it was raging for the first time in his sorted life.

"You like her, huh?" Bob grinned. "You've got a way with women. The kid, the doc… by the way, how was she?"

"I forgot you're a spook. But to answer your question, she was fine."

"*Fine*, huh?"

"Yeah, fine. And you won't get any more details. Except for the chandelier we pulled out of the ceiling." Both men shared a laugh.

They arrived back at CIA. It seemed to both like they had been gone for months. In truth, it had been less than forty-eight hours since this latest turn of events had occurred.

"Sampson, we've got to finish this quickly. You know that."

"Yes, I do. I don't think the killing is over. Not by a long shot."

The remainder of the morning and early afternoon moved along at a snail's pace for Sampson. He was tired from his lack of sleep due to the good goth doc, and his thoughts constantly drifted back to the little girl. Why did she feel so familiar? Literally like family. Or did he just long for more intimacy, kinship wherever he could get it in his cold, surreal reality?

CHAPTER 27

Cates and Whisnant met in another out-of-the-way diner in suburban Virginia. Cates was the first to arrive and had only a moment to order coffee before Whisnant's arrival. Cates had known Whisnant a long time and was well-aware of his many qualities, both good and evil. He was always punctual for better or for worse.

They hunkered down in an isolated booth in the far corner of the diner. Both men sat silently, looked at the greasy laminated menu, and ordered a late lunch consisting of cheeseburgers, fries, and Cokes. As the waitress completed the order and retreated to the kitchen, the men finally looked at each other and were prepared to start a conversation. Cates punted the first words to Wiz.

"Colonel, the work we've done seems to be ready to pay off. I understand the FBI and the CIA are meeting with the airlines shortly."

"That's what my sources, which are probably not as good as your sources, are telling me. Surely you're not surprised that they went to the police."

"No. In fact, I would have been much more surprised if they hadn't gone to the authorities. Well, no matter. It doesn't change the decisions they need to make. It just adds a little pressure for them to say no. But in the end, they won't say no. They will say yes, hoping their planes won't be shot down and, worse yet, their ridership decline. They'll pay, Cates, mark my words, they'll fucking pay."

"Seems that way to me also. I might do the same thing. I also must tell you that I have about had it with this Sampson guy. You will not have to pay me to take care of him next time. That one is on the house." Cates was annoyed, angry maybe, and Wiz needed to make sure that he did nothing to upset their delicate plan that was intact so far.

"Look, Colonel, don't worry about him. He hasn't hurt us, and everything we have tried to do, we've done. He's a nuisance; a housefly that will land on a pile of shit soon. He can't hurt us. Don't waste energy thinking about him."

"All right," Cates said flatly. But Wiz wasn't convinced. He'd have to give this more thought. If Cates started on a vendetta, this whole thing could explode. Wiz was concerned. The look on Cates's face told him that trouble might lie ahead.

They struggled with the dripping burgers in silence as both men thought of their next moves. Cates would head back to his house, and Wiz to a greater house… The White House.

CHAPTER 28

At about four o'clock, five of the most powerful men in the world were assembled in the windowless conference room of an unassuming boutique hotel in the suburbs of Virginia. The men all knew each other but had seldom spoken outside of public social occasions. All lived in fear of a government-sponsored collusion investigation. Each knew how to play the game well. If they wanted a competitor to know something, there were private and secret ways to disseminate info. They all knew why they were here today. What they didn't know was what they should do about the catastrophe. They individually hoped answers would come from another in the same sinking boat.

Bob and Sampson met briefly outside the room. "Sampson, I'll take the lead. Just follow me. Remember they are powerful men, entitled and used to getting their own way. They don't take direction well. They can't be threatened. Let's tread as light as Fred Astaire."

They walked into the stonily silent room. After introductions, Bob began.

"Gentlemen, thank you for coming. I am Agent Robert Becker, and this is Agent Sampson. This is our case. The matter at hand has national security issues, and that's why the CIA is involved. We are co-operating with all of the other government agencies, but make no mistake, we are the lead dog in this investigation." Bob stopped and caught his breath. Surprisingly he seemed to have their full attention. He continued.

"What I am going to tell you is quite confidential, and I will ask you to keep it that way. We believe what happened in Syracuse today is linked to the series of assassination attempts on Senator Grant. The first attack, as you know, was the bombing in Syracuse. I was there, along with Agent Sampson. It was done professionally. There were no clues left at that scene at all. It was something of a miracle that the senator was not killed. But let's not forget that a lot of innocent people died from that explosion."

Bob moved on. "Senator Grant was also targeted at his estate in Virginia. Four government agents and four mercenaries, hired gunmen, were killed. Again, no evidence was left behind. A young woman was killed in suburban Washington just a couple of days ago, and we think there is a link to this case (he decided not to tell him that his psychic partner was the only reason that they even thought she was involved). Lastly, and the reason we are here today, the downing of the Mohawk Airlines flight in Syracuse. We still don't know everything. All but one toddler died in the wreckage."

Sampson surveyed the conference room. As if in a trance of horror and disbelief, the participants sat with stony expressions on their faces, no one moving at all.

"We're fairly certain that the aircraft was hit with a surface-to-air missile, probably a Stinger. It appears to be a U.S. government-issued device, based on a shell casing we recovered. The gunman, or gunmen, knew what they were doing. The shell hit the left wing, which triggered a cataclysmic explosion that caused the crash. We're not optimistic about learning too much more. We know it was professionally done, just like everything else we've encountered so far. That brings us to the case at hand. We have heard the tape each of you received. I also need to tell you that at least one news organization already has the tape, and it will be public by the six o'clock news tonight. That's what we know. Agent Sampson and I will be glad to answer any questions you may have."

"Sir, I have some questions." The voice was that of the CEO of Marine Airlines, a Dallas-based carrier, the most powerful of the airlines and men represented here. He was a tall, angular and thin man who spoke with a slight drawl. "My assessment here is that we are boxed in real tight in this. If we don't pay, this nut will shoot down another plane; on the other hand, he may do that anyway. On the other side, our revenue stream is in big, big trouble either way. People won't fly until they feel more comfortable. From what you just told us, you're not too close at all to solving this. I'm not a brain surgeon, but it seems unreasonable to think that the police, the FBI, the CIA, whoever… can safeguard the 300-plus airports in the U.S. Plus, you just said this monster is a professional, not amateur, so it's probably a longshot that you'd catch them in the act. In short, gentlemen, *we're fucked right up the ass*." He accentuated his last words as if this disaster weren't dramatic enough.

Sampson jumped in, "Your assessment, sir, is very good, but we do have some leads and remember, this is the CIA. We have the best talent in the business, and the best tools. We'll find them. I'm sure of that."

"Son, no disrespect, but we ain't got time," the CEO shot back.

"I understand, sir, but—"

"No buts, son. Agents, would you leave us alone? We need to talk about this privately." The four pasty-faced, white-haired CEOs nodded in unison like a group of robots.

Once outside the room, Bob breathed and exhaled deeply. "They are right, you know. They can't win."

An hour later, Sampson and Bob were summoned back to

the conference room. The Texan spoke for everyone as if on cue. "None of us are used to losing, and we can't win here. We've talked our options through. Our strategy is to minimize damage in this situation. We're going to pay. Tell the public we paid. We hope that that will keep the public flying and our planes in the air."

Bob and Sampson gawked at each other. That was it? No other context or sentimentality played up for the loss of life. In this simmering pot, these lobsters opened and closed their mouths to chew on the loss of revenue only.

Bob replied, "You know, your plan is a bit flawed. You are assuming this group won't take your money and keep blowing away planes."

"No, sir, we don't know that. But short of you finding this group, we don't have any other alternatives. If we don't pay, no one will fly and on top of that, our insurance carriers will drop us. In short, we go out of business, our people lose their jobs, and our shareholders lose the money they've invested in us; not to mention the reality of what happens to the U.S. economy if our business travelers can no longer travel for business."

It was Sampson's turn. "We thought you'd get to this point. While we can't recommend one way or another, we support your decision. What we'd like to do now is work with you on all the details. Maybe we'll catch a break."

The Texan nodded in agreement. "Son, we'll do whatever you ask."

Those instructions would take the next several hours to shape and share. Still, Sampson and Bob were not entirely sure about their plan.

Bob yawned and shook his head. "Tomorrow, we've got to sort out what we're going to do with Binky. I think it's time to rattle that cage."

"I agree. Well, goodnight. See you in the morning."

Sampson gathered his stuff and started out the door to his car. He had no intention of going home. He drove straight to the safe house, with his protective detail behind to be sure no one followed him. After showing his identification, he was let in. He found the little girl on the couch watching "Barney". When he caught her eye, she ran to him shouting, "Sam!" Her hug was like nothing he had ever experienced in his life. He felt warm, safe, and familiar with the little girl. She led him to the couch and curled up in his lap. They watched "Barney" giggling for half an hour before Sampson got on the floor and pretended to be the goofy purple dinosaur as Becca squealed with delight.

"Agent Sampson." Sampson looked up to see a female agent standing near a sofa. "It's almost 10:00. We should put her to bed, sir."

"Oh, God, you're right! I'm sorry. I've never had kids. I've always just been a kid. Should we feed her?"

"You really don't remember being a kid, do you? Kids eat dinner at 5:30 or so. She ate hours ago."

"Oh. Well, if you'll help me, let's get her ready for bed."

The female agent led Sampson to the child's bedroom. Sampson was amazed. A stylish toddler bed was set up. Five or six outfits, sneakers, and a hat, all lay on the bed. The agent caught him marveling at the items. Would he shop for all this one day?

"We went shopping today. She is a great kid, chose all her own outfits!"

Sampson's face lit up with talk of her independence. He couldn't claim "like father, like daughter," but it came to mind strangely.

In ten minutes, the child was changed and wearing pink fuzzy pajamas with feet. She looked adorable. They played for a few more minutes until she began to yawn and rub her eyes.

"Tired, huh, kid? I have a gift for you!" Sampson handed her the Elmo doll he had purchased for the girl. She immediately hugged the doll.

"It's Elmo."

"Elmo!"

Sampson scooped her up, and she nestled into his shoulder. Nothing had ever felt better to him. He gently rocked and walked back and forth, and within minutes she was asleep. He placed her gently in the mini bed and kissed her goodnight on the forehead. He pulled a light pink blanket up around her. Sampson left the room, closing the door behind him. He spoke briefly to the agents. They seemed nice; he trusted them. He was tired and headed for home.

Sampson opened a beer and sat quietly on a couch, trying to figure out what to do with Becca. This was now his role—to do something with the little girl. His brain already burning from the other topics of the day, Sampson fell asleep without a blanket, which never happened.

While Sampson slept, Cates did not. He was not pleased with his meeting with Whisnant. He could see the doubt in the man's eyes, despite his conciliatory words. Cates had never been beaten; not ever. He had been in combat many times and had always won. He had been a mercenary for five years and had never been beaten. Now, this Sampson person was beating him, and the beating would have to end.

Cates spent the entire evening on the phone. He worked every contact he had at the CIA and the FBI. He learned more than he would need to know to settle his score with Sampson. And the score would be high, even at the price of others in the freak's circus tent.

CHAPTER 29

Back at The White House, which seemed to be hosting a bunch of crusty, old senior citizens today of all days, Wiz briefed the President, who seemed uninterested in the good news. The airlines had complied, and the money was sitting in an untraceable account in Switzerland. Fifty million dollars… fifty million tax-free dollars… which would certainly ease their retirement worries. On top of the money, the polls were swinging back in the direction of the President and his "softer" stance on terrorism. In essence, the whole goddamn plan was working, and no one seemed to give a shit. The President didn't give a shit, that crazy merc, Cates, didn't care a bit.

Wiz stormed out of the White House, taking out a few walkers and canes in his haste, unbeknownst to the President.

In truth, the President did care and pulsed underneath with satisfaction. He was just thinking of other things that were more pressing. He decided he would have dinner and thank Wiz tomorrow night. He should have been more thoughtful.

Morning came quickly for Sampson. He showered, dressed, and was at his desk by 7:45 a.m. Progress needed to be made today, and he was determined to close this case.

On the drive in he thought of Susan, and decided before the

day got too busy, he would see if she could join him for dinner. For a split second, the gothic doctor jumped his thoughts, but he didn't feel the warmth, emotional resonance, that he did when he thought of Susan. He began to perspire as the phone rang. To his surprise, it was Susan who picked up the phone on the second ring.

"Susan Grant."

"Counsel. Did you miss me?" She instantly recognized the voice, and it brought a bright smile to her lips.

"Well, sort of. I thought our last date went so well... you know, dead bodies, police and all."

"Yeah, that was probably not the greatest date of all time for you. So, I have another proposal. Something normal. Same black dress, different occasion. Besides, I'd like for you to meet someone."

"I hate double dates!"

"I know. You want me to yourself."

"Not exactly."

"Trust me."

"All right." Susan really did want to see him. The short time they had spent together were pleasurable moments for her. She liked him, and wanted to see where this would all go.

"I'll get you at 5:00 p.m."

"That's early."

"I know. We've got to be somewhere at 5:30 sharp."

Susan agreed and they hung up. Susan adjusted her glasses and smiled for the first time that morning. She was in immense pain from uveitis, eye inflammation, again. She had a figure from hell, a sophisticated wardrobe to match, and incessant eye issues that prevented her from seeing the full ensemble for longer than a few moments in the mirror. Her mother's doctor wanted to put a steroid shot straight in her iris, but Susan almost fainted at the thought of it. She refused the treatment, knowing if the problem persisted, she could go blind. Sampson seemed like the kind of guy who would be nurturing, but she had to be sure. Mulling it all over, her smile remained.

Sampson was smiling as Bob's very serious presence in the doorway shook him to his senses. "Sampson, it's time to shake the tree. I've got a warrant to search Binky's." Go time.

"This should be fun. Let's go. Hopefully we'll wake them up," Sampson eagerly responded.

They arrived at Binky's in twenty minutes. Bob had requested a backup unit and was pleasantly surprised to see an unmarked Ford Taurus waiting half a block up the street. He pulled up alongside and rolled down the window.

"Sampson and I are going to go in alone. We don't expect any trouble. I'd like you guys to find the parking garage exit. No one gets out until we finish. I have some fear the rats may try and leave the ship."

The agents nodded affirmatively, and Sampson and Bob drove to the entrance, parked, and walked to the front door. They found the door locked, and were surprised to see a surveillance camera trained on them. They smiled and waved at the camera. A thin, scratchy voice emerged from a nearby intercom.

"Can I help you, gentlemen?"

"Yes. We're here to see Binky," Sampson wryly replied.

"Do you have an appointment?"

'No, the U.S. government said we could just show up." Sampson flashed his CIA badge at the camera. "We have a search warrant. I want this door open right now, or I'll take it down myself."

About a minute went by during which the agents assumed that Binky was being notified that he was about to have his day ruined officially. Too bad it had to occur so early. A buzzer sounded. The agents walked through a glass door to be escorted to Binky's office. They were met by a bearded, round man who asked them to sit across from him at a desk. The agents took in the surroundings—functional, but not overpowering office. Leather chairs, high-end PC, a widescreen TV with a laptop connected to it. Why that? Seems out of place. *Probably nothing*, Sampson thought.

Bob took the lead, "Mr. Binkoski, is it?"

"Yes."

"May we call you Binky?"

"Yes, why?"

"Oh, nothing."

"I'm Agent Becker, and this is Agent Sampson. We are with the CIA. We have a search warrant." Bob slid it across the desk. 'We are going to search this building in some detail this morning."

"But why?" Binky gasped. He was a trained liar. He approached the situation calmly and was already playing the part of the martyr. Bob moved forward.

"We believe you were involved in the death of this woman." He slid a photo across the desk of the woman lying on the medical examiner's table. Binky looked at it, wrinkled his brow slightly.

"Never seen her before." As he said it, his mind raced ahead to how he would or could preserve that lie. He wasn't sure how he would hold up. He knew under scrutiny that his girls would not hold up.

"Now, you're sure about that, sir?"

"Yes. Am I under arrest?"

"No, not yet. You'll know when that happens."

Sampson stood up and walked behind Binky and placed his hands on the shoulders of the broad man. "Binky, I think you know what happened here. I think you're not telling the truth. Now, who did this to the girl?"

The man was silent, but his thoughts were clear, and Sampson concentrated with all his might. He saw the face of a man he knew from the news, he heard the name 'Wiz"...

"Sampson. *Agent Sampson!*"

Sampson broke the connection and looked at Bob. Bob motioned toward his nose, and Sampson instinctively touched his, only to find it was moist and crimson. He quickly applied his handkerchief and noticed he had also dripped blood on the shoulders of the man below him. No matter: he had gotten the information he needed.

"Agent Becker, I'd like to see you privately for a moment."

The men stepped outside the door. "Bob, we've got what we need. Let's do a quick search, tell him we're sorry that it was a mistake, and get out. We need to preserve doubt in his mind that we have him nailed. Trust me."

Without hesitation, Bob agreed.

They went back in the room. Sampson looked directly at Binky. 'We want to search the place. Would you show us the rooms, sir?"

They spent about an hour searching every room and corner. The agents were shocked at the crop of elegant, gorgeous women who worked for Binky, a stout mouse of a man, at least on the exterior. None of the women appeared trashy or cheap in any way.

Sampson and Bob found bits and pieces of information, but never let on about any discoveries. Within three hours, they left the building and headed to their car. They drove to the rear of the building and thanked the other agents, who looked incredibly bored waiting in their car.

"Well, that was fun, Bob. Where do you want to start?"

"Well, how about what we found through conventional methods, absent the psychic shit?"

Sampson smiled. "So, start with the old-fashioned shit, eh?"

"Yup."

"First of all, if I die, I want it to be there in her arms. *Her* could be any of them! My God, did you see those women?" Sampson exclaimed.

Agent Becker's mind was on the round man though. Any man in that position, no matter how meek or polite he came off, was used to hiding things.

Sampson continued, "I saw quite a bit that interested me. Let's start with the basics. It's a high-end brothel. He has a dozen girls designed to meet all tastes. More importantly, the bedrooms are all arranged the same, furniture in deliberate places. I couldn't spot them without being obvious, but I'll bet there are cameras someplace. One other thing. Did you notice that false wall in Binky's office early in the tour? If the carpet hadn't been matted, I'd have missed it. But I'd like to see what's in there. That's it for the visual. What'd I miss?"

"Nothing. You caught what I caught. Tell me about the supernatural stuff."

"I guess in my previous life you saw me work an audience. Remember every once in a while, you saw someone who just connected with me. I got to their thoughts in a heartbeat. Well, that's this guy. Clear as a bell and quick as a sprinter. Sit tight. The guy we want is none other than John Whisnant. Ring any bells?"

"Wiz? No way, can't be. He's…"

"Oh, it is him, it's him. No doubt. I saw him clear as a bell. He killed the girl. Binky knows it. Binky is sure of it. No mistakes here."

"Fuck, fuck, fuck. I'm not sure how this information was obtained will hold up in court. Binky didn't tell us this—you took it. What do we do with this? Goddamn!"

"Hey, he's a bad guy with a big title. We bust his ass, plain and simple."

"Easier said than done. He's basically the number two guy in the White House, tightly connected with all the agencies. If he smells this coming he'll squash us big time. Maybe worse. Partner, we've got to do this on our own. No one else can know. It could be life threatening to us."

"Maybe I'll go back to doing my little shows," Sampson huffed.

"No way. I am not doing this alone!"

"All right, partner. What do we do?"

CHAPTER 30

As soon as the agents left, Binky phoned Wiz and was surprised to reach him on the first ring. "Wiz, it's me. We have a problem. We should get together."

"I'll be over in two hours."

The line went dead. Binky was dreading the meeting, but he knew Wiz would find out what happened earlier in the day. He had no desire to anger this man. He was volatile and dangerous, all in one package. Binky knew Wiz would be furious that the law was getting a bit close. He would have to think about how he positioned what was discussed.

In exactly two hours, Wiz was escorted into Binky's office. The dreaded moment had arrived. What Binky didn't know was that Wiz already knew most everything. And more importantly, that this was a test for Binky. Would he tell the truth? Would he hold up if things got a bit rough?

"Binky, how are you?" Wiz smiled and extended his hand, which Binky weakly shook. Wiz found his hand warm and sweaty. Not a good sign.

"I'm fine, Wiz. We need to talk right now." Binky was antsy, and a fine line of perspiration was forming above his bushy brow.

Wiz wanted to talk to Binky, but on his terms and his timing. Control was critical, and he intended to be the lead dog, and wanted Binky to clearly get that message. "Binky, I'd like to, uh, relax a bit first. How about you get me an hour or so with one of the fine ladies that reside here?"

Binky wanted no part of waiting, but he knew better than to cross this psychopath.

"All right. Let me see." He banged the keyboard and dreaded the answer. *Not her. Not her.*

Please, not her! Alas, the only available girl was Caryn. Caryn had been his personal favorite for the year and a half she had been with him. A tall, dark-haired, twenty-two-year-old who resembled Cindy Crawford, both in looks and mannerisms. Binky had come across her through an acquaintance and liked her instantly. She lugged around a tough life. An only child, her parents were killed in a car accident on her nineteenth birthday, a day she would never forget. Her parents had been poor and basically, after funeral expenses, she was left with nowhere to live and about $2,000 to her name.

Caryn had taken to waitressing and while the money and the hours were okay, she didn't want to sling plates and glassware for long. She drifted toward acting and modelling and found that to be a dead end for her. No job offers knocked on the door like the horny agents promised and in four months, her savings burned through. That's when Binky and Caryn happened upon each other. Binky took to her instantly. Besides her obvious looks, she had a sparkling personality. They struck a quick business deal.

She approached her business as a CEO. When she was with a man (and a couple of lucky times, a woman) she was single-mindedly focused on pleasing the client. She approached the video teaching sessions that Binky provided with the same passion. She soaked in his teaching and put it to practice in the very next session. She learned quickly and was without a doubt, the best woman in his stable. The thought of putting his favorite with this madman was beyond comprehension. Binky had no way out. She was the only option, other than saying no, and that was not an option.

"Caryn is available. She is delightful. Let me take you to her."

Binky had already alerted Caryn via the computer that he was on the way up. He sent his files to her and while she would only have a moment to review them, he knew she would be ready. As they knocked on her door and the door opened, Wiz was delighted with what he saw: a statuesque dark-haired beauty. Caryn was dressed in a tight white halter-top and spandex pants and was wearing a pair of white Keds. She looked like a college senior who just returned from a class where no male in the room, including the professor, could concentrate on anything except her beauty.

"Well, thanks for the ride, Binky. I'll take it from here." Wiz placed his hand around her waist and closed the door behind them. Wiz liked the feel of this woman.

Binky raced to his study, desperately wanting to watch this, but totally unsure of what he could do to stop this if anything went wrong.

"Would you like a drink, Mr. Whisnant?"

He chuckled to himself. Not only did she look like a coed, but she was also going to play coed. *Well,* he thought, *this could be fun. Why not?* "Sure. How about a vodka martini. Will you join me?"

"Yes on both counts."

As Binky tuned in, he watched as Caryn made the martinis and moved to the sofa near Wiz. They made small talk for a few minutes while each finished their drinks. Caryn inched closer and gently began to kiss Wiz's neck. He responded by pulling her closer and gently caressing her breasts. In seconds, they were passionately kissing one another, and they moved quickly to the bedroom.

His heart fluttering, Binky prayed this would be quick and his angel would be safe.

Wiz lay on the bed with Caryn straddling him. She pulled her top over her head and revealed full breasts with round, hard nipples. Wiz devoured all her beauty with his alert, darting eyes. Next, she removed her sneakers and shorts, then began to undress him. He was amazed at how excited he was about this woman. For brief moments he was able to forget his troubles and really concentrate on this woman.

Caryn straddled him and slid his ample manhood inside her. They moved rhythmically for a long period of time, his eyes open and watching every minute. Abruptly he shifted, and he was now on top of her. She noticed his facial expressions had shifted from soft pleasure, to a focused, maybe angry, look. Wiz felt it happening again. As he neared climax, he felt me must kill this girl just as he came.

Binky could see it all and was mortified. He spoke to his screen, "Read the signs, Caryn. Read the signs!"

Caryn noticed what was happening. She also knew what Binky had taught her to do. In her line of work, sometimes the customers got rough. "Oh, Wiz, please go slower. This is the moment of a lifetime. I've never felt like this."

She looked directly at him, and it had the desired effect. He blinked and slowed. She could tell moments only stood in the way of climax, and she just needed to ease him through.

His thrusts slowed. As he began to moan, he placed his hands around Caryn's neck and squeezed. While he wanted to kill her, he would not. It would raise his risk profile. Wiz finished the act unceremoniously, rolled over, and went to shower. Ten minutes later, Wiz winked at Caryn while breezing past her naked body on the bed and exited the room.

Eyes glued to the screen, Binky released a high-pitched laugh from the relief and glee he felt. It felt like a holiday—a happy hooker one. Caryn, as savvy as she was, would never know how close she was to being destroyed by this maniac.

In minutes, Wiz and Binky were squirreled away together. "That girl is good, Binky. I want her next time." No words sounded sweeter to Binky, but he would have time to plan and protect his best girl next time. "Well, hit me with the details."

For the next thirty minutes, Binky shared the details of his unsettling meeting with the agents. That damned Sampson was really something. His mind seemed to be on overdrive taking in every nook and cranny of his whore house.

Wiz said, "Look, they have nothing. I know that because I checked with the bureau… discreetly. If you don't say anything else, this goes away in a matter of days. And Binky, let me be clear. If you do something stupid, I will hunt you down like the dog you are and butcher you. You do understand that, don't you?"

Sour sweat dripped into his mouth. "Look, Wiz, I understand the score. We have history. You know you can count on me."

"You're right. I do count on you—for ample ass when I want it. I just don't know about this situation. Tell you what. Let's talk this through over a steak at Jimmy's tonight. I'll pick you up out front at 8:30."

"All right. Sounds good," Binky lied, but he had to play this game out.

It was always interesting how a meeting between two people could be interpreted in totally opposite ways. Binky left feeling like he had survived; Wiz left knowing Binky would never see another steak in his life.

CHAPTER 31

Sampson arrived at Susan Grant's workplace at 5:20 and was escorted to her office. He found Susan with her head down busily writing on a pad. For a moment, she did not notice him, and he was struck with just how lovely she was. Her office was immaculate too. A big corner office, solid cherry furniture, and even a couch and chairs in the far corner. Susan suddenly looked up. "Hello, sailor. Need a date tonight?"

"Yup. Anybody in mind?"

"Yup. Me, and we are going to have fun!" She stood up, removed her big block glasses and came around the desk to kiss him fully on the mouth. Sampson was pleasantly surprised... and caught off guard. He stammered a bit and said, "Look, lady, I want you to know that I'm not easy."

"Good to know." She gave him a throaty laugh. "Shall we?" But in all her enthusiasm, she winced in shrieking pain. *Fucking eye.* Sampson noticed the change in Susan's demeanor as she put her glasses back on. He wanted to inquire, but also craved to make this a seamless date. He hoped to know her inside out soon enough.

They walked out of the building and into Sampson's car. Susan smelled gourmet food and was surprised to see two upscale, gold takeout bags nestled in the back seat. "Oh, I can't wait to hear this—and taste that!" Susan was smiling, and Sampson was relieved that she would be a good sport.

"Well, let me tell you a little tale. You remember that picture of me with the little girl that I found in the plane crash in Syracuse?"

Susan looked directly at him. "Sure, I do. I'm sure everyone does."

"Well, we have her tucked away in a safe house. I kind of bent the rules to make that happen. It seems there is another woman in my life, and it's a two-year-old! Her name is Becca. You see, she is an orphan with no one in the world, no relatives. When that plane went down, she was on her way to an orphanage. When I found out I was… well… sad. I thought maybe I could at least buy her some time in a safe house. But now… don't laugh at me… I, well, like her, and I'm thinking about trying to adopt her. I know you'll think I'm crazy."

Susan's eyes welled with tears and stung with pain as she studied Sampson's face. Her heart melted. "I think that is maybe the finest thing I have ever heard from any man. You are something else."

The real something awaited them at the safe house. Sampson and Susan, making an arresting pair, greeted the other agents. Sampson handed them one of the gold bags, which they happily accepted. "Guys, enjoy the food. Susan and I would like to have dinner with Becca in the kitchen if you don't mind. Where is she, by the way?"

The female agent smiled. "Watching 'Barney' in the den. Agent Sampson, you are a quick study…one tip on feeding time and you caught on!"

Susan took in her surroundings. The female agent winked at Sampson as everyone scattered to unpack the delicious food.

Sampson and Susan went to the den. The little girl was

oblivious to them entering the room. Susan held Sampson's hand and squeezed it a bit. "She's beautiful."

"Becca," Sampson uttered.

The little girl turned, and a huge smile came across her face as she stood up and sprinted toward them. "Sam!" she beamed.

Sampson and the girl hugged. If the feeling could be replicated, it would be the hottest attraction at Disney World. As she squeezed him with all her might, Sampson made up his mind that he would find a way to be with her forever.

"Becca, this is Susan. She is a friend. You'll like her."

Becca eyed her with a child's caution and continued to hold tight to Sampson. Susan's smile drew the little girl in. "It's nice to meet you, Becca. You are very pretty."

Sampson guided them all to the kitchen. He was reluctant to let go of Becca but placed her in a booster chair, which was clipped to an island counter, and Susan and Sampson took chairs on either side. Susan was smitten by the extravagance when she began to unpack the bag of food: truffle macaroni and cheese, truffle fries, bison burgers, lobster fettuccine, assorted cookies, milk, soda, orange juice and a pink lemonade Snapple. "Sampson, there is enough food for a family here!"

The word made him tingly. "So, let's be a family tonight! I'm hungry. Besides, I didn't know what Becca would want to eat."

"You're giving her a demo in gourmet junk food."

Susan took over and made plates for everyone. They talked and laughed as they ate. Becca warmed quickly to the stranger. She launched into nonstop chatter that the adults found both funny and interesting while devouring the delicious food that surely was never served to her before.

As they finished dinner, both were shocked to see that it was already 7:30 p.m., and obviously nearing the toddler's bedtime. "Hey, Becca, how about I give you a bath and we'll make

Sampson clean up." The little girl's eyes lit up and she shouted, "Baf!"

"Do I get a vote?" Sampson uttered.

"No, slave. Clean the kitchen. Come on, Becca." Susan was happy when Becca held her hand, and they waltzed to find a tub. Sampson was happy, but hurried to clean the kitchen as he had no intention of missing bath time.

Bath time was as much fun as dinner, and the only regret was that it was time for bed. They tucked her in, and both kissed her goodnight. She curled up, and they could tell she would be asleep in only minutes.

At about 8:30, they said goodnight to the agents and strolled toward the car. Sampson was pleased that Susan had grabbed his arm, and they both strolled happily. He opened her car door and closed it as she sat down. He went to his side and got in. He looked over at her.

"Thanks. I'm sure you had better plans for tonight than this, but I enjoyed it."

He noticed her eyes were moist again. "Come here." She reached across, and pulled him toward her, and they kissed the most passionate, wet kiss Sampson had ever experienced. He became instantly aroused, and he knew she felt the same way. Sampson was the first to speak. "Want to go parking?"

"How about we park at my place? I'd hate to leave footprints on the ceiling of your car." As Susan was saying this, she expected a laugh or at least a witty Sampson comeback. Forgetting about her own eye pain that evening, she looked in his eyes and they were glazed.

He could feel the pull. He saw colors, flashes, and bright lights. He felt danger and sensed a need to drive. He could see the course in his mind, and he could see the destination. It was the place they planned to visit tomorrow, but it could no longer wait until tomorrow. It must be tonight; no, it must be *now*.

Sampson felt the tugging on his arm, and suddenly saw Susan with a frightened look on her face. "Are you okay? You're bleeding again."

Sampson felt consciousness envelope him; fuzzy at first, but clearer each few seconds. The routine had become routine. He knew he was bleeding from his nose at a pretty good clip. He also thought he felt blood in his ears. He could see the fear in Susan's eyes. He was certain she couldn't understand this. Hell, he couldn't understand it. As a sense of clarity came to him, he reached for the cell phone and punched in ten digits.

"Hello?" Bob answered with haste.

"Bob, Sampson. No time to explain. You've got to get to Binky's now."

"Sampson, do you know something?"

"I feel something. It's bad and it's imminent. I'm with Susan, and I'm going now. You better get the locals as backup." Sampson slammed down the phone, threw the car in gear, and sped off. Sampson looked across at Susan and saw her near tears. Who could blame her? Spending time with him was like a train wreck. "Look, Susan, I'm sorry about this. I'll drop you off at a hotel on the way. I'll be back as soon as I can."

"Oh, no. I'm going with you. Someone has got to look after you."

"Look, I don't know what we'll find, and I don't want you hurt."

"I'm resourceful. I'll manage."

He wanted to argue, but he didn't have time. They were within a minute of Binky's. "Susan, in the glove box is my gun. Will you hand it to me?" She did as she was asked. He was not surprised that she showed no fear of the weapon. *What a remarkable woman*, he thought.

As they rounded the corner, and within a block of the building, Sampson could see a lone figure standing curbside. He could tell from the build it was Binky. The pain shot through Sampson's head like a bolt of lightning. As he looked at Binky, he felt, smelled, and heard death. The man was going to die shortly.

Sampson gunned the car forward in the direction of Binky and skidded to a halt just short of the man. "Binky, get down." The man froze in his tracks like a deer in the headlights of a car. It was a mistake.

Sampson opened the car door and dove towards the man. As he became airborne, he caught from his peripheral vision a muzzle flash from directly across the street. As his hands just touched Binky, he heard *thunk*, and saw Binky's head explode like a melon struck with a baseball bat. It was a surreal experience, which Sampson knew was not over. His body's momentum propelled him into Binky, and they tumbled to the ground, with Sampson coming to rest on the dead man. Sampson rolled quickly, all the training coming into play from somewhere in a distant, forgotten area of his brain. As he moved, he felt a sting in his left arm from the impact of the tackle. Sampson came into the firing position and squeezed off three rounds into the precise spot where he had seen the muzzle flash. No fire returned. He dove to the safety of the car and was relieved to hear nearby sirens.

"Susan?" He looked inside the car and could see her curled up on the floor of the car. He dove on top of her and was surprised to hear a groan.

"I thought this was what you had in mind for later?"

"Shit, thank God. I thought you were hurt. Are you?"

"No, except for the ribs you just crushed."

A strange voice came from behind him. He knew he had forgotten his training. By covering Susan, he had given the shooter time to circle behind him. His stupidity would kill them both.

"Slowly back out of the car, and I want to see your hands."

Sampson breathed a sigh of relief when he saw it was a pair of uniformed officers. He had caught a break. He moved slowly out of the car with his gun resting on one finger. He heard the officers shout, "Gun, partner!" He had anticipated that and wanted to do nothing to intensify the situation.

Calmly he spoke, "Officer, I am CIA. My ID is in my coat." He felt the gun removed from his finger, and he was pushed roughly on the hood of the car. He was thoroughly frisked, and the officer found his ID. From the corner of his eye, he could see Susan emerging from the car, only to be roughly pushed toward the car. He knew if he said anything at all, the situation could escalate. He prayed they wouldn't hurt her. He was relieved to see Bob making his way through a small crowd, toward the officers. Fortunately, Bob knew one of the men. Within minutes, he and Susan were free from the armed horde.

Sampson rushed to the body of Binky. Blood and brain matter littered the sidewalk. As Sampson lightly touched Binky's hand, he saw the face of John Whisnant yet again. He also saw the chiseled face of a gorgeous girl he had seen at Binky's. Sampson could get nothing else from the dead man.

Cates was surprised, to say the least, as he saw the car roar up next to Binky. What would be a simple kill became a bit complicated. He knew his first slug had taken out Binky but was shocked that he had missed the other man. Cates was even more shocked that the man had returned fire. Cates felt the first bullet sail past his head, and the other two embed themselves in a wooden crate, which he had been leaning against. Cates was even more amazed to see that it was Sampson. He had little time to dwell on the situation as the approaching sirens told him it was time to cut bait and get out of Dodge. Cates was a thorough man, and his escape route had been well-configured. Within minutes, he was in a car and miles from the scene, at least physically. Mentally he was someplace different altogether. He was seething. This damned agent was driving him absolutely nuts!

CHAPTER 32

Sampson and Bob learned little, as they expected, at the crime scene. They had searched the area that Sampson had fired at. All three slugs were easy to find, but there was no blood, which meant Sampson had probably not hit the intruder. It became obvious to Sampson that they would be here all night, waiting for another search warrant and scouring Binky's establishment again.

Sampson found Susan in the backseat of a squad car. The uniforms had been kind enough to give her a blanket, and she sat quietly, staring straight ahead. She jumped as he opened the door.

"Sorry. You okay?"

"Oh, yeah. I get shot at and get to watch a guy's head explode almost every night." Sampson knew this was not her usual sense of humor, and he decided not to push.

"Sorry. Dumb question."

She looked at him with glassy, sad, irritated eyes, and the expression on her face changed from anger to sorrow. "God, I'm sorry, Sampson. This is not your fault, and I shouldn't have snapped at you."

"Forget it. I'm not doing a great job in terms of dates, am I? But, how about diving on top of you? That's got to be worth something?"

She smiled. "Well, it was pretty brave, but it also hurt. Could you dive a little softer next time?" They both chuckled. Sampson reached across the seat and pulled Susan towards him. They kissed slowly and sensuously, both deriving great pleasure.

Sampson was first to pull away. "Look—"

Susan interrupted, "I didn't say I was through with you."

"Oh, hmmm, sorry. Bad news, though. I'll be tied up here for quite a while. I'm going to ask a uniform to take you home."

"Oh, great. My neighbors will love that. I'm sure the press will love to see the senator's deadbeat daughter in the back of a squad car. But I accept. It's the best alternative."

"I'm sorry. Can I call tomorrow?"

In response, Susan pulled Sampson towards her and firmly planted a delightful, moist kiss on his lips. What the hell was she getting herself into? The last boyfriend had been so simple, too uneventful, despite all his silver and gold. Boring trust fund baby. She couldn't dismiss the sense of adventure and intimacy she felt with Sampson. And the way he doted on that little girl was nothing short of adorable. Her assessment of Sampson was that he was a great man—with a highly dangerous job.

As Susan departed with a rookie officer, the search warrant arrived. After a ton of bickering between the various agencies that had responded to the murder, the CIA had rightfully won the lead-dog status for searching the building. Bob summoned a team of fifteen men with all the various specialties, and they converged on the building. Sampson and Bob were anxious to find what lay behind the door they deliberately overlooked yesterday. They also wanted to do that privately so, in Bob's instructions, he personally deployed men to specific parts of the building.

Bob briefed them on what the "business" was all about, and what they were likely to find. He instructed them to interrogate the women for everything they could, and then tell them about Binky. He expected they knew little.

Sampson described the woman he saw through Binky's

eyes. He asked that she be questioned and then brought to him. He didn't know what she knew, but he felt certain there was something.

The agents went to work. Sampson and Bob headed toward the room they knew the untrained eye would miss. They entered the room that contained the hidden space. Both men looked for a way to open the panel. They felt along the wall, with no clues. On hands and knees, they searched the carpet area and found nothing. Sampson scrutinized the walls nearby. He spotted a wall-mounted gold-framed light, the kind with funny, twisty bulbs. He moved toward it and noticed one arm of the light was a bit greasy, while the other had a fine layer of dust, almost invisible to the eye.

"Think I got it, Bob. Stand back."

Sampson tugged gently on the arm, and slowly the wall slid back about four feet, revealing a compact room filled with high-technology camera equipment. Sampson sat near the control panel in amazement. As he played with the knobs and buttons, different rooms and bedrooms came into full view. "Goddamn, Bob. This is spectacular."

"Shit. Big Brother's watching."

After they satisfied their curiosity with the technology, they searched the room, turning up very little. They closed the room back to its original position and moved back into Binky's office. Ninety minutes had passed during the search, and they heard a tap on the door just as it opened. A young agent with bright red hair came through, followed by the woman Sampson had seen in his vision.

"Agent Sampson, this is Caryn. I thought you might like to speak with her, sir."

"Yes. Thank you, agent." On cue, the dismissed ginger exited the room.

"Hi, Caryn. I'm Agent Sampson, and this is Agent Becker. We're trying to figure out what happened to your… boss."

"He was my friend and my boss." Sampson could see by the moist eyes that Caryn was close to tears. Her emotions seemed genuine. She looked like someone who had, indeed, lost a close friend. He wondered to himself if they had been more than friends… lovers perhaps.

The woman was stunning. Though it would be hard to find anything but absolute beauty at Binky's, this woman was the best of the best. Supermodel material.

"Caryn, what can you tell me about Binky?"

"Everything, anything. I knew all about him. He was my…" She broke down crying. Not just a sob, but a raking cry. Her body trembled. Sampson reached to comfort the woman and while it violated his own principle of reading others' thoughts, he could easily justify it. Murders were happening at a frantic clip, and the perpetrator (or perpetrators) must be found.

As Sampson channeled his thinking, he began to pick off random thoughts from Caryn. He could tell instantly that she would be a difficult subject. Her thoughts came to him in jumbles and fragmented pictures. Still, it was something, and whatever he picked up would help. He could also tell that she was genuine in her sorrow. He could feel that to her core. He caught images of them together. It was a father-daughter relationship. They had not been intimate. He felt she was not involved in his death, but she knew something.

He let go of her hand and broke the connection. As he looked up, he dabbed his nose and happily found nothing. He realized she had stopped crying and was staring at him. He almost wondered if she knew what he was up to. He had found in his shows that sometimes some people did seem to know. "Caryn, tell me what you can about Binky."

She rambled on for twenty minutes and while the information

was at times interesting, it was worthless to the case. She painted him as a good man, a committed man. She described the business and reiterated he was not a pimp; he was a businessman. The girls were his well treated employees.

Sampson interrupted her, "Caryn, what is the room all about—behind the wall back there?" He knew she knew, so no valuable information would be passed along.

"Binky would watch us. It was mostly a security system."

"Security from what?"

"The customers. Sometimes it could get rough."

"I'm surprised. Your clientele was so… upscale?"

Caryn huffed at his ignorant response. "That doesn't change anything. A man's a man. Many men are angry. Many like to hit women. It really doesn't matter if they are important or rich. It's something good or evil inside."

"Who were the clients?"

"Lots of people."

"No, no. I mean specifically."

"Oh, sorry. We are forbidden from sharing details like that."

"By whom?"

"Binky."

"Caryn, he's dead."

"Hmm." She pondered that reality. "I suppose that changes things. But am I in trouble?"

"No. We are not interested in anything you did here."

"So, no matter what I tell, I don't get in trouble?"

"Yes, as it relates to the prostitution."

"I suppose it doesn't matter now, does it?"

"I wouldn't suppose."

Caryn stood up with and walked with grace behind Bob, who was seated in the far corner of the room. Both men watched her like hawks move to a bookcase. She reached under a shelf, and magically the bookcase slid to one side revealing another room.

The agents followed the woman inside. The room was bathed in a warm, fluorescent light. What the men saw startled them. Racks and racks and racks of small jump drives each marked with a last name and a date. All were alphabetized, and the men could not believe the names! A who's who of politicians, CEOs, ambassadors, and movie stars.

As Sampson scanned another rack, he came upon a tape labeled "Grant, Alan" from five years ago. His stomach sank. This would crush Susan. Without thinking, he picked up the jump drive and slipped it in his pocket. He made sure no one, including Bob, saw that action. Sampson moved back to finish the scan of the drives. Towards the end he found "Whisnant, John".

"Bob, take a look at this one."

"Hmm. That's a common thread, isn't it? I've got an even bigger one. How about his boss?"

"No way! Is it current?"

"Try less than a month."

As they fawned over all the goodies, they realized Caryn had retreated to the other room and was sitting in a chair crying.

"Bob, these drives need to be tucked away, particularly the President's. Releasing, or even letting their existence out, would wreck lives, hurt the country, and if they have no material value to the case…?"

"What you say seems right. Let's box these up and ship them back. If things cool down, we can get rid of them. But we need to see what Whisnant and the President were up to."

"Agreed. Let's close the room up and pack it ourselves after everyone goes. We've got less risk that way."

They left the room, and Bob reached to the same spot he had seen Caryn reach to. He felt a steel switch, which he flipped, and as from a "Harry Potter" movie, the bookcase closed.

Sampson went to Caryn. "Thank you for being so honest. One last question. Did you know Mr. Whisnant?"

No more hesitation on her part as the vicious death of her friend and employer set in. "Yes. He was here earlier today. In fact, he was with me. He is creepy. I also bet dangerous. In fact, I thought I might be in trouble with him today. Watch the tape. You tell me."

They thanked the woman and told her she was free to go back to her apartment. She seemed relieved in one sense and disappointed in another. Probably didn't want to be alone right now, Sampson guessed. He wondered how many psycho fucks like John Whisnant had paid a pretty penny to invade her path, her beautiful garden.

CHAPTER 33

Cates had left the scene of the gory killing and grew angrier by the minute. He knew he was not slipping with age. The problem was this psychic. And the psychic was making him look bad.

It was time to go on the offensive and punish this sideshow freak. He needed to be punished and then killed.

From his car he made a few discreet calls that led him to the information he needed.

A day later, Cates sat outside her apartment watching and waiting. He knew she was in there, but he was in no rush. This would be payback, and it would be sweet.

He left the car and silently approached the building. He worked his way around toward the back, relying on the cover of bushes and trees, which had grown to unmanageable heights.

The night was cold and silent as Cates assessed his situation. From the farthest and darkest corner, Cates could see the woman in her bathrobe patiently putting a coffee cup and saucer in the sink. He watched as she moved toward the bathroom, and he could see her starting the shower, the steam gently rising above the tub.

He watched as she removed her robe. Cates found it oddly exhilarating, a new sensation for him, and strangely one he was enjoying. He watched as the open robe fell to the floor. The woman stepped into the tub and closed the curtain.

"Showtime," Cates whispered to himself as he adjusted his pressing erection. He rose from his crouched position, and moved toward a window, which he presumed was a bedroom. With a thin knife, he jimmied the lock and raised the window. As a skilled spider, it took him only a moment to climb through the opening and into the room. He lowered the window and walked from the bedroom toward the bathroom.

On this cold evening, the steam created a shroud of fog, which was undoubtedly delightful for the poor soul who was showering. Cates reached in his belt and removed a Smith and Wesson 45. He affixed a silencer, walked stealthily into the bathroom and ripped open the shower curtain.

At first, the woman did not quite know what was happening. She had been shampooing her hair, and as she tried to focus on the intruder, bits of soap dripped in her eyes. The pain caused her to blink but in short order, she assessed the situation as not good.

"Nothing personal, ma'am," Cates said as he leveled his pistol to her forehead. Like a deer caught in the headlights, the woman froze. Cates placed the slug directly in her forehead. The woman crumpled into a ball in the tub.

Cates left the water running and walked to the kitchen. He found a white cordless phone and punched in the ten digits. The phone rang three times, and a groggy Sampson finally said, "Hello?"

"Sampson, old buddy. You missed me last night."

Sampson shuffled to sit up and tried to focus. "Who is this?" He knew but wanted to buy time to think.

"It's me, you prick. You will regret you have chosen to tangle with me. You are good, but you are out of your league."

"What—"

"Don't interrupt me, prick. I want you to know I'm coming

after you myself, and soon. Just to let you know how serious I am, I killed your girlfriend. She's dead in the tub. I will see you soon." Cates uttered the last sentence in the most cold and menacing voice Sampson had ever heard. As the phone clicked dead, Sampson's thoughts flew to Susan. He had gotten her killed. He should never have gotten involved with her or the goddamned CIA.

He scooped up the phone and called the DC police. They would respond immediately. He phoned Bob and gave him topline.

Sampson dressed and was out the door in ninety seconds, speeding towards Susan's house. He had tucked his weapon in his trousers and pulled a loose sweater down to conceal the gun. He raced the car to the extreme. His thoughts continued to Susan, who was so special. They had a major connection. He would rip apart anyone who ended that chance of intimacy in his life. It was simply unthinkable.

As he pulled up to Susan's house, he could see three squad cars, lights flashing. Arriving at the same time, a SWAT van screeched to a halt. Eight fully clad officers jumped from the van and began to deploy around the house. Sampson sprinted from his car toward the scene. He was able to quickly spot the lead officer who was busy barking orders at the other officers. He rushed to the man. "My name is Sampson. I called this in." He fished out his ID.

The officer seemed vaguely interested. "Yeah. Tell me what you know."

Sampson recapped the telephone call, as the officer's face and demeanor never changed. "Officer, I have a relationship with this woman. I want to go in now. The killer is long gone. Trust me. He is smart and would not stay here to risk being caught."

"Look, we'll handle this."

"Officer, no disrespect, but she may be in there bleeding to death. Time is critical."

"Look, I understand. Hold tight. SWAT is going in any minute. Watch." He pointed toward the men who were huddled together. He watched them deploy around the house with precision. It seemed like a dream sequence with the players all moving slowly at first.

He could see the front door being rammed down, and SWAT carefully rushing in. They were inside for what seemed like an eternity. Sampson's heart raced so hard he worried he might have a heart attack.

He was broken from his trance by a strong clap on the shoulder. "Sampson, what have we got?"

"Bob, I'm glad you're here. Not a thing. SWAT just went in. Fuck, this guy's killed Susan.

Goddamn it. It's my fault!" Sampson shouted dejectedly.

"Let's wait before we go there." Bob tried to be convincing, but he didn't believe it himself. He knew she was dead. He just hoped it wasn't a terrible death. He suspected it would be though. This guy was not right, and he had a full-blown vendetta agenda with Sampson. This would be bad, and it wouldn't end here. It would end only when they caught this bastard, or he killed them. They waited side by side for what seemed like hours, but in truth was only minutes.

Both men saw a flicker of activity from the front door as two SWAT agents emerged. But something was wrong, delightfully wrong. The agents were smiling and giving a thumbs up to the lead officer. Sampson and Bob charged forward and could overhear the conversation, "She's fine. She was in bed…"

Sampson ran towards the house, up the steps, and nearly knocked down the bathrobe-clad and beautifully disheveled Susan emerging under escort from Washington's finest.

"I should have known you'd be involved in this."

"Are you okay?"

"Uh, yeah. I was just sleeping."

Sampson moved toward her and hugged her tightly. Susan could sense his concern, his genuineness, but couldn't resist her normal sarcasm, "Sampson, you could have just called. You didn't have to try to make such a big impression."

This brought a smile to everyone's face but snapped Sampson back to reality. As suddenly as Sampson's elation had begun, it drifted away just as quickly. "Susan, stay with the officers."

"Where—"

Sampson walked quickly toward Bob. "She's fine. Something's not right."

Bob looked equally puzzled. "Sampson, it doesn't fit, not at all. This is not a guy who fools around. He wouldn't fuck with you. Doesn't fit the profile."

"I agree, but what does he mean?"

Both men pondered the situation. "Sampson, you told me you haven't had a girlfriend, at least, not recently."

"No, Bob, I've been a recluse. In fact, Susan and I have hardly been an item. In fact, the past year I've only been with one other woman…" His words trailed off. He was certain he knew the answer. His training told him and somewhere in the distance, his powers told him.

"Sarah Axel, Bob. The woman in Syracuse. The doctor."

Bob remained calm, which was easier for him to do. He too figured the doctor was dead, and this would weigh heavily on anyone's conscience. "Look, we've got to move on this. I'll call the Feds. You call Sergeant O'Reilly in Syracuse. We need to get them quickly."

Both men worked their cell phones in a fury. Within five minutes, an army of locals and Feds would be re-enacting at the doctor's house what had just played out at Susan's house. The ending would be different, however. Horribly different.

Both men waited. "Sampson, I've got a plane standing by. If this plays out, we go right away."

"Yeah. Look, I'm going to see Susan. I'll be right back." Sampson walked back toward the house and found Susan in her living room flanked by DC police. "Guys, would you give us a minute?"

The locals left the room, and Susan looked at Sampson in a frightened and curious manner. "Look, Susan, I'm sorry about what happened today. I can't tell you how glad I am that you're okay, though."

"Sampson—"

"Let me finish. I'm mixed up in something nasty right now. I don't have time for all the details, I'm afraid. But suffice it to say that someone is trying to hurt me, and we thought he had hurt you. He didn't, thank God. But we think he did kill someone else."

Susan's eyes darted over Sampson's shoulder, and he knew someone was there. Bob. "She's dead, Sampson. We've got to go." Bob left as silently as he had entered.

Sampson's face lost color. "Look, I'll be back tomorrow night. I want to see you and Becca. More of those truffle fries, huh?" Sampson laughed nervously, but as they embraced, Susan sensed he was on the verge of tears. Who died, she wondered.

"Tomorrow," he whispered as he pulled away from her warm chest.

Bob was waiting in his car. As Sampson closed his door, Bob threw on the lights and siren, and they raced to the airport.

Once on board, Sampson was the first to speak, "What do we know?"

"It is Dr. Sarah Axel. Dead, found in the tub." Sampson grimaced.

They were at the scene in forty minutes, thanks to the speed of a government jet given full priority clearance all the way to

Syracuse. The scene was alive with activity—police cars, TV crews and cameras everywhere. A murder in DC was not a big thing, but in Syracuse…"

Both men clipped their badges to their pockets and had no trouble entering the activity. They signed the logbook and moved to the house. Sampson felt nauseated, but knew he had to go inside.

"Ah, the spooks are here."

"Hello, Sergeant," Bob uttered. "What have we got?"

Even O'Reilly knew this was no time to play games, and he started into an efficient summary. "Dead woman, Dr. Sarah Axel, thirty-two. Nobody saw or heard anything. Neighbors says she kept to herself most of her time spent at work. Co-workers said she was an excellent doctor. No arrest records. In short, she's clean, and we have not a fucking thing to go on."

"You won't, O'Reilly. Another professional job." O'Reilly did not seem surprised at all. "How'd she die?" Sampson asked.

"Forty-five-caliber, close range to the head. If it helps, she didn't suffer. She was taking a bath. Looks like he stood and watched outside. We found footprints. He came in through the bedroom window. His tracks inside suggest he went right to the bathroom, took her out, and left. It doesn't look like anything is missing, but we don't know for sure."

Sampson jumped in, "Sarge, he's not a thief."

"No, doesn't sound like it. I'd like to know what you know, Sampson."

"Yes, but first I need to see the victim." Sampson saw no reason to tell O'Reilly just yet that he knew the victim. He felt an urgency to get to Sarah. "Please."

"Sure, spook. Come on."

O'Reilly led the two agents toward the bathroom. For a small house, the bathroom was quite large. There is no horror worse than a murder. This was no exception. Sarah lay naked in a pool of crimson, bloody water. Sampson could see the bullet entry point. A clean hole. But my God, the back of her head was gone. The force of the bullet. Another head exploded. Gruesome sight like the one at Binky's.

As he looked at the rest of her body, Sampson recalled their intimate moments only days ago. He had truly liked her. What a woman. Now, what a dead woman, thanks to him.

"O'Reilly, you know enough about me to not ask a lot of questions, right?"

"Spook, I got the T-shirt from our last event together. What do you need?"

Sampson motioned to O'Reilly and Bob to follow him to a quiet comer of an adjoining room. "I need to touch her. I sometimes have an ability to see things. I know you must preserve the evidence chain, so you and Bob can stay, but I'd like everyone else out of the house; if you could."

O'Reilly scratched his face, hesitated, and moved toward a group of officers. He mumbled something, and they moved toward the front door. Sampson was grateful for O'Reilly. He was a rough and tumble guy, but he had good instincts, and Sampson knew he could trust him.

In a few moments, the house was deserted except for Sampson, Bob, and O'Reilly. They followed Sampson as he moved toward the bathroom and knelt next to Sarah. Sampson stayed motionless for a couple of minutes as he tried to clear his thoughts. As he touched Sarah's left hand, he knew he had made a connection. He wanted to tell her how sorry he was, but he knew she was dead and would not hear his words. She could help him find the killer though. He concentrated and bore down. Flashes of images. Some made sense, some didn't. One image was as clear as day. As if looking from Sarah's eyes, in slow motion he saw the killer level the gun and fire the bullet that took her life. He had his man. He had the killer, and he would devote his life to finding him. There was to be nothing else to learn from Dr. Sarah Axel. He had gotten her killed and nothing would change that.

Sampson broke the connection and tried to regroup himself. He half-staggered to the back of the room and stood silently for a few moments in front of Bob and O'Reilly. "I know who did this. We need to match a name to a face." Sampson wanted to cry, and he wanted to punish the man who did this.

Bob sensed the anger and frustration. "Sampson, you have to stay focused. This isn't over."

"I know. O'Reilly, you got a sketch artist?"

"Sure, spook. Come on. I'll run you downtown right now." O'Reilly looked at the other agent. "Come on. I might as well take both of you."

They arrived at the Syracuse Public Safety Building within fifteen minutes and were ushered directly to the artist. Sampson couldn't help but think she looked like an artist: short and thin, wearing thick glasses, a bit unkempt; but after just a couple of minutes, he discovered she was a highly talented individual. In five minutes, the picture was very good, and in fifteen minutes, it was damn near perfect.

CHAPTER 34

Cates had time to think on his return to Washington DC. He reached the conclusion it was time to tidy up the loose ends and move on. His military training had taught him that when a spot gets too hot, to get out. Only fools would stay and fight a fight you can't win.

And this is too hot.

Go to the house, pack, get the books.

Destroy the house; can't leave evidence.

Speaking of evidence, can't leave Wiz around.

Give yourself twenty-four hours and get the fuck out!

Bob, Sampson, and O'Reilly were huddled in a room. Bob walked to the front to take the lead. "So here is what we know so far. Our perp is a bad dude. But he used to be good. Without boring you with the details, his name is Cates. He was a full bird colonel, special ops. Highly decorated; highly effective. He's retired now and does 'special project' work. This is where we leave fact and move into rumors and second-hand information. So, take it for what it's worth. The book is he does all kinds of freelance work for very big dollars. He never had much of a conscience, so there are not a lot off limits to what he does. We couldn't prove this guy had done anything. He's that good. We also know he has friends inside the Pentagon, the FBI, and even CIA. He is always one step ahead. The last piece of information I have on this guy is that he is close friends with the current dictator of Haiti. We've known all along that's where he'll head when we get close to nailing him. They don't extradite, and he'll live like a king there."

O'Reilly shook his head in disgust. "So, you spooks do nothing about this guy?"

Bob looked frustrated. "Not much. You'll love this, O'Reilly. I've even heard CIA has used his services."

O'Reilly looked dejected. "What a fucked-up place!"

Bob was a bit defensive. "Some of it is fucked up, but most of the people do really good work. Most really care. We're like every other organization; we have weak spots."

Sampson chimed in, "I think we're done here. Bob, I'd like to get back to Washington. This is hot, and I'm anxious to close this down."

"Yup. Let's go. O'Reilly, thanks. You were a big help." Bob smiled at the beat cop.

"Same here, O'Reilly," Sampson extended his hand.

"Don't come back, spook. But, if you need help catching this son of a bitch, let me know." O'Reilly smiled.

Sampson knew he meant it.

The flight back was uneventful. Both men discussed the options for catching Cates. And there weren't many answers. It seemed the next move belonged to Cates. Neither man could even guess how this would all play out.

Meanwhile, Cates knew his time was short, but he was unfazed. He thrived on pressure and lived for adventure. But he felt troubled by what he had done today. Why had he chosen to kill the lover of his rival instead of the rival himself? He could not answer the question. Perhaps he was losing his edge or maybe his perspective. Regardless, it had been a stupid act, which he reasoned, would only weaken his position. The CIA would not stop their search for him now. And he knew in his heart that Agent Sampson would not rest until Cates was in jail or, more likely, until he killed Sampson. That thought did appeal to him on many levels. But it would have to be measured against his personal risk. While death as a warrior was acceptable, capture and jail time would not be an acceptable alternative.

As Cates thought deeply of his options, he knew only one man had evidence of his wrongdoing, and that was John Whisnant.

CHAPTER 35

Sampson phoned Susan upon his return to Washington. He did not know what her reaction to him would be after more scandalous events, but he couldn't wait to see her again. He noticed in her the same kind of longing for intimacy. It was time to let go of any cliffhangers. Perhaps being close to death so often as of late lit a flame in his heart to feel more and act on those feelings.

He picked her up at 6:00. Didn't sense any residual hesitation in her luscious kiss until they accidentally banged heads in their urgency. She winced a little. Sampson rubbed her forehead tenderly. "No, it's my eye. I have a rare infection." Sampson's face showed concern. "I've been putting off surgery. Would you still have me blind?" Susan chuckled nervously. "Helen Keller said, 'The only thing worse than being blind is to have sight but no vision.'"

Oh, he certainly had visions. If she only knew. "Honey, I'm so sorry. Is there anything I can do? Do you want me to find someone to take care of it?" As the words tumbled out, he wanted to laugh at his stupidity. She was the daughter of a powerful senator! The family had the kind of health care only the two percent had access to.

"Just don't mind me if I have my aviator glasses on sometimes. They seem to prevent the irritation from flaring up."

"You look hot in them. Wear them to bed if you'd like!" With that, Susan punched him gently on the arm and they headed to the safe house in total silence. Susan held his hand the whole ride.

As they reached the house, Sampson's spirits were buoyed. They reached a new high as they opened the door and Becca ran to his arms, shouting her characteristic, "Sam! Sam!"

"Hello, love bug. Boy, did I miss you!" They both held tight and hugged for a full minute.

"Do you remember Susan?" Becca lifted her head and shyly smiled at Susan. Susan responded by tickling the little girl in her ribs. She giggled and reached to be held by Susan. Sampson held tight to the little girl's midsection while he and Susan played a game of give and take with Becca. She started a belly laugh, which made everyone in the room laugh. Just what they all needed.

The evening went as every moment with Becca for Sampson—perfect. He decided that the little things were the big things in life. Eating and playing with someone innocent who had no agenda except to love and learn was what it was all about. Sampson, through the trauma of the past few weeks, had come to realize that he had not been living his life for many years. His spirit had died. He had been on autopilot. There was no way to change the past, but he could damn well affect the future. Starting today, he would. Two things had become increasingly clear. First, he would adopt Becca. This would not be easy, but he would leverage his CIA connections and he was sure that he could finagle a way to make this happen. Second, he needed to find out if Susan and he were a match. All systems said "go" but in truth, they had spent very little time together. That needed to change.

Both Susan and Sampson hated to put the little girl to bed at 9:00 p.m. But she was yawning to beat the band, and it seemed cruel to keep her up any longer. They tucked her in and kissed her goodnight.

Susan beamed. "She doesn't even fight going to bed. She is the perfect kid!"

"Yeah. I've taught her everything I know."

"Uh huh. How's about a beer and a little television at my place? I've got to be in the office early tomorrow, but I'm too wound up to sleep right now."

"Is that a proposition?" Sampson inquired.

"No. Why is it that men turn everything into sex? Can we be beer buddies and binge on Netflix too?"

Damn, that actually seemed like a fine idea. Sampson couldn't remember the last movie he watched, let alone with a "friend". Would there be fuzzy pajamas too?

Sampson said goodnight to the two agents who were looking after little Becca, and he and Susan rode to her place. Once the beer top popped off, Susan began the conversation. "Sampson, what is going on?"

Sampson paused thoughtfully. "Well, it's simple and complex, and it all ties back to your dad, believe it or not. Your dad is a real threat to become the next President. Someone in the government, way up in the government, doesn't want that to happen. Your dad's stand on terrorism was winning votes. That plane in Syracuse was shot down to make him look bad and lower his popularity. It backfired. We know who did that. We haven't caught him yet, but we're close. We know this plan was hatched way up in the government, and we have a good handle on where. But Bob and I are flying solo because we just don't know who we can trust or better yet, not trust. The government is a spider web of connections, and the people that are involved are deeply connected." Sampson took a deep, exasperated breath. "That's the business portion of the explanation. Now there's the personal side. The mercenary is a guy named Cates, and he has a personal thing with me right now. He's a professional, agency-trained, with lots of military experience. He's the one who took some shots at us. Nice guy."

"Oh, God." Taking in the gravity of it all, Susan looked like she would pass out.

"Susan, we're close to this guy. We'll get him. My guess is in the next couple of days."

"Aren't you worried or scared?"

"Oh, yes, but Bob and I will get him." Sampson tried to reassure her.

Susan had tears in her eyes. "Why did the police come to my house?"

"Cates called me and told me he was with my girlfriend and would kill her. I thought it was you. My God, that scares me." Sampson paused. "But thank God, it wasn't you! But he did kill someone… a woman, a doctor actually… in Syracuse. Her name was Sarah Axel. I met her the day of the plane crash. She had helped with Becca. We… well, we spent the night together." Sampson bowed his head in embarrassment. "As I said, Cates is wired in and to strike back at me, he killed her. The bastard shot her in the head as she was corning out of the shower. It was my fault. I caused her death."

Susan sipped on her IPA. The fresh, cold hops hitting her throat made her close her eyes to savor the layers of taste. The content was a lot to digest. "Sampson, her death wasn't your fault. How were you supposed to know?"

"I met her before you and me…"

"Sampson, stop. You don't need to apologize to me. I'm not exactly Sister Mary Alice from the convent nor is there a ring on that finger."

"Susan, this will be over soon. I will get Cates myself, and then you and I need to spend time together. I think you are pretty special."

"Yeah, I sorta like you too." Susan cupped his face in her hands and gently kissed him.

Sampson did not want to intrude on her personal thoughts but couldn't help himself. It did confirm what he was feeling. Susan really did like him. Maybe even love?

She looked at him with a wry smile. "You were reading my mind, weren't you?"

Sampson stumbled, "No. I mean, yes." He continued to stammer. "Yes, I was. I want you know that you shouldn't be thinking what you were thinking. I have no desire to take you up into your bedroom and have sex with you all night. No, ma'am!"

Susan shook her head and laughed. "Your wires are crossed. That wasn't quite what was on my mind, although it's not bad. But not tonight. I've got to be into work very early tomorrow."

"Hmmm," Sampson muttered, a bit unhappy with the less than perfect outcome.

"Don't be disappointed. Good things are worth the wait, my love," Susan fired back.

"I hate waiting," Sampson pouted. "And what about that movie?"

"You think we'll make it through a chick flick tonight? Rain check!"

"All right, Sister Mary Alice."

Susan shifted the conversation. "You've made your mind up with the little girl. It shows.

Are you working toward adoption yet?"

"No, but I want to."

"Tell you what, let me poke around today and see what I can come up with."

Sampson squeezed her hand with an outpouring of gratitude. What a woman.

CHAPTER 36

Cates was surprised how well the call had gone. He had reached Wiz with little difficulty, and they agreed to meet for lunch tomorrow. Cates felt pangs of regrets, maybe even second thoughts. Wiz had been a business partner, a friend… or as close to a friend as one gets in this business. He reasoned he could safely, to a degree, leave Wiz alone. But risk was something Cates calculated. If Wiz was found out, Cates would be his trump card to cut a deal. Nope, couldn't risk it. Sorry, Wiz. Cates jotted the address next to the phone. They had agreed to meet at 11:00 a.m. in Lakeland Park, which would be convenient for both men. Quiet and secluded.

Cates organized his critical belongings, which included a dozen passports all under different names, as well as his bankbooks and a few other essentials. He had planned for this moment for many years, and each detail was crisp. With one twist….

Sampson managed to get six reasonable hours of sleep. He dressed, showered, and reached the office by 7:30 armed with a mile-high list of actions.

By 9:30, Sampson realized that the team of researchers who had worked all night had come up with very little useful information. Then as depression was setting in, Bob burst into Sampson's office.

"Sampson, we have a break! It came from an unofficial source—actually, an official source, one of our sister agents caught with his hand in the cookie jar. He started singing about a lot of things to avoid long jail time. One of those songs was about Cates. We've got an address." Bob smiled.

Sampson could taste the closure. "Bob, if it's reliable, this is the home run we were waiting for."

"It's a good tip, all right. I'm sure."

"Let's go."

"Not so quick. This could get hot. I want to make sure we have some help; actually, a lot of help."

"Bob, we can't lose time."

"We'll lose only a few minutes. I don't want anyone killed; not after all this."

It took longer to assemble the team than Bob or Sampson would have liked, but they both agreed that a well-conceived plan with plenty of support was the best shot of safely capturing Cates. In total, thirty-three agents would be involved in the raid. As they met in the briefing room, tension was high. Each knew enough of Cates to know that he could match wits and skills with any of them.

The group had been assembled in a way that would preclude any conversation after the briefing, to avoid any leaks to Cates. Partners were randomly assigned and given strict instructions about the communications blackout. Everyone in the room knew why.

The raid would be straightforward in its approach. First, neighbors directly adjacent to the Cates house would be evacuated. Two trucks bearing the name of the local cable television company would be dispatched. The drivers, wearing bright red jumpsuits, would go door to door cautiously explaining that a police situation existed, and ask that they leave the house by car or foot, and proceed to a safe location a couple of blocks away. History had shown that most people willingly complied. This exercise would take forty-five minutes to an hour. During that time, the perimeter of the house would be quietly surrounded. Snipers would be placed in advantageous positions.

Last, all the local streets would be sealed off. Bob had already placed a team in a house directly across the street from Cates. The owners were not home, and it took only seconds to gain entry. If the owners complained, and they rarely did for obvious reasons, the words, "national security", would absolve them of any wrongdoing.

The early reports from the house were not promising. The agents had detected no activity. Most of the windows were not shaded and with powerful field glasses, they had good views inside. All reports indicated the house was empty. The briefing concluded on a positive high, but Sampson noticed a heightened degree of nervous energy in the room. Not surprising. This was risky.

The agents were dispatched to the scene. Action ensued.

It took thirty-four minutes to contact and relocate the twelve neighbors closest to the Cates home. This went without incident. The seven snipers were positioned, and a green light given back to Bob. In the briefing they had determined that a simple approach would be best. First, a phone call was placed to Cates home. There was no answer or detectable movement in the house. Bob and Sampson donned brightly colored bulletproof vests with the inscription "CIA" embossed on the front and back. They led a small team of agents toward the front door. Two agents carried a battering ram. That would make short work of the front door. The others, including Sampson and Bob, were heavily armed with automatic and semi-automatic weapons.

They reached the front door and on Bob's signal, the two

agents rocked the ram back and forth, and on the fourth revolution, the ram slammed into the door with such a loud *thwack* that the door gave way, splintering as it crashed to the ground.

"CIA. Cates… come out now!" Bob's voice boomed. But there was no response.

On Bob's signal they cautiously moved room to room and determined the house was empty. They regrouped in the living room. Bob radioed outside that the house was clear, and they would begin a search.

Bob was the first to notice Sampson, who appeared ashen in color. He went to him and could see Sampson's disoriented stare. He could see blood trickling from Sampson's nose and eyes. The other agents stared in confusion and disbelief. "Sampson." Bob gently shook him. "What is it? Where are you, man?"

Sampson came around as if removed from a spell. "Fuck, everybody out now!" In the confusion, everyone stood motionless until Bob took charge and screamed at everyone, "Get out. Now!"

The men ran from the house, and Sampson was able to see the baffled looks of everyone on the street. He could hear Bob yelling for them to get down. Some began to comply, but most simply stood still. This time warp lasted only seconds. Behind them they heard a *whoosh*, and all seven agents were blown down by a jet of hot air that washed over them. Sampson and Bob landed twenty-five feet from where they had been standing. While both were shaken, neither was seriously hurt.

From their positions on the ground, they looked back at the house, which was no longer there. Nor were four homes that stood adjacent to the property. In fact, debris was everywhere but there were no fires.

"Sampson, what was that?"

"God knows. Bob, I felt it. We tripped something."

"Sampson, thank god you felt it. We were toast otherwise."

"I could see a wire and a device, and felt it was a bomb. There is nothing left."

The two men sat up and surveyed one another. Each was a bit bloody, but no lasting injuries. Neither man was ready to stand up. "Thanks for dragging me out."

Bob uttered in a scratchy voice, "He's moving."

"Why do you say that?" Sampson wiped his face with his sleeve.

"He's gone. He knows we were close. Maybe even tipped off about the raid. We tripped a wire. I buy that, but that house was going down soon, I'd bet my life. That bomb, or whatever the fuck it was, I'm sure was there to destroy evidence. We may have hastened things, but it was there to clean up any evidence."

"I'd say it worked."

"Seems that way. Well, partner, let's see if our legs work, and try to see if anything survived."

Slowly both men got up, each grunting and groaning, but moving, nonetheless. As they reapproached the area where the house used to stand, a lone uniformed police officer confronted Sampson and Bob. "Thank God you boys hollered when you did. It gave us a couple of seconds to get down, and that's a damn fucking miracle. Looks like no one was hurt other than scrapes and cuts. We were lucky."

Sampson and Bob knew it was not luck at all. They owed their lives to a science experiment gone bad, and the CIA. Then again, if not for the CIA, they wouldn't have been put in this spot.

As they walked throughout the scene, both were aghast at the destruction. Cates's house was gone. What amazed the men was that no sizeable debris remained. The biggest fragments were no bigger than a toothbrush, and there weren't many of them anywhere. All that remained of one neighboring home was a section of a chimneystack. Both men were disturbed by the severity of the blast. In the distance they could hear sirens which both men found ironic. Within seconds, several bright red fire engines approached the scene. Sampson sighed. "Unless they build houses, there isn't much they can do."

In short order, the two men left the scene. It was confirmed there were no serious injuries, and both were thankful for that. It would also ease the pressure they would feel from the higher ups about a mission gone bad.

Bob and Sampson stood silently for a brief time. "Sampson, you know this is going down fast now, don't you?"

"Yup. It's gonna be tough to get ahead of him now."

CHAPTER 37

Cates was driving in his car when he heard the report on the radio: "Just a little over an hour ago, a home exploded in the Lynwood section of Washington. Initial reports have confirmed that police were on the scene prior to the explosion and able to evacuate all residents. Police have indicated a ruptured gas main was responsible for the incident, which leveled four homes. Miraculously, no injuries occurred, thanks to our local police. Hats off to the boys in blue."

Cates grimaced. "Gas, my ass!" Cates was troubled. They were close, having missed him by only a couple of hours. They wouldn't get him. He wouldn't allow that. And he had a score to settle, warrior to warrior.

At the appointed hour, Wiz maneuvered his car into a remote part of the park. He had taken care to ensure his appearance was well-altered. He wore oversized dark sunglasses and a wig with a graying ponytail. He looked like a modern-day hippie, but it was perfect. No one would give him a second look and if they did, they would simply think they saw some weird dude.

Wiz meandered a dirt path but saw no one. He knew Cates was there… listening, watching. But this was one cagey nut. He would not reveal himself until he was damn sure there was no one watching.

True to form, Cates emerged from the shadows and momentarily took the breath away from Wiz. "Why do you have to do that? You know I'm not going to bring anyone with me."

"Wiz, by now you should know I trust no one… except myself," Cates chuckled.

"Christ, whatever. Look, I'm pulling the plug on this thing. It's getting too hot. I heard about your house. You know they're close, too damned close."

"Yup." Cates said nonchalantly, "But they're not good enough to get me. Look, Wiz, I like you… and I'm sorry." As the last word was uttered, Cates pulled a pistol equipped with a silencer out of his pocket and before Wiz could utter a sound, a bullet lodged in his forehead and exploded as it exited his head. Wiz slumped to the ground, a puzzled look fixed on his face. He hadn't expected this act of disloyalty. It was ironic to think you could trust a paid killer—a fatal mistake.

Cates left the park as silently as he had arrived. He was seen by no one. There would be no witnesses to this crime, no connection to Cates. Killing over. He was scheduled to depart for Grand Cayman in just a little over six hours. He had a couple of passengers to pick up on the way. He would be in the Caymans long enough to gather his money and deal with a little problem. And then, off to Haiti while things cooled off. He was mixed about Haiti, but it offered his best haven. His friend, Thomas, would take great care of him. They had been close friends and allies since their days in the service. Both had profited from gray-market activities along the way, and neither man needed any money to sustain a lavish lifestyle. Cates was under no illusion that, while Thomas was anxious to see him and renew their friendship, Thomas had other plans. Life as a dictator could be a short-lived experience—insurrections and the ongoing battle of others trying to overthrow you. Few could sustain power the way a Fidel Castro could.

The economy of Haiti was difficult. Most of the world powers did little to cooperate with the island nation. This meant, with no trading power, the island would have to rely primarily on its own natural resources to sustain itself. Difficult, to say the least.

Two things were changing under Thomas's leadership—one good and one bad. Thomas had pushed hard to promote tourism for the island that held a mystical, and even frightening, appeal. He had persuaded two of the largest global hotels, Hyatt and Marriott, to invest in the island. This arrangement got done with the same trickery, cunning, and deceit that had earned him his dictatorship.

Cates laughed as he replayed the conversation with Thomas in his mind. "… it was great, Cates. The suits came down and we treated them like royalty. Two men and two women. We toured and pitched our hearts out. I showed them the beautiful beaches we would lease to them. They seemed interested, but I had to be sure. After dinner I told them that I had something special in mind, that I wanted them to meet some of our people and get a real flavor for the island. I told them that I had arranged for each of them to meet with different groups of people for a few hours, and then we would reconvene around 11:00 a.m. the next morning and have a final discussion.

"Okay, Cates, here's the best part. Each of them is escorted to a different part of the palace and the fun begins. We've developed a drug, well actually it's an old Haitian herb. This is the damnedest drug. You need only a tiny amount, like a teaspoon. At first you feel as good as you ever felt. You literally don't know anything is going on. You start to feel high or a bit drunk, but it doesn't affect your personality at all. You don't slur your speech, but you do talk a bit more than normal. But what happens is that you virtually always agree with suggestions that appeal to you.

"The two people from the Hyatt were my favorites. Both were in their forties, and both good looking. We slipped a little magic in their drinks, and *voila*! The natives took over. The woman had her clothes off and was being ridden in no time flat. She responded to everything. She had more sex that night than she probably had in the past twenty years. It was great!

The guy from the Hyatt performed equally well on three gorgeous women. But we didn't stop there. We got the man and the woman together. They seemed to like it. Of course, we taped it all. Great footage, Cates. With the tapes I owned the hotel chains.

"The next day was beautiful. We made sure each awoke with an attractive partner next to them. We made sure they were sticky and smelled like a night of sex. Funny thing with this drug… you wake up feeling great, but your memory is fuzzy. It really wouldn't matter 'cuz I have a great video of it ready to be released on the Internet. These are smart people. No need to even mention the video. Next day, we shake hands and *bang*, we have a deal. We did the same thing with the Marriott people… brilliant, huh?"

Cates could only laugh. Jeez, what a scam!

So, the good was tourism. The bad was drugs. The climate of Haiti was perfect. All sorts of drugs grew everywhere. Thomas controlled the drug trade and profited wildly from these activities. But he also used portions of the profits to do things for his people. Thomas had asked Cates to join him many times to head his national security force. Essentially, this meant he was the guy to stop anyone who had any thoughts of trying to do anything negative to Thomas. Essentially, he could do anything he wanted as he would be the law on that island. Cates could do the job, and the lifestyle would be good. It might even be fun. The U.S. government could not extradite him. His only risk was Sampson. The guy would not let go over time. Cates was sure of that. So… he would be eliminated.

He grabbed his cell phone and punched up a familiar number.

"Sampson."

"Hello, Sampson. It's Cates. How ya doin'?"

Sampson quickly cupped his hand over the phone and whispered to Bob. Cates sensed what was happening. "Sampson, let's not waste time. I'm on a cell phone. I'm moving and you can't trace it. Remember, I'm a spook too. Look, you and I must meet soon. I'll call you. Keep your phone on. But first head over to the northwest corner of Lakeland Park. Go up Finch to Steeles. I left a little something for you."

The connection broke. Sampson sat in silence. What did Cates mean? Sampson replayed the conversation to Bob, and they soon wheeled the car toward the park, and radioed the information to the locals and other agents. They reached the park along with a dozen other agents and officers in fifteen minutes. They were prepared for a slow and methodical search, which turned out to be unnecessary. They spotted the familiar shape and size of a body.

"Shit! You know who that is?"

Sampson grinned. "Yup. Cates is closing off his trail. The son of a bitch is good."

CHAPTER 38

Cates was already working on round two. He sat outside the house, looking closely with binoculars. Three agents, all expecting nothing. Stupid… and easy. Cates screwed a silencer on his 357 and approached the house. It was dark outside by now and in the quiet neighborhood, he cut a silent path. With the agents downstairs, he decided to enter from upstairs. An old, large tree limb hung close enough to shimmy across to a window that was open a crack. He climbed the tree and made his way across the branch and was able to grasp the windowsill and pull himself inside without a sound. He was startled as he heard a rustling to his right. Instinctively the gun was pointed at the source of the noise. The little girl sound asleep.

Cates lowered the gun, his reflexes relaxing, and crept towards the stairs. He could hear the agents in the living room, which was not visible from the staircase. Cates crept one stair at a time, gun drawn.

At the base of the stairs, Cates stopped and drew in a deep breath. He wheeled to his right and drew his weapon down on the first agent. With a *thwack* the first bullet caught a young agent in his thirties squarely in the head.

Cates continued to walk forward, gun pointed ahead. By now, the remaining two agents were beginning to react. Cates drew down on his second victim, a forty-year-old Black male. He had his hand on his weapon, which was still holstered. As he fumbled to release the gun, he felt his head explode and his consciousness slip away. His last thought was of his two-year-old girl, then… blackness.

The third agent was a female. Early thirties, dark hair, and in very good shape. She had assessed her situation quickly and accurately. As Cates was drawing down on her fellow agent, she spun to her left and dove for cover as she clawed for her weapon. Cates was aware of these movements from his peripheral vision. As he released the shot into the agent, he spun to his left out of the sight of the female agent and stood still. Predictably, the female agent stood to release a bullet at the spot where she had last seen Cates. She realized her mistake. Cates had moved… had outsmarted her.

Not a word was spoken. The agent had time for one last breath as a bullet caught her in her right temple. Ironically, her last thought was one of praise for the way she was outdueled by this intruder. So much for training….

Cates viewed the carnage and felt nothing. This was not personal to him. The agents had been sloppy. They should have been more alert, and they had paid the ultimate price for their stupidness and laziness. Cates walked over to an inexpensive, tan landline phone and punched in ten numbers.

"Sampson."

"Hey, freak. How's it going? Find my package?"

"Cates, goddamn it…"

"Testy, testy, testy," Cates teased, "Let's not get hostile, baby."

"Cates—"

"Hey, don't cut me off. I really don't have time for a discussion right now. I've got someplace to be."

"Cates—"

"I'm serious. Shut up. Time to go. Listen, pal, that little girl of yours is cute. I'll call you and let you know next steps…"

"Cates, if you hurt her…"

"You'll what? Shut the fuck up and wait for my call."

Sampson heard the line disconnect and felt his heart sink. He knew exactly what had happened. How stupid he had been! He left her alone. Damn it!

Bob could see the look on his face. "What?"

"Shit, this is bad. Cates says he has Becca."

Bob wasted no time. He picked up his radio and called in the emergency. He asked to be connected to the safe house. The phone rang and no one picked up. Both men had grown to know Cates, and they knew what was likely to have happened. Cates got inside intel, which told him Becca was a point of leverage.

They rode silently to the house, which was an agonizing, thirty-minute drive. As they arrived at the scene, there was chaos. The locals flooded the scene with squad cars. No weapons drawn. Bob knew this was a bad sign or certainly not encouraging. It either meant everyone was okay, or more likely dead.

Their worst fears were realized as they approached the house. A young, local police officer with a dark complexion shook his head despairingly as they walked past him. Inside the house looked orderly, almost clean, except for the bodies lying face down. Two dead agents were sprawled on the floor near a sofa and coffee table. Both were lying in a murky red pool of blood. Sampson could tell they were ambushed or surprised by the attack. First, their weapons weren't fully drawn and, second, they were too close together. Their training instinctively would have told them to separate at first sight of trouble. It was simply harder for an intruder to hurt two men or women separated by distance.

The female agent was a different story, however. She was found fifteen feet to the side of the men. Some magazines and pillows were scattered on the floor near her feet. Bob guessed she had jumped or rolled to avoid the gunfire. Sampson noted her weapon was drawn. In fact, she died with it in her hand with her index finger on the trigger.

"Shit, Bob," Sampson exhaled.

"He made quick work of them. These two didn't even see him coming," he pointed to the male agents. "She looks like she made it interesting, but I don't think she was able to even get a shot off. It's the JV versus the Varsity. He is fucking good." Bob looked tired and frustrated. He felt depressed and angry.

They continued past the bodies and scaled the stairs. There was nothing to see except an empty bed. Sampson could smell the little girl. He reached for her pillow, desperately hoping to pick up something… some vision… some thought. But there was nothing. As both men breathed deeply, Sampson's phone chirped.

"Sampson."

"Hello, freak. Find my presents?"

"Cates. You want me. Name the time and the place, but let Becca go. She's done nothing. You're a soldier!" Sampson knew he had to slow down and concentrate. This nut had control of the most important package in his life. He had the girl.

"Sampson, my thoughts exactly. Ironic, eh? I do want to see you. But from here on out, everything… and I mean everything… is on my terms. Understand?"

"Yes, but…"

"No buts. My terms." Sampson could hear Cates slow his breathing and assume the position of the dominator. "I want you to meet me in Grand Cayman. There's an America Airlines flight that leaves Atlanta in four hours. Be on it. Oh, by the way, you alone. Clear?"

"Yes…"

"No, I mean it. I will check all my contacts, and you know they are deep. If one agent, one cop, one friend is on that flight, she dies. I will kill her quick, and she won't suffer, but I will kill her. And then our game will go on in another venue. Time to go, Sampson. Missing that flight will be fatal for someone. Bye!"

The phone went eerily dead. Sampson knew he could say little to Bob in public. It was possible Cates was listening, or worse yet, a disloyal agent, a traitor, might overhear.

"Bob, outside," Sampson whispered. The men went quickly downstairs to an area distant from all the others.

"He has her. He's given me special instructions on everything. I have to be in Atlanta in four hours to catch a flight to Grand Cayman."

"Why Grand Cayman?"

"Don't know. He says I must come alone. He'll use his sources to watch. Any breach, he kills her."

"Okay, first things first. I'll have the company plane get you to Atlanta for the commercial flight. No way to get weapons through conventional channels on this short notice, but—"

Sampson interrupted, "Bob, we've got to play this square up. He is connected, and he is deadly serious. All I want to do is get the girl to safety. The rest… well… we'll see."

"I don't like it, but I'm in the same spot as you. Get in the car and go. Sampson, you are a skilled agent and on top of that, you have some great gifts that he doesn't. Stay cool and use your head. Remember he is one of us. Do the unexpected."

The men shook hands. "Bob, one thing. Will you tell the senator's daughter that I said she was something special?"

"Sampson, you can do this. You can get the girl and get Cates." Both men smiled. Both knew it was a long shot. Cates held all the cards. Bob watched Sampson go, and hoped it was not the last time their paths would cross.

Bob thought, *I've got to even up the odds, but how?* Anything would risk Sampson. He remembered his own words. *Think unconventional. Cates thinks like us.* And it hit him like a ball off

Aaron Judge's bat. No one would ever be looking for a grumpy beat cop from Syracuse.

It took Bob twenty-five minutes to track down O'Reilly.

"O'Reilly."

"O'Reilly, it's your old pal, Agent Becker."

O'Reilly recognized the voice and jumped in, "Great, it's Halloween. The spooks are here."

Bob explained the gravity of the situation to O'Reilly. He was grumpy, but Bob could tell he was concerned and would help. There was something about this guy he really liked. This would be a guy you would want on your side if things broke bad. They planned to get O'Reilly on the flight through the Syracuse Police Department. Bob was certain Cates would not connect with this.

First, he had to look like a tourist with little time to do it. O'Reilly ran to the property room, grabbed a beat-up suitcase. In a pile of clothes currently held as items of evidence, he found shorts, a T-shirt, and a pair of cheap flipflops. *Perfect*, he thought.

A fellow officer raced O'Reilly to the airport, and he made the flight by minutes. So, he now had two hours to figure out what he could do to help… and stay alive. Hmm… all without a gun.

O'Reilly boarded the plane unseen and unnoticed in Syracuse and found his seat. The flight carried a light load, and he was able to be seated alone in a row of three seats.

He had many concerns. First, he now knew enough of this Cates fellow to know that this matter could not be taken lightly. He felt his disguise would be enough to get him aboard the plane unnoticed. His biggest concern was that he was traveling alone to a vacation island. This was somewhat unusual, he reasoned, but not so out of the ordinary that he would stand out for sure. He would try to blend into a group if the opportunity presented itself. The next issue was firepower. He would be without a weapon, which was a strange feeling for an officer accustomed to always carrying a gun. If time permitted before the Cates/Sampson showdown, he would find some "supplies". Working with the local police would be too difficult, and who knew how deep Cates's connections ran. Absent a gun, there were some easily attainable items that the average citizen could get ahold of. O'Reilly knew them well. Some obvious; some not. He would find a fishing/hunting store if one existed on an island like Grand Cayman.

O'Reilly was a blue-collar man's blue-collar man. He was a thinker with a practical edge. He was a survivor—a man with honest determination. His few closer friends came to understand his temperament and knew that his generally nasty behavior was nothing personal. It was merely him.

As a member of the Syracuse Police Department, O'Reilly was highly respected. His arrest record was second to none, which surprised no one. His work habits had dictated his success. He worked six days a week, and never less than fifteen hours a day. He had been much less successful in his personal life. He was the consummate bachelor. His apartment was small and always cluttered. He never, ever cooked a meal at home. He took all his sustenance from a reliable circle of diners, sub shops, and an occasional Chinese takeout restaurant or pizza joint. His love life was quite another matter, which he couldn't quite figure out. While not the most attractive man in the world, he was never hurting for female attention. He never quite understood this. He had been told that women were attracted to his stormy personality. He chose to think it was his honesty. Of course, he was a police officer and "badge bunnies" did really exist!

He was always up front with his dates—"not looking for a long-term commitment, no intention of getting married, ever." Stupid lines, but they worked. Dating required no initiative on his part. Women usually asked him out, and he almost always said yes. Surprisingly to him, most were pretty good looking, some outright knockouts. Like used cars, they came in all different ages, styles, and colors.

While O'Reilly always found it interesting to be with a woman in her twenties, he preferred his dates a bit older, except in bed, of course. *Nothing beats the thrill of bedding down a twenty-five-year-old beauty*, O'Reilly mused.

As his flight touched down in Atlanta, O'Reilly took a deep breath. He grabbed his belongings and followed the line off the airplane. The gate for the flight to Grand Cayman was only a short walk. He thanked God he didn't have to trudge through the Atlanta airport's miles of terminals and cumbersome, but efficient, monorail system.

O'Reilly was certain that Cates or one of his people would be watching the flight. There was no point in trying to spot the person (or persons), not to mention the risk factor of being obvious in trying to spot someone who may be observing all the passengers. Instead, he concentrated on finding a way to board the plane inconspicuously.

He spotted an elderly couple in their seventies at a corner of the waiting area near the gate to Grand Cayman. He walked to the couple and made eye contact with the gentleman. Softly he said, "Hello, sir. My name is O'Reilly, and the gate agent is a friend of mine. I'm going to Grand Cayman, and he asked me to give you a hand getting on."

The gentleman extended his hand, and both he and his wife smiled brightly. "Isn't that nice, Tom?" the grandmother cooed.

"Sure is, Sue, sure is." The couple seemed pleased.

For the next fifteen minutes, O'Reilly worked hard at making conversation with the grandparents. He needed to project an image to the watcher that these folks were with him and not total strangers. From time to time, he would laugh a little louder than normal. He made a point of touching their arms and shoulders; not too much, but the kind of touch a relative or close friend would do. He had easy people to work with. They seemed to take to him immediately, and they were exuding warm trust. *Perfect*, O'Reilly thought.

The agent began to call the flight, and offered preboarding for those who needed a little extra time. O'Reilly scanned across the boarding area and did not see Sampson. As he rose from his chair, he motioned at the couple. "Time to go. Let me get those bags." With that, he scooped up two carry-ons and helped his new companions to their feet. The couple shuffled to the gate and, as they handed their boarding passes to the agent, the grandfather blurted, "Young man, you were nice to ask your friend to help us."

The agent looked perplexed. O'Reilly smiled warmly and winked at the agent. Luckily the agent smiled back, assuming only that he was a relative or good samaritan helping an older and confused couple. "Have a nice flight, folks," he uttered. With that, they started the painful and slow-shuffling journey to the aircraft.

The grandparents were in 13B and 13C. Once he had them settled, he told them he would help again on the other end. He took his seat in Row 34, Seat A, right next to the galley and the bathroom. The smells would not be good, but it was a perfect spot to see everyone getting on board the aircraft.

As the remainder of the passengers came aboard, he spotted no one who looked evil. But who was to know? Sampson was one of the last to board the plane. O'Reilly was relieved to see him, but quickly slumped and turned away. Sampson would be more relaxed if he was not aware of O'Reilly's presence. Sampson was seated near the front of the cabin; O'Reilly guessed around Row 10 or so.

The ground time was short. They taxied out and were airborne in twenty minutes. The captain made his announcements;

they would be cruising at 35,000 feet, and the flight would be about two-and-a-half hours.

When the seatbelt sign dinged off, a couple of people stood and moved back toward the restrooms. Soon, two more followed them and stood patiently next to O'Reilly's seat, waiting for their turn. Momentarily, O'Reilly's view of the forward cabin was blocked, but soon, the line moved, and O'Reilly could again see the entire plane. As he looked toward Sampson's row, he could see a flight attendant bent down in the aisle speaking to a passenger. O'Reilly looked more closely. She was speaking to Sampson, and something seemed wrong. The expression on her face was tight, not smiling, concerned.

Shit, he thought. *What now?* He waited and watched for another minute or so, and nothing changed; still the concerned face.

He weighed his options and decided to stand and go to the grandparents. He could do this without causing a commotion and probably not blowing his cover. As he approached them, he could now see more clearly. Sampson was in trouble. There was blood everywhere. But how? He had heard or seen nothing.

He moved to Sampson but was stopped by the flight attendant. "Sir, please return to your seat. We have a medical situation here."

"Ma'am, this man is an acquaintance of mine, and I've had some medical training. Please step aside."

She began to protest, but he brushed her aside and knelt next to Sampson. He could see blood pouring from his nose, but no other injuries were apparent. Sampson appeared disoriented and dazed. O'Reilly grabbed him by the shirt and shook him gently. Sampson briefly appeared normal.

"O'Reilly… what?" His voice was hoarse.

"Spook, what is happening here?"

Sampson swallowed deeply and fought for consciousness. He

knew he had to find strength and breathe. O'Reilly's shaking of him had allowed him to 'let go', and he knew the episode was over. "O'Reilly… Syracuse again. Same feeling. Bomb." Sampson was drained of strength. He knew it would be thirty minutes before some degree of normalcy occurred.

"Shit," O'Reilly said. He looked at the flight attendant. "I need to see the captain right now." She fought back. "That's not possible, sir. FAA regulations—"

O'Reilly jumped in and moved closer to the woman. He pulled his shield from his pocket and stuck it in her face. "Now. Right now."

They walked forward and he was asked to stand near the lavatory in the First-Class section while she spoke privately with the pilot. He could sense concern mounting with the passengers but within a minute, the pilot appeared from the cockpit. He was a tall man, 6'1 or 6'2, maybe early fifties with gray around the temples and bushy brown hair elsewhere. "I'm Captain Briggs. What—"

"Captain, my name is O'Reilly. I'm a policeman. The man back there is CIA. This is a long story, and we have no time. So, make up your mind right now whether you trust me or not."

The captain's expression changed only slightly. "Go ahead."

"Look, this plane is in trouble. My guess is a bomb. This is tied to all the trouble recently in Syracuse. We have very little time. I'm going to find the bomb. You need to get this plane on the ground now, in the nearest spot you can, and I mean the nearest thing you can… a street, a field, or a fucking driveway if you have to!"

The captain backed up in shock. "You realize I'm going to trust you, Officer. This will likely cost me my job. Regulations say I should ignore you."

"That, sir, would be a death sentence. That man back there bleeding is a straight shooter. There's no bullshit here at all,

Captain, I promise you. But we have problems, you and I… big problems."

O'Reilly's expression softened. "Captain, we need to get on with this. Let me find the bomb. You figure out where to put this damn thing down."

"All right. You're on. I'll need about ten minutes," he huffed. With that, the tall man headed back to the cockpit.

O'Reilly knew time was running out on them. He looked back at Sampson, whose color had returned slightly. He judged Sampson wouldn't do him much good for the next little while.

Suddenly O'Reilly blurted out, "Shit!" and ran towards the cockpit. He began banging on the door until it opened. He could see that the door was opened by a young co-pilot, and he saw the captain beginning to speak into a microphone. "Captain, no!" O'Reilly reached forward and pulled the microphone and headset from the captain.

As the co-pilot reached to restrain O'Reilly, the hand of the captain came up to ward off the co-pilot. "Let him be. Officer, what now?"

"Chances are they're listening. They may be able to detonate this thing remotely. You've got to trust me on this."

"Officer, I've just told Miami Control we have a situation. I was about to tell them more when you… well, interrupted me."

"Captain, make something up, please," O'Reilly pleaded.

"Very well. Miami Control, this is American Airlines 221. Our situation is under control. We had a bit of air rage on board. A passenger was being difficult with a flight attendant. Fortunately, we have an off-duty police officer on board who corrected the situation. I will advise the Special Constables in Grand Cayman to meet the plane if necessary."

The captain held his breath. His story was fishy and if he had an experienced air traffic controller, he was toast. The wait was short but intense.

"American Airlines 221. Roger."

"American Airlines 221." The Captain smiled and turned to O'Reilly, "We're off the hook, Officer."

"Find a place to set down. I'll be back in five minutes."

The captain nodded, and he and the first officer began reviewing flight manuals.

O'Reilly dashed toward Sampson. Sampson looked up weakly at him. "It's that way, I think. I just can't tell. The one in Syracuse was in a lavatory. Start there, but hurry. I can tell time is tight."

The other passengers on the plane were, by now, in a very mild state of panic. O'Reilly ignored them. While he understood their concern, he had no time to deal with it all. He sprinted toward the three rear lavatories. He started to his left. He carefully opened the door and with a rapid visual inspection, saw nothing. He moved toward the waste bin. Except for one paper towel, it was empty. He checked a towel dispenser, the toilet paper roll… nothing.

Time was critical. He moved on. In the second lavatory he found an empty waste bin. He carefully felt around the paper towels… nothing. But something was not right. What was it?

The Kleenex dispenser was different. No, it was empty. He peered between the empty slots, and he could see a small red light flashing. He decided to look more closely. He removed the plastic cover to reveal a bomb; not a big bomb, but a bomb, nonetheless.

"Shit," he muttered under his breath. He had a small amount of training with explosives, but not enough to deal with this. He studied the bomb. Simple design. A compact plastic explosive connected to a timer with an LED readout that said, "24 minutes". There didn't appear to be any other trip devices. This made sense. Nothing fancy because Cates didn't expect the device to be discovered.

As he emerged from the restroom, he found the flight attendant who had confronted him earlier. "Miss…" he could see the disgust on her face from him addressing her as such, but he just didn't give a shit. "Miss… keep the seatbelt sign on, and don't let anyone in that middle bathroom." She began to object, but O'Reilly stared at her, and she thought better of it.

He started up the cabin to Sampson. "Sampson," he whispered. "You were right. Small device. Looks straightforward, and we have twenty minutes."

Sampson wanted to help, but physically wasn't able yet. "Can you disable it?" O'Reilly shook his head no. "Well, that leaves two choices: land and evacuate, or get it off the plane, I guess."

O'Reilly nodded his head in agreement. "That's all I could come up with, too. The captain's looking at the first option. I'm going to him right now."

"O'Reilly, by the way, what are you doing here?"

"Vacation… or maybe your pal, Bob the spook, sent me to help. Take your pick." O'Reilly laughed and moved toward the cockpit.

A flight attendant ushered him in straight away. He closed the door behind him. "What have you got, Captain?"

"We have two options. As you can see, below us is nothing but water. There is an abandoned air force base on an island not too far from here. It's tight, but I think I can get it down safely. Option 2 is to try and land in Cuba. No guarantees, but they might let us in."

"How much time?"

"Forty minutes to Cuba; thirty to the air base."

"That's it? Nothing closer?"

"Nope."

"Fuck! No good, no good! Look, we have a bomb on board. I've found it. It goes *kaboom* in fifteen minutes. There won't be a plane left to fly after that."

"Officer, there is nothing. We are in the middle of the ocean."

"Can you land in the water?"

"If all else fails, that is an option, but that's a real long-shot to survive."

"Okay, so we've got to get rid of the bomb. Captain, I don't suppose we can open a window and throw it out, can we?"

The captain chuckled, "No. It's not that simple. Anything you throw out gets sucked into the engines. Plus, if you open a door… well, you've seen that scene on TV."

"Okay, give me another solution." When he received nothing in return, he bellowed, "Fuck! We're dead then."

Silence filled the cockpit until the second officer addressed the captain. "Sir, I spent some time months ago touring the Boeing plant that made this plane. During the tour, I met with one of the assemblers responsible for the landing gear. He gave me a private tour. There is a lot of room down there, and you can get at it through baggage, and you can get to baggage through the galley. The point is this: from the landing gear we could drop the bomb. It's below the engines. It might not get sucked in."

O'Reilly jumped in. "Let's do it!"

"Not so fast," said the Captain. "I don't think you understand the risk. Once those doors come open, even at the slowest speed, there will be no air, the temperature will be close to fifty below zero, and you'll probably get sucked out to boot.

"It's the only option, and we have ten minutes. Give me the portable oxygen you have on board, and a piece of rope to tie me down."

"Officer…"

"Let's go. If not, this whole plane goes."

"All right. The first officer will show you down. Good luck. As soon as he's back, I'll open the gear up, you drop the bomb. I'll slow to 180 knots, which is just above a stall, and I'll get down close to the water. That will help with the temperature."

"Okay, here we go." The first officer unbuckled his belt as he spoke.

They made their way toward the rear of the plane. The first officer grabbed a green cylinder of oxygen meant for emergencies and completed the short journey to the galley. He pushed a button, and a door opened, revealing a narrow ladder leading down below.

"This is it," he said to O'Reilly.

"All right. Let me get our little friend."

O'Reilly could feel his heart beating and thought he might just have a heart attack. He focused his concentration on the bomb now before him. Well, one good thing was that the explosive and the timer were wrapped tightly in black electrical tape, so he would only have to delicately handle one secure package. He allowed his hands to explore the outer edges of the device. Again, he felt no trip wires. He held his breath and gently hoisted the bomb. Nothing exploded. *Yes, dear God*, he thought.

He backed out of the lavatory and headed to the stairs. The flight attendant and the co-pilot now saw firsthand how grave the situation was. He approached the stairs but found no way to climb in and hold the bomb. *Shit!* He looked at the first officer. "Put your hands out and hold this."

He did as he was told, and O'Reilly climbed to the ladder. The co-pilot handed the bomb back as a hot potato fresh out of the oven, and O'Reilly very carefully climbed down. He was vaguely aware of the pilot making an announcement but paid no attention. He reached the bottom, and the co-pilot climbed down behind him. He moved forward. 'We're going to have to climb over and around the bags and cargo. We've got to get mid-compartment, which is about thirty feet that way." He pointed over what looked like a pile of suitcases, crates, and God knew what else.

"We've got to do this fast. What we'll do is this. You go as far as you can and still reach back. I'll hand you the package. Then I'll pass you and do the same. We'll play leapfrog till we get there, okay? *Go.*" The co-pilot climbed straight up about six feet. "Okay, hand it off."

O'Reilly reached up and made the handoff. They continued along for five minutes without incident. Both men were sweating profusely, a combination of nerves and exertion, when they reached a small hatch in the floor marked in black letters, LANDING GEAR - NO ACCESS. The co-pilot looked at the panel. "That's it." He grabbed the handle and started to manually unscrew the panel. It took only a few turns before the hatch opened. Both men felt the cold instantly and even with the gear doors shut, it felt like a giant vacuum trying to suck them down to earth. Both men wondered what would happen when the doors were fully open.

"Okay, now what?"

"You should be able to crawl down there. Stay way to the right. Everything else will be exposed when the door opens. I grabbed this piece of cargo netting. Tie it on and around your mid-section."

O'Reilly did as he was told. "Pass me the bomb and go. We've only got a couple of minutes."

"What about the oxygen?"

"No time. Button up the hatch. Open the gear fully and then close it. I'll handle the rest.

And by the way, come get me quick. I'm not ready to die yet."

"I'll be back, Officer. Here's the package." The men exchanged the bomb. O'Reilly nestled in, and it became eerily dark. Once secure he climbed over the cargo and up the stairs. He moved with haste up the aisle and into his co-pilot's chair.

"Captain, he's ready."

"Okay, let's go to 300 feet and 180 knots. I will now bullshit the passengers." He pushed the intercom button on the microphone. "Ladies and gentlemen, I'm sure you've noticed that we have had a couple of small incidents during the flight. Nothing serious, I assure you. One of the issues was a medical condition with a passenger. We've spoken with a doctor on the ground, and he believes the passenger's condition was caused by the altitude we were flying at. As such, we are going to significantly lower our altitude for a little while as we work on the passenger. Just wanted to let you know so you wouldn't be alarmed."

He clicked off the microphone and the co-pilot smiled at him. "You fooled everyone except any doctors, nurses, or paramedics on board."

"Yup. Oh well. We're at 400 feet and the air speed is low."

O'Reilly waited patiently in virtual dark. He was afraid to move for fear of when the doors opened he wouldn't be ready. He worried about oxygen. He felt he could hold his breath for sixty, maybe ninety, seconds. He wondered how long it would take for the gear to go down and back up again. Surely no more than ninety seconds, he hoped.

O'Reilly had plenty of time to think through the options that might play out for him in the moments ahead. He had resigned himself to the reality that if he had to, he would die to save the passengers on the plane. He didn't have a lot to live for, but he did love life in his own sort of way. He really hoped it wouldn't come to that. *Shit*, he thought, *should have been a priest; better shot at heaven.*

His private thoughts vanished as he began to hear a motor nearby spring to life. He hugged the bomb like a football and took a deep breath just as the doors began to open.

The experience was nothing like he had ever felt before. He felt his entire body go airborne, and he began to bang from side to side. He hugged the bomb to protect it from accidental detonation.

He was shocked by the cold. He began to shiver and did what he could to protect his hands. As the doors fully opened, he was able to lean forward and though his hands were now numb from the cold, he could pitch the bomb out just as the doors started to close. He was not able to see the path of the bomb as it passed outside the plane. Just as the doors were about to fully close, he could hear and feel the explosion of the device. Not five seconds had passed.

As the doors closed, O'Reilly exhaled and gulped for air. He coughed, but the air was like a drink of water to a very thirsty man. He soaked it in. Within a minute, he could see the co-pilot staring down at him.

"Wow, you cut that close!"

"Yeah. Get me out. I'm freezing." O'Reilly managed a smile having cheated death again.

The cockpit had become very interesting for the captain. He was an honest man and hated lying but if the officer was telling the truth, what choice did he have?

"American Airlines 221. This is Miami."

"American Airlines 221."

"American Airlines 221. What happened? You went off our screen."

"American Airlines 221. We hit a wind shear. No injuries. Climbing back to 35,000."

"American Airlines 221. Climb approved."

"Roger that. American Airlines 221."

Good. Another lie completed, and one more to go. He pressed the intercom button. "Hello, everyone. This is the captain. Just wanted to give you another update. Our medical emergency has cleared, which is great news. You may have heard and felt an explosion moments ago. We just passed a U.S. Navy training exercise and due to our low altitude, which the Navy knew about, we were able to hear some of their activity. Anyway, sorry for all the inconveniences. We are now on our way to Grand Cayman, and we should be there in about two hours. Enjoy the rest of the flight."

O'Reilly, with help, squirmed out from his tomb. He could feel warmth surging through his near frozen body, but he was alive!

The two men made their way back to the cabin of the plane. O'Reilly stopped and saw Sampson smiling brightly. "Way to go, flatfoot!"

"Easy on the jokes, Seinfeld. But, yes, I am a hero. Send money. But we've still got work to do. Let me talk to the pilot, and then we got a few hours to plot the future."

"Great. And seriously, great work. You are a hero."

"Aw, shucks. Thanks, spook. I'll be back."

O'Reilly was back with Sampson in ten minutes. "We're cool up front. The pilot and the co-pilot are good guys. I assumed someone might be tracking this flight, so I had them basically lie about everything that has gone on so far. We will need your connections to make sure these guys don't get fired."

"That won't be a problem." Sampson felt strong again.

"Here's what I think. Your pal, Cates, will know the plane survived. He'll either think the bomb was a dud or, more likely, he'll know you did your mindreading thing yet again. Whatever… no matter. The plane will be watched when we land, so I'll have to be careful but trust me, I've got a good cover going. You'll have to get word to me when Cates contacts you."

Sampson shook his head no. "No. He'll kill her, and I won't risk that."

"Sampson, you can't take him alone. You know that, don't you?"

"No, I don't know that."

"He is one of the best. Two of us stand a much better chance of getting her back than just you. Let's play the odds. He won't spot me, I promise."

Sampson mulled this over and grudgingly agreed. "I know

you're right, but I won't lose that little girl." *My daughter*, he thought.

"You won't. Look, your room may be bugged, so here's what we do. I'm sure the Marriott has a restroom in the lobby. Leave me a note in the stall closest to the door. Pull out the toilet paper, write the note, and roll it back up. Go there tonight and I'll leave you my room number. Every time you are about to leave the hotel, dial my room, let it ring once, and I'll head to the lobby. I've done this before, and it works great."

"O'Reilly, I do trust you. And I'm glad you're here. Do me a favor. My bag is right above me. Bring it down and throw me a clean shirt."

"You got it."

Their plans set, they decided it would be best to take their seats and relax and look inconspicuous for the rest of the flight.

An hour later, Cates received word through his network that the plane was proceeding straight into Grand Cayman. He learned that the pilot and Air Traffic Control had a series of strange discussions, but the plane was due to land in thirty minutes. Cates had half-expected this outcome. In an odd way, he had come to respect this man for a talent he couldn't understand. Cates also knew this man to be resourceful and quick on his feet. Killing him would be more of a sport, and riskier that he first imagined. Still, the competition would be fun. Time to prepare.

CHAPTER 39

The plane landed without incident. Sampson had decided to let the plane empty before he left. He watched O'Reilly begin his charade with the old couple, and he had to admit it was convincing enough to at least cast doubt if anyone was watching. He had misjudged O'Reilly, and he hoped he had time to tell him that he was sorry. As the passengers moved down the aisle, Sampson grabbed his bag from the overhead bin and walked forward. He saw the pilot and co-pilot smiling as he approached. Sampson reached his hand out and shook hands with both men.

"Thank you, guys. Look, I can't dawdle here as it's likely someone will be watching as I leave. I'm sure I'm out of favors but do what you can to not tell the truth. I promise I'll sort this out for you as soon as this is over. It won't be long, I think."

"We'll take care of it. Good luck." The pilot smiled and they shook hands again.

Sampson scurried down the jet bridge and glanced around as he entered the terminal. He saw tourists, no businesspeople. No surprise, since this was a vacation resort. Nothing else jumped out at him. He saw a couple of maybes… a man dressed casually in khaki shorts and a Grand Cayman T-shirt. He was texting on his phone. He never really looked up, and Sampson believed him to be a tourist.

The other suspect was a young woman in her late twenties

and dressed casually. She was seated at the far end of the waiting area, reading a paperback novel. Unlike the man, the woman looked up a couple of times and while never making eye contact with Sampson, he would bet she was watching him. *Ah, maybe I should have some fun with this*, Sampson thought. *No harm one way or the other if I catch her eye and wave back. Or, better yet, if I could touch her just maybe I'd see something.*

Sampson stopped at a snack shop located at the center of the waiting area. He browsed a moment and selected a Gatorade, the original green/yellow, of course, and a bag of Lays potato chips. He paid the cashier and sauntered over in the direction of the woman.

As he came upon her, he made eye contact and asked, "Excuse me, ma'am, is this seat taken?"

She looked straight into his eyes and replied, "Why no, I don't think so."

She put her eyes back on the book. Sampson opened his drink and chips, and calmly ate a portion of the snack. "Where are you heading, if you don't mind me asking?"

The woman peered over the book. "Oh, nowhere. I'm picking someone up. His flight is delayed."

"Oh, too bad," Sampson idly said. "But it's not a bad place to wait."

"No, it's not. I just hope it won't be much longer."

Sampson finished his snack and began to get up. *Now for the fun part.* "Nice to meet you, ma'am," he said as he extended his hand.

Instinctively the woman reached out, and Sampson could see her hesitate. She was watching, and that bastard, Cates, had told her not to touch him. But she was stuck, no option. She and Sampson came together, and he saw flashes in his head. First, it was now clear she was watching him. Other images came in flashes. He saw Cates in a bright light silhouette and a strange image. He saw brick pillars with a white fence atop a concrete structure and on one of the pillars, a word: *XANDRIA*.

Sampson broke the connection. "Thanks for letting me sit down. I really learned a lot." He wanted her to know he knew. He was banking on the fact that she wouldn't tell Cates that he had spotted her. He hoped she feared him as much as he did. He sensed he was right, but the truth was it wouldn't matter much either way.

She smiled a knowing smile at him as he strolled down the corridor. Once he was out of sight, she moved to a phone booth and dialed a series of numbers. Predictable. "Cates, it's Marcia. The target was acquired without incident. All appears well."

"Thank you." And the phone went dead.

She worried about lying but feared telling the truth more. She had dealings with Cates for years. He was a smooth, mean son of a bitch who had no human feelings at all. Killing was a project to him, no different than some people cleaning the basement. She had no desire to tell him she had been made. She certainly wouldn't tell him that she had been touched. She remembered his words, "Under no circumstances, no matter what, are you to allow physical contact. Are you clear?" He glared at her with vampiric eyes the color of smooth black stones. And sure enough, she had blown it. Bad enough she was spotted; it was worse she was touched. His touch had been an odd sensation. She had felt her mind racing, and she knew her thoughts, private and public, had entered his mind. She fucked up. Now, would she pay with her life?

Sampson retrieved his bag from a belt, along with the other tourists. The belt was in an openair area, and it was hot and muggy. He spotted O'Reilly still playing his charade with his new mom and dad. The perfect family. The guy was a trooper, Sampson had to admit. He had really underestimated this guy.

On his way toward the cab stand, he stopped at an information booth, the kind you saw in every tourist airport around the world. Sampson was always amazed, on the few vacations he had taken, how wonderfully, in a brochure, someone could describe a dump. He had long ago learned that you should never trust the marketing spin. He decided to take one of each brochure. It would provide him some intelligence about the island. The young lady manning the booth smiled at him, and he smiled back. Every bit the tourist, he played along.

"Can I help you, sir?"

"Why, yes. I'm here for a couple of weeks and I'd like to see all the attractions in Grand Cayman. Any suggestions?" He surveyed her features. One side of her face had been severely burned. How painful that must have been. Could have been the victim of domestic violence, and now, the poor thing was working for a mundane hourly wage.

"Well, yes. Do you like to snorkel?"

"Sure do."

"I would recommend a trip to Sting Ray City. You can swim with the rays. It's fun.

Your hotel can arrange it. Also, the Turtle Farm. Some think it to be boring, but I like it."

Sampson feigned interest in the materials. He looked up and made perfect tourist eye contact with the woman. She had been a beautiful woman. His heart raced, assuming she was the victim of a stalker or abuser. *Have to know.... Goddamn it, Sampson, and what are you going to do for her? Stick to the matter at hand.*

"Hey, let me ask you a question."

"Sure." The woman brightened and sat more upright in her chair.

"A friend of mine was here and asked me to see Xandria. Said I would enjoy it. Any idea where I would find it?"

"Hmm, no. Doesn't ring a bell." She was still smiling brightly.

"I'm off the next couple of days. I wouldn't mind showing you around."

Sampson smiled. "Thanks, really, but I'm here with my wife."

The woman looked dejected. "Oh, I didn't see a ring. Sorry."

"No problem. I just don't wear one."

She smiled back in a sincere way. "If you change your mind and need a break from the wife, call me anyway. I think you'd have a very good time." She handed him a piece of paper with the name, "Catina", and a phone number.

"Thanks, Catina. You're very nice." He pulled out a one-hundred-dollar bill, dropped it on the counter and walked away briskly. He didn't have to envision what had happened to Catina, he just knew from intuition. Maybe if he weren't trying to track a killer, he would take her out to dinner to show her kindness.

Sampson made his way to the cab line. He noticed he had begun to sweat in the tropical heat. The line wasn't long, only four tourists in front of him. He was pleased to find his driver was an old timer, a Black gentleman in his late sixties. They made small talk as they wound their way through the town on route to the Marriott. Finally, Sampson threw it out. "Driver, you don't know a place called Xandria, do you?"

He didn't answer right away as he thought. "No, I don't think so... no, wait, yes I do. Why do you ask?"

"Well, it's a long story, but a friend said I should check it out." Sampson smiled brightly to encourage a response.

"Who is your friend? Better yet, you should be careful of your friend," he said, with a stern face.

"Why's that?" Sampson shot back.

"Xandria is a difficult place, my friend. It is out on the far end of the island. I only know it because it was a place I played at as a child."

"What can you tell me about Xandria?"

The driver became silent. Sampson decided to trust the man

and tell him what he was up against. Again, he had nothing to lose. At the end of his explanation, he waited. The driver said nothing for two minutes.

"I have learned to trust my instincts as I grow old. I do not think you are one of them. I will trust you. Besides, I am an old man… little scares me anymore."

Sampson felt a wash of relief come over him. "Thank you. This is really important to me."

"I see that, young man. Let me tell you about Xandria. When I was a young boy, there was a beautiful piece of property on the far side of the island that belonged to a reclusive, old man who obviously had no financial worries. When he died, which was probably fifty years ago, maybe more, he willed it to Cornell University. They constructed some buildings and sent students down who studied the fish and wildlife as part of their veterinary program, I think. Anyway, that's when I got to know the property. I was sixteen or seventeen, but I looked a bit older and well, I dated a couple of the coeds through the years. Oh, those were fun years."

Sampson chuckled to himself. He could see the old man reliving his younger past and really enjoying it.

"Well, about ten years ago, the school decided it was just too much, and they sold the property to a private individual. As it turns out, this individual is a part of a larger, in fact very large, organization who makes their living in, well, shall we say, in the pharmaceutical business. Now to be fair, they have been good to the island. There haven't been any shenanigans at all. Rumor is that their muckety mucks use the place as a vacation spot, and to take advantage of the liberal banking laws of the Cayman Islands. Not an unusual situation at all down here. So, that's what I know. I'm real sure no one is at the house right now, except maybe some of the help. The family was all there last week, but they left a few days ago. I saw them myself at the airport."

"So, it's a drug business?" No reply came back.

Sampson's mind raced forward. Cates must have called in a favor from a connection. Regardless, Sampson needed to get to Xandria and sooner was better than later.

Sampson jumped in, "I've asked enough already, but I need another favor. Could you sketch out what Xandria looks like?"

"Young man, it was a long time ago. I've forgotten some, I'm sure."

Sampson laughed. "Sir, I really don't think you've forgotten much, particularly about the coeds." They both snickered. "Suppose I buy you lunch, and you tell me what you can?" The old cabbie was not about to pass up a free meal and a beer, which rarely came along. It turns out the driver's name was Benjamin, and he was almost eighty but to Sampson's delight, he remembered everything. Benjamin shared his past with Sampson at a hip café packed with locals, no tourists. While the two looked out of place, no one seemed to mind. Sampson was taking two calculated risks. First, he assumed no one would follow him from the airport. Given his surprise encounter with the woman, this seemed a safe bet. And two, that what Benjamin was describing was mostly still accurate. This was probably also a safe bet, Sampson theorized. People usually clung to the past. People loved history. It was likely the new owners of the estates would have kept the existing university structures, and merely gutted the insides to suit their unique needs. Sampson prayed this was true. He had a chance if he could move unnoticed inside the compound and if Cates was there.

Benjamin's mind was bright, and his outlook on life even brighter. "Ben, you have been very helpful, and I hate to impose again, but I have no one else to turn to."

Ben sat stone-faced and attentive. "Go ahead. As I told you, I am old. Besides, this is kind of fun… and an old man needs that."

"Thanks, Ben. I mean it. There are two of us here. We need

to get out to Xandria tonight. Right at dusk. If I am to have any chance at all getting my little girl back, it has to be tonight. We need a ride and a distraction; not much, just enough so they take their eye off the ball for a second. I can't risk being seen getting in a cab at the Marriott. Would you mind picking me up at the Hyatt in the parking lot at 6:30 tonight?"

"No problem, mon. You and your friend. We can discuss the rest in the car on the way across the island. It will take an hour, which should put us there at dusk." Ben smiled warmly at Sampson.

"Thanks again, Ben. You're a good man, Sir."

Little was said between the two men on the way back to the Marriott. Ben could sense the swelling tension in Sampson, but he knew there was little he could do to help. He would do what he could. He intuitively liked Sampson, but what would his chances be of handling this alone?

"Sampson, why not go to the police here on the Caymans?"

"Ben, I wish I could, but the risk is too large. If one person makes a call to Xandria I could lose her forever. I've got to do this pretty much on my own."

"Hmm. I see what you are saying, but what is your plan? Surely they will have more men, and I'm sure they'll have plenty of weapons."

Sampson's jaw clenched tight. "Ben, I don't have a game plan. I'm pretty much going to have to make this up as I go. Bad strategy, I know, but it's the best I can come up with."

Ben straightened in his seat. "Mmmm. You'll win, young man. I know it. Good conquers evil. It's been that way since the beginning of time."

As the car pulled up to the Marriott, Sampson handed Ben his fare. "Thanks, Ben. You're a good man. I'll see you tonight."

"Okay, my friend. Rest this afternoon."

Sampson walked to the lobby of the Marriott. It was plain as lobbies go—marble floors, oak tables, flowered sofas. Sampson made his way to the check-in desk and was greeted by a pretty, dark-haired woman. At a closer glance, the young woman resembled Dr. Sarah Axel. His heart dropped.

"Welcome to the Marriott, sir."

After awkward silence, Sampson smiled warmly and replied, "Thank you. The last name is Sampson."

With a click of the keyboard the woman looked up, "Yes, sir. We have your reservation.

This says you will be staying with us indefinitely."

"Correct."

"Will you require a key for your wife?"

Embarrassed, Sampson stared into her eyes, but could see a wry smile on the woman's lips. "Oh, I'm not married."

The woman smiled brightly. "Oh, well, that's good for us single girls." Sampson blushed a bit.

"You flatter me."

"We aim to please in the Islands. Here are your keys, Mr. Sampson. If there's anything I can do to make your stay more pleasurable, be sure to let me know."

Sampson fully understood what she meant. "Oh, I will. Thank you." *What gives*, he thought, *I've never been hit on by so many women in my life! Got to love the Caymans.*

As he headed toward the elevator bank he scanned the lobby, looking to see if he was being watched. To his delight, the lobby was deserted. He reasoned that Cates knew he was here and would, from time to time, keep tabs on him, but it was encouraging and helpful that he was not under surveillance fulltime.

Cates sat at a table under an umbrella drinking a Red Stripe beer. He liked Xandria, having been here on five or six occasions in the past. Its owner was a Colombian named Juan Gonzales. Juan made a big-time living in the drug and guns trade. To his good fortune, Cates had worked several critical jobs for Gonzales over the years, and each job had been executed perfectly. This earned Cates a mountain of respect, which had translated to an allyship of sorts with Gonzales. His plan was to let Sampson stew in his hotel room for a couple of nights. Cates had taken the liberty of bugging his room and his phone, in case the CIA agent was stupid enough to try something. Cates didn't have a specific plan for the much-anticipated murder. It had to be a quirky method for the quirky freak himself. Still, the act wouldn't diminish what was happening to him. He would be forced into hiding for at least a couple of years. *There are worse things*, he thought.

He had no plans to kill the girl, a mere child who could barely string a fucking sentence together. What kind of men murdered children? He didn't have much of a heart, but he did have more pride than that. Xandria came equipped with five women who lived there in the lap of luxury. Their only job was to meet the needs of the men who came in and out as guests. The women had flocked to the child when Cates arrived, and he had not been bothered by her since. Frankly, he was getting bored with this whole charade. Time for the last murder and move the fuck on.

Sampson threw his bag on the floor. He was tired, and really wanted to collapse on the bed, but he needed to find out just how prepared Cates was for his visit. First, he checked under the bed for bugs and bombs. Nothing. Next, the phone—a bug. He stopped there. If there was one, there were more. It didn't matter anyway. He had no intention of saying anything that could jeopardize Becca. He had to assume that he was being monitored, so he had to play it cool. He flicked on the TV and flopped on the bed for a moment.

Sampson knew he had to get to O'Reilly and give him as much time as possible. The phone bug complicated that matter a bit. He played the options in his mind. For sure he couldn't call from the room. Calling from the lobby would be too risky. *House phone*, he thought. Every good hotel has a house phone in every hallway. They are there for two reasons: first, to provide extra security and second, to help the guests who lock themselves out of their rooms, which happens a lot in the hotel industry.

Sampson recalled a rather embarrassing moment in his past when he had gone to set a tray from his room service delivery outside his room, only to inadvertently lock himself out. If that wasn't bad enough (which it was), he was locked out wearing only his underwear. He remembered his sense of panic, and relief when he had spotted the house phone. That was his answer.

He headed out the door and took the elevator up two floors. He wasn't sure if Cates would have wired the hall house phone near his room or not. The son of a bitch was smart, so he could take no chances. The doors opened and Sampson headed to the phone. He examined it for bugs, found none, and reached for the receiver.

"Hotel operator."

"Could you connect me with Mr. O'Reilly's room, please?"

"Certainly, hold the line, please."

After a brief pause, the line connected and the phone rang once, and Sampson hung up. He prayed O'Reilly was there, but he knew he would be. The guy was nothing if not a professional. Sampson headed for the lobby. He wandered to the gift shop. Sampson picked up a *USA Today*, a pack of Dentyne, and a box of Altoids. *Good tourist stuff*, he reasoned. He paid the cashier and sauntered towards the men's room off the lobby.

Following the plan, Sampson went to the stall closest to the door, and scratched a message out on the toilet paper, "Located package, I think. Meet tonight 6:00 p.m. Hyatt back parking lot… and thanks. PS - My room is bugged. Be careful."

Sampson left the washroom and made his way back to the lobby. He casually strolled past the front desk and was not surprised to see his friend, the hot desk clerk, smiling at him. He gave her a slight wave and smile, nothing suggestive, and made his way back to his room.

He had about four hours of time to kill. He flicked on the TV and absentmindedly watched the screen. Zombies. Just what he needed to relax! Sleep was fitful. Thoughts of Becca continually made their way to his level of consciousness and disturbed his sleep pattern. He was glad, however, that this was corning to a conclusion. He wanted a life back. He wanted his life back, and sooner rather than later. He wanted to be with the little girl, and he thought he wanted to be with Susan also. They would make his perfect family.

Sleep did come eventually, and Sampson was startled awake by the alarm. He made his way to the shower and let the warm mist and water wash over his body. He found a bar of flowery French soap and scrubbed himself clean. The shower felt as good as any shower he had ever taken.

Sampson could sense his nervous energy approaching. He wasn't surprised, and deliberately slowed his breathing to a normal pace. He toweled off and searched his luggage for proper clothing for tonight's adventure. He found his old blue jeans, a black T-shirt, and a pair of dirty, battered hi-top Converse sneakers. He shook his head in disbelief that this was how he had to battle Cates. He worked for the most sophisticated agency in the world, and here he was with nothing.

With his room bugged, Sampson could do little more than leave the television on and hope that would at least confuse those who were listening. It wouldn't for long, but there was nothing more to do. He dressed. He silently left his room and walked up one flight of stairs, down a corridor to another set of stairs at the far end of the building. He walked silently and found himself at a landing which left him with two choices: back to the lobby, or out to the beach. He chose the beach, carefully looking about for anyone who might be watching.

No one, he thought. He darted up the beach through a path that led to a street, which he followed north to the Hyatt. He was just a little early, and carefully chose a spot that concealed his presence well.

"Evening, spook!" Sampson was as startled as he had ever been in life. Not four feet away, literally inside a row of bushes, stood O'Reilly.

"You scared the fuck out of me."

"Pretty good, spot, huh? Not bad for a Syracuse beat cop, huh, spook?"

Sampson had to chuckle when he saw O'Reilly's face. He was grinning ear to ear, bearing a striking resemblance to the Cheshire Cat. Sampson was also surprised to see that O'Reilly was clad in green and black camouflage pants and a baseball cap.

At that moment, the cab pulled up. "Our ride is here, flat foot."

"Oh, great thinking, spook. A cab. No one will notice that."

"Hey, it's that or walk."

"All right. Let's go. You weren't followed. I kept an eye on you."

"My guardian angel." They emerged from their hiding place and jumped in the car.

"Hi, Ben. This is my friend, O'Reilly. Thanks again for coming." The old man nodded and drove off.

O'Reilly opened a backpack he was carrying. "Spook, I got us a couple of goodies." He began pulling things out of the bag. "First, here's some camouflage stuff. Should fit." He thrust the clothing at Sampson. "Next, we're gonna be light on weapons, but these will help." O'Reilly pulled out a couple of knives, good size hunting knives, and two canisters of mace. Both men chuckled. "That's it. Couldn't get a gun or anything like it. These are crude, but they'll have to get the job done."

"O'Reilly, you are the best. I mean it."

"Don't get misty on me." He shook his head.

Sampson looked up at Ben. "Ben, any thought on how to get into Xandria?"

"Ya, mon. Pretty simple. I talked to a couple of the cabbies. Nobody big is there. They mostly left a couple of days ago, which means small stuff, not much in the way of guards. The road bends about 100 feet in front of the gates to this place. They can see the lights but if you guys jump out as I slow, not stop, mind you, you only have to travel 100 feet or so in the woods on the right. I'll drive to the gate; confuse them with a cab. They'll send me away."

Sampson interrupted. "Then what, Ben? You said there are fences and gates. Then what?"

"Simple, mon. When I was a kid we played in a drainpipe. If that drainpipe is still there, it's a way in."

"Where is it?"

"Near the main gate, to the right. At the very end of the brick facade, you can find a drain cover. Slip it off and climb in and crawl south. It comes up about 200 feet inside the gate in a cozy courtyard near the main house. When you come up, walk straight in. That is, well at least was, the main living quarters. It could have changed, you know. This is old, old information."

"Ben, it's great information and I am very thankful."

"Ah, 'scuse me," O'Reilly motioned to the driver. "You were a kid and you fit in this pipe.

We're adults. Some of us are big adults," said O'Reilly, looking down at his ample size.

"I see your point, mon. You'll fit. She'll be tight as a new bride, but you'll fit, mon. You'll fit." Ben laughed uncontrollably.

"I hope to fuck you're right, old man," O'Reilly grumbled.

Ben laughed a deep belly laugh. "Oh, I'm right, I'm right."

The remainder of the ride was silent until they were a short distance from Xandria. "Gentlemen, I will slow at the corner. Good luck."

"Show time, spook." O'Reilly opened the door and rolled out, followed closely by Sampson. Both men survived the exit without incident and moved swiftly to the cover of the woods. They both moved with cat-like quickness toward the gate. The cover was mostly pine trees, which proved easy to navigate. They reached the gate close enough to hear the conversation between Ben and the guard at the gate.

"No one ordered a cab here."

"Dammit, Mon, somebody did. I just drive all the way out here. You must check."

"There is nothing to check. There's hardly anyone here, and everyone is staying here. Go away now."

"Shit, mon," Benjamin protested.

O'Reilly and Sampson stayed low. They could see the guard settle back down in his shack. He was reading what appeared to be a newspaper, and they could also see the flicker of a television. Sampson contemplated an encounter with the guard. "O'Reilly, I vote we leave him alone. No point in making noise right now."

"Agreed. Let's find that pipe."

With keen focus, they searched for the pipe. The area was as Ben described it, but it was very overgrown. Over time what was once grass was now thick with underbrush.

"Spook, got it!" O'Reilly whispered.

Sampson moved toward his partner. The odd pair pushed brush aside, and it took the two of them to remove the lid, which came off with a muffled creek. At the first sound of a scraping metal noise, both men dove for cover. They could see the guard look up and scan the area, but clearly he saw nothing. They waited five minutes and then finished removing the plate. Both men were anxious.

"Spook, this is tight, small, and dark."

"Are you describing your girlfriend?

"Funny. Let's get on with this."

Sampson crawled in first. He took a breath only to inhale a musty and stale odor. *Something died*, he thought. The pipe was smaller than he had imagined and as he lay on his back, he could move his knees only in a twisted way, lift and push forward with his butt. It would take time, a long time, to complete the journey.

Sampson could hear O'Reilly behind him. It took forty-five minutes to reach the end of the pipe. In the darkness, Sampson could only reach and feel for a pipe cover. It was there, but he feared the noise it would make as he opened it. Carefully he pushed upward and lifted the steel cover. He was able to push it up and aside with only a faint noise. The mystery was, what was outside? He sat up in the pipe and was able to scan the area. As Ben had said, he was indeed in a courtyard, and mercifully it was empty.

He pushed the cover completely to the side and shimmied out of the pipe. O'Reilly followed in a few seconds. They replaced the cover and moved to their left in the shadows of a small structure that looked like a gazebo. The structure offered little cover but allowed them to silently survey the area. They saw no movement and heard no sound. The men remained motionless for two minutes. Convinced they had entered unseen, they looked at one another.

"O'Reilly, so far so good. According to Ben, they're probably holding her in the main house." O'Reilly could see Sampson motioning to a building about 500 feet through the courtyard. The building was brick with green ivy climbing the three-story structure. Most troublesome to both men was the fact that the house was well-lit, as well as the surrounding area. There was no cover at all from where they stood to the outskirts of the building. There was no hidden approach. Both men grimaced.

Each knew the element of surprise was critical. They did not know how many men were in the compound, and they didn't know where the little girl was. Both knew that stealth was critical. They knew time was also critical. Eventually they would be spotted, and each moment they wandered the compound posed great risk to themselves and more importantly, to Becca.

Satisfied that their target was spotted, both men looked at one another, nodded, and moved single file directly toward the corner of the brick house. Sampson dreaded the move. Even in camouflage they were sitting ducks if anyone was watching. Sampson was conscious that he was holding his breath. He exhaled and concentrated on breathing slowly and normally. Crouched low with their backs against the wall, they shimmied to a window and shared their first peek inside the house. They could see two men sitting at a table eating some kind of food. They were big men, young, and both wearing shoulder straps that held guns. They could see the kitchen area and a third figure in a distant corner.

Sampson scanned the room for other men, or other signs or clues. On a table not far from the very window where they stood, was a sign he was looking for—a sippy cup, a baby cup. She was here! O'Reilly made the same connection. They sought cover below the window.

O'Reilly spoke first in a hushed tone. "I spotted three, all armed. I'm sure you saw the cup."

"Yup. We've got to get in. We're sitting ducks out here."

They moved from the far end of the house. The lighting was a bit darker here. Both men felt windows to their right and left but found each locked. They continued to their left around to the other side of the building and found no luck with any of the windows. They came upon a doorway with deep shadows. Instinctively both men climbed down three stairs and hid motionless in the dark caverns of the stairwell.

Sampson looked with a grin at O'Reilly as he reached for the door handle. "Probably wishful thinking that this will be open," he whispered. True to form, the door was locked.

"Maybe these will help," O'Reilly uttered with a smile on his face.

Sampson was surprised as he reached to his left to accept a leather-bound set of burglar tools. "You are a genius, O'Reilly!"

"I know. Open the fucking door." O'Reilly passed the tools to Sampson. "We do have some risk, though. It might be alarmed. But, regardless, we've got to get in, and I don't see another way. Let's hope."

Sampson had already begun working the tumblers. He knew O'Reilly was right on all counts. They had to get in, and there was no other option. It took less than a minute for the tumblers to click a final click, and Sampson could feel the door give way slightly. He hesitated to fully open the wooden door. Both men knew there would be an alarm of some sort.

Sampson held his breath as he pushed the door open. No noise. Both men hustled into the dark room lit only by the thin streak of light passing under a nearby door. O'Reilly closed the door behind him and bolted the door shut. *Leave it like you found it*, his training echoed in his head. The two men heard nothing above them.

O'Reilly motioned Sampson to the door, then pushed it open. To his surprise, he saw a man fast asleep on a couch, and a wide-screen TV with a baseball game blaring. The man sensed a presence and came awake with a start. Sampson took a running start and hit the man squarely in the chest as he struggled to rise from the couch. There was the unmistakable sound of bone breaking as both men fell to the floor.

O'Reilly surveyed the damage. "Good tackle, kid."

Sampson replied, "Yeah, I hit him a bit harder than I planned."

"I'd say. Let me see what I can find to tie him down just on the odd chance he actually survived that hit." O'Reilly returned in less than a minute with a familiar gray object in his hand.

"Duct tape. Did you know it fixes everything?"

"A comic cop. Interesting concept," Sampson shot back.

With mutual assessment, they determined they needed to climb the lone staircase to the first floor. Still, they had little to work with. The guard had been carrying a small handgun, which O'Reilly pocketed. They both realized stealth was their only weapon, and the only question was, how long could they work their way through the house without being found? Probably not long, they feared. They left the basement and started the perilous climb of twenty-two stairs to the top; Sampson had counted. "You ready, O'Reilly?"

"Yeah, let's do it. Take this, spook." O'Reilly passed the gun to Sampson. "I'm more comfortable with knives anyway. Hey, do me a favor. Don't fucking tackle anybody else, all right?"

They both smiled. Sampson chuckled.

O'Reilly felt the door handle. It turned without effort and without any noise. O'Reilly peered through the space and saw nothing… a dangerous nothing. He opened the door enough to squeeze through and found the hall empty. They could see two staircases, but the house was silent.

"Sampson, it's too quiet. They know."

"Yup." O'Reilly cautiously nodded his head.

"I'll go left, you go right. Whoever finds her just goes and doesn't look back." Sampson nodded. They looked at each other, both men drowning in mutual respect. They moved with sheer caution. Sampson climbed slowly to the second floor and peered beyond a doorway. Again, an empty hall. He could hear faint voices from behind closed doors. A female voice and maybe a man or two.

Sampson was concerned that he could not see O'Reilly. He moved down the hall and listened as he moved. He was able to determine that the voices came from midway down the hall to his left. He focused his mental concentration but found nothing… not a clue. *I'll have to do this the old-fashioned way*, I guess, he thought.

Sampson approached the first door and found the room unlocked. As he opened the door, he found the room empty and dark. He closed the door and moved further down the hall. He could feel the *tick, tock* in his head. He knew each minute exponentially lowered his chance of success.

He felt a light sweat on his brow begin to take hold. As he inched down the hallway he came to another door. Again, he found it unlocked, and slowly opened the wooden door. A smile came to his face. Directly across from him, in a white wooden crib, was his little angel sound asleep. Her little body looked oversized in the crib, but at least someone thought to secure her, keep her warm.

Sampson rushed towards the side of the crib, anxious to hold the little girl… his little girl. From his left side he sensed movement; a movement he had no time to deal with, and he knew instantly that he had violated his training rules. He also knew it was a fatal mistake.

He felt a sudden sharp pain on the left side of his head and neck. He was vaguely aware of a warm sensation and struggled to bring focus to his eyes. Weak, but not dead, it became all instinct to Sampson. He needed time to recover, which left him only two options: run, but that would leave Becca alone and exposed. His only choice was to wound the hunter and strike a blow to buy time. He would need only seconds until he had recovered enough to fight.

From deep within his belly, he howled and threw himself at the spot where he guessed the enemy would be. Evidently, the attacker was caught off guard. Sampson's lunge caught him squarely in the chest, and propelled both men backward until they contacted a glass bookshelf which shattered on impact. Both men felt sections of the glass tear into their flesh. The pain seared.

Both men struggled on after the impact. Sampson regained some strength. The attacker was strong and delivered a series of blows to Sampson's face and mid-section. Sampson went down.

The battle was short. Sampson saw his attacker. Colonel Cates. Cates, now the victor.

Sampson lay on the floor, blood streaming from a deep cut over his right eye. Cates towered over the wounded agent; a revolver trained on Sampson's forehead. "You are a tough son of a bitch, Sampson, but this game is over," Cates scowled.

"Why? Tell me why." Sampson possessed only the hope of time, so stalling was a necessity. He also felt a burning passion to know why this all happened.

"You caused it, you idiot. This was all about getting our beloved President, Austin Feeney, re-elected. If you hadn't gotten involved, a couple of people would have died, Alan Grant would have disappeared as a candidate and *bang*, it would be all done. Except for you. But you did, and then it got personal. I wasn't about to lose. As it is, I'm going to have to go into hiding for a while."

"But..." Sampson tried to string it out.

"No buts, and no more stalling. Bye."

Sampson held his breath, waiting for the sound of the gun. His eyes stayed focused on Cates. *Becca.* He would die failing her?

From behind, he heard a *whoosh* from the doorway, and could see the expression on Cates's face change. Sampson blinked furiously, blood seeping into his eyes and causing immense pain. Was he seeing what he thought? Cates had taken a step back. Sampson was staring at a man who was dead but had not yet fallen. Stuck in his chest, in his heart, was an arrow... a great big arrow.

Cates fell to the floor in a heap. Sampson struggled to sit up.

"Spook, you okay? I leave you alone for a minute and look what happens. You fucking spy guys are soft."

O'Reilly helped Sampson to his feet. From his pocket he pulled out a handkerchief, which he placed over Sampson's eyes to quell the bleeding.

Sampson couldn't help chuckling, "Who are you? Tonto? Christ, can't you get a gun and be a real man?"

"Oh, you're one to talk." They both laughed.

"I found the bow and arrow in the hall closet. It makes a nice, quiet weapon!" O'Reilly chuckled.

"Okay, Sampson, here's the deal. The house is secure. There were two guys. I got them. There are a lot of buildings that may have people, not to mention the guard at the gate. I think we should get out of here now."

"Yeah, you're right. Let me call Agent Becker. Maybe we can get some help." Sampson picked up the phone and punched in the numbers. The call routed to his partner.

"Hello."

"Bob… Sampson. I could use some help."

'When?"

"Now."

"Two minutes, okay?"

"What do you mean?"

"Is it clear for me to come in?"

"Yes, but…"

"Two minutes."

Sampson checked his watch. Within ninety seconds, both men could hear the roar of engines. A helicopter, perhaps two. As they looked out the window, they could see two black Bell Ranger helicopters circling the courtyard, and two teams of agents disembarking. All were heavily armed.

"The cavalry is here, O'Reilly. Clever, huh? Kind of keeps with the cowboy and Indian theme you started."

O'Reilly looked stumped. "How did they get here so quick?"

"I don't know."

"Sam." From behind Sampson came the smallest, sweetest voice in the world. With all that was going on, the little girl had been startled awake.

Sampson ran to her, grabbed hold of her, and gave her a bear hug. "Becca. I missed you.

You okay?"

Bob and his men burst into the room.

"Easy, spook. No bad guys in here, at least none that are alive." Bob eyed O'Reilly and the arrow protruding from Cates' chest.

"No, it seems you handled that." Bob shook his head.

"Bob, how did you know we were here?"

"Satellite. We tracked you all the way, partner. I pulled strings on the satellite. You cost the taxpayers a bundle, but… anyway, let's get the three of you out of here. There shouldn't be trouble, but who knows. Hi, little girl." Bob winked at Becca. She smiled shyly and buried her head in Sampson's shoulder.

Within minutes, Becca, O'Reilly, and Sampson were airborne.

Bob finally broke the silence. "You two guys are quite a team. Just one question. What's with the arrow?"

Sampson laughed. "Oh, that was Tonto over there," pointing at O'Reilly.

"I never liked you two spooks." A thin smile popped up on O'Reilly's face.

The helicopter took them directly to the airport, where they boarded a small Challenger aircraft for the flight back to the U.S. Bob explained that he wanted the three of them out of Grand Cayman before the local officials were notified. No reason to get caught in any local political or extradition issues. They agreed to make Syracuse the first stop. Sampson and O'Reilly exchanged words and even hugged. They had shared an eventful experience;

one that neither would ever forget. The men promised to stay in touch, but both knew that, given the distance, it was unlikely.

On the way back they discussed next steps. Sadly, they knew the evidence was thin.

They would have an uphill climb to build a case against Feeney.

Sampson arrived back at his apartment, threw his coat on the sofa, and collapsed on it with Becca. He closed his eyes and was startled awake at some point by the sound of running water coming from his bathroom. He rose, covered Becca with his coat, removed his gun from his holster, and tiptoed to the bathroom. It was the shower. As he peaked around the comer, he was struck with a striking sight.

"Hey, secret agent man. Join me."

"Well, ma'am, I'm a bit shy."

"Now," she said in a commanding, husky voice.

"Okay."

They caressed one another for what seemed like hours. The warm water and steam rejuvenated both of their bodies. Sampson looked into her eyes and was awestruck. "You are beautiful."

"Yup, I know. Men tell me that all the time," Susan laughed.

Sampson's face went serious, and Susan became worried about the words that would follow. "I've got some news for you."

"Oh?"

"Don't interrupt," he said playfully. "This is big news. Your dad will be the next President. You'll find out tomorrow."

"But… how do you know?"

"Trade secret. But trust me."

"I do actually. It's hard not to trust a naked and bruised man."

"I see."

"Well, I've got news for you, too," Susan interjected. "Remember a few weeks ago I said I'd look into the adoption of Becca for you?"

Sampson's face lit up. "Yes?"

'Well, I'm thirsty. Get me a drink."

Sampson held her tight. "Later. Tell me."

"She's yours. All yours."

Sampson and Susan both beamed. Sampson had never experienced a better moment in his life. Such promise, love, endless sunshine ahead. "How, Susan? How did you get it done?" Tears flowed freely. She was touched by his wave of emotion. And this man clearly deserved some happiness in his life.

"Well, my dad did. He's well-connected, you know. Anyway, it's done. You're a dad, pal!"

The sound of those nectarous words was sliced in half by a dark feeling. Sampson had to check on his daughter—now. Slipping away from Susan before she could process their jeweled spell being broken, Sampson ran down the hallway only to see the atrocious sight taking shape. His sweet, little girl sitting up in a trance with crimson liquid dripping from her tiny nostrils.

About the Author

Tom Markert is a highly accomplished businessman, author, writer, and public board director. For 30 years, he has held senior positions with some of the world's most respected companies including Procter & Gamble, Citi, Ipsos, Nielsen, and Office Depot. Tom also has extensive sports marketing experience having worked domestically with Stewart-Haas Racing, Miami Heat, NBA, and the American Basketball League.

Tom served on the Board of Directors for State Auto Financial Corporation (STFC/NASDAQ) for twelve years and The True Value Company for five years. Tom is currently the National President of InfraGard, a partnership between the FBI and the private sector dedicated to sharing information and intelligence to prevent hostile acts against the United States. Tom also serves as City Commissioner in his hometown of Delray Beach, Florida, where he lives with his wife, Sarah. He has four grown children. He is a 2022 graduate of the FBI Citizens Academy and DEA Citizens Academy.

Tom is the author of *Death Watch*, a thriller, and two business books, *You Can't Win a Fight with Your Boss* and *You Can't Win a Fight with Your Client* (Harper Business).

www.ingramcontent.com/pod-product-compliance
Lightning Source LLC
Chambersburg PA
CBHW060539310726
48982CB00009B/1315/J